LEGIO...

...ST

STAND

■ ■ ■ ■ ■ ■ ■ ■ ■

Luis took to the stairs and put on a burst of speed. He reached the fourth floor in the middle of a nasty firefight.

Znnap! An AK round snapped past his head and took another Legionnaire in the neck. He turned back to the fight in time to see a Soviet-made M-10 grenade rolling along the corridor, directly toward him.

He barely had time to drop to the floor behind his buckler when the shield slammed against his head and shoulder. Dazed, bleeding from nose and ears, Luis rose unsteadily to his knees. A quick glance showed him to be the only living Legionnaire in the hallway. An instant later the dust-laden air filled with automatic fire as the Panamanian rebels charged...

★★★ THE ★★★
LIBERTY CORPS

#3 CANAL ZONE CONQUEST

Also by Mark K. Roberts

The Liberty Corps
The Liberty Corps #2: Maracaibo Massacre
The Liberty Corps #4: Korean Carnage*

Published by
POPULAR LIBRARY   *forthcoming

★★★ THE ★★★ LIBERTY CORPS

#3 CANAL ZONE CONQUEST

MARK K. ROBERTS

POPULAR LIBRARY

An Imprint of Warner Books, Inc.

A Warner Communications Company

Special acknowledgments to G. M. Hoover for his research and creative participation in this work.

This volume in the operations of the Liberty Corps is dedicated with honor and respect to a great American, Lieutenant Colonel Oliver J. North, whose spirit, it is hoped, is embodied in the American Foreign Legion. *Legio Patria Nostra!*

—M.K.R.

CHAPTER ONE

Captain Robert Fuller of the American Foreign Legion thought over the last words he had said. From the looks of their situation, he indeed might never get to taste the results of the fledgling Legion brewery. This can of loose bolts was doomed. He ran short, blunt fingers through his black, curly locks and produced an idiot, "What, me worry?" grin. Hell, he'd far rather jump than crash-land at sea in this decrepit bird. The C-130D wallowed like a drunk in a windstorm. The lower they got, the more the turbulence increased. Well, he allowed, these were his men and it was up to him to do something to keep them calm.

"Listen up!" Fuller called out. "The co-pilot told me they had a ship in sight. We're going in, but we'll be picked up fairly soon. They'll fire flares before we ditch."

"Yeah, if *they* work," a disgruntled voice answered him over the roar of the laboring aircraft.

The crew chief, a burly master sergeant, appeared in the doorway of the bulkhead that separated the flight deck. "Everybody strap down good and tight and assume the position. We're going in," he commanded in a stentorian voice.

A pair of dull thumps sounded as the flight engineer fired distress flares. These arched high into the air to either side of the failing aircraft and burst into bright showers of red. The water came closer. Heaving seas could be seen through the ports. A rending sound, much like the tearing of tightly stretched canvas, came from beneath them, followed almost at once by a violent thrust toward the nose of the plane. The

1

crippled craft lifted a moment, then slammed down hard. Spray rose past all ports and a giddy, jouncing began, to end far sooner than it seemed. Wing tips awash, the C-130 settled in the water.

"Up," the co-pilot commanded. "Everybody up and open the escape hatches. Get on the wings and begin to inflate rafts."

A confused babble of voices rose inside the metal tube, until Bob Fuller commanded quiet. Hatches popped open and the Legionnaires began to file out onto the wings. Working in desperate silence, they inflated and launched rafts, then loaded into them. Three Legionnaires and the crew chief had been injured slightly in the crash landing. They were handed out with as much tenderness as the situation allowed, and placed in rafts. By the time the last rubber boat, with Bob Fuller aboard, edged away from the doomed aircraft, an ominous burbling rumble sounded from within.

"Any idea where we are?" Bob asked the navigator, a young kid from Nebraska.

Dubiousness lighting his eyes as he studied the tattoos on Bob's forearms, the kid cleared his throat. "If you want an instrument reading, forget it," the youthful navigator responded lightly. "If you want my considered opinion— guess, if you prefer—I'd say we're somewhere not too far off the coast of Central America."

Small whitecaps washed over the bow of the raft and Bob Fuller tasted the salt spray on his lips. Already their clothing had become saturated and most had ditched their helmets in favor of boonie hats that provided eye shade and lightweight protection from the weak sun that burned through the high clouds. Fuller raised himself and looked around. A thin black smudge on the horizon ahead and to their left indicated the location of the ship. He could see nothing else.

"What part of Central America?" he asked, sounding a bit uneasy.

"Costa Rica," came the reply. "Maybe Nicaragua."

"Oh, great. Just what we need. A little sojourn in *Señor* Sandino's hell will do us wonders," Captain Fuller came back.

"Not necessary," the navigator explained. "We saw that

ship before we ditched. It's now turned toward us. We'll be picked up long before we can drift into Nicaraguan waters."

Fuller gazed askance at him, his dark eyes and beetled brows intimidating. "You're sure we'll not wind up in Nicaragua?"

"As sure as I can be. I grew up in Nebraska on a farm. As a kid I went hunting and fishing a lot. Even got caught out in some snowstorms. I developed a strong sense of direction. It's only a gut feeling, but my gut isn't often wrong. We're far west of where we should be, but not so far as to encounter Nicaraguan patrol boats."

Satisfied for the moment, Fuller let it ride. His thoughts turned to the fierce fighting in Venezuela. An army is an army, even if it is run by drug producers playing at being a government. The Colombians fought hard and well. The Legion had taken more casualties than they could afford. A lot of equipment lost, too. He knew that Colonel Watie intended to put him in for a citation for that end run and attack in the rear that broke the Colombian First Infantry and Third Armored.

That didn't amount to a pinch of coon shit when he started mentally ticking off the names of those who had died in the engagement. He'd have to knock off that sort of crap, Bob chided himself, or he'd become some kind of peace creep. He rummaged in his uniform pockets and came up with a trail bar from a forgotten combat ration. With the solemnity of unveiling a great monument, he peeled off the wrapper. Eyes closed in anticipation, he bit into the concentrated energy stick.

Even the bittersweet chocolate covering couldn't disguise the flavor that he always thought of as sawdust and metal filings. Fuller chewed slowly, making the iron ration last half an hour. By then, the ship they were counting on had breasted the horizon. It came toward them, tall and beautiful, painted an immaculate white. Fuller's spirits lifted. Ten minutes later it had steamed close enough for him to make out the name, done in bright red letters near the bow.

пбвлеземля

"Pohl' yeh-z' yehml' yah," Fuller pronounced the Cyrillic characters. *"Meadowland*, in English," he went on to say. "Not exactly the folks we want picking us up, either. Everyone," he called out loudly to the lashed-together rafts, "ditch your helmets and all Legion identification. That's a Russian ship."

"Aw, shit!" Legion Sergeant Paul Challenger expressed the sentiment of all. His blondish, curly hair, which had a tendency to be too long, fluffed in the breeze as he removed the crested headgear and tossed it over the side.

By now the Soviet freighter had turned broadside to the rafts, the moderate wind stiffening the large, blood-red flag with its hammer and sickle. Boats were being lowered and a man in an officer's uniform came to the rail with a bullhorn.

"Veeya v spasaht' ihlynuhyu lohtkuyere...."

"You in the lifeboats," Fuller translated for those who did not understand, "stand by to be taken aboard."

"Gahvahret' yeh lee vee pa ahngleeskee?" Captain Fuller called back.

"Da. I speak English," the tinny reply came from the bullhorn.

Fuller quickly ordered the men to get rid of their weapons and any ammunition. The last splash had barely dissipated when the first boat arrived. The dowsed men clambered aboard and were propelled by sputtering motors to the side of the Soviet freighter. After that the transfer went swiftly and without injury or loss of life. Within twenty minutes, stocky, muscular, thoroughly wet Bob Fuller stood on deck.

"You are in charge?" the young Soviet officer inquired of him.

"More or less, yes," Bob allowed.

"We heard broadcast, American aircraft missing and presumed in distress. Belongs Foreign Legion. You are that aircraft?" The latter came more as a statement than a question.

Bob Fuller took a deep breath and swallowed before answering. "We are people in distress, in international waters. The majority of us are United States citizens and request to be taken to the nearest American embassy or consulate."

"We will talk with captain," the officer responded flatly.

"Lieutenant Chapenko." Fuller had read the Cyrillic name

inscribed on a plaque on the officer's right breast pocket. "International maritime law clearly states that we are to be afforded the protections of any persons downed at sea."

"You tell Captain," Chapenko said curtly.

On the bridge, introductions were made quickly. Captain Vorshavski listened to a brief recitation of his subordinate's conversation with Fuller, then turned to the soggy American.

"I should use your rank, but you didn't give it to me. So, then Mr. Fuller, you and the men with you are prisoners, I'm afraid. Contact with your embassy or consulate is out of the question."

"By what right and for what reason are we prisoners?" Captain Fuller demanded.

Vorshavski's gray eyes grew icy. His voice had a quality like the wind off the Siberian steppes. "You and these men are mercenaries. Members of the American Foreign Legion, I believe. As such, you are outside the law and have no protection under international agreements."

"Whose authority places us outside the law?" Fuller demanded, temper rising.

"That of the Union of Soviet Socialist Republics and its allies. You will be held aboard until a decision is made in Moscow. Chapenko, take him below with the others and secure them in a hold."

"Da, tovarish kapitan," Chapenko responded with a crisp salute.

After the Legionnaires and flight crew had been roughly shoved below and securely locked in a small, smelly hold, Captain Vorshavski made a precise entry in the official log, the one shown to his Soviet superiors, not the one seen by international maritime officials.

"At 1039 hours (local), took aboard survivors from crashed American Foreign Legion aircraft. Forty-three men and flight crew of five. Position: 11 36′ 8″ north, 81 42′ 5″ west. Proceeding to destination."

Lieutenant Chapenko entered the captain's quarters, his bearing far from that of a servile junior officer. Although he didn't wear the red collar tabs of a major in the KGB, his attitude exuded his true rank admirably.

"I'll need a copy of your report to send to Central, Comrade Captain."

"Certainly, Comrade Major," Vorshavski responded obediently. "Also a transcript of our conversation with this, ah, Fuller."

"Yes. May I have it all in half an hour?"

"At your disposal, Comrade Major," the ship's captain acknowledged.

Down in the hold, Captain Bob Fuller held a quick council of war. "There's no denying we're in deep shit. We're being held prisoner on a Soviet freighter headed south to who knows where. Worse, there's a boatload of Nicaraguan troops and equipment aboard."

"Are you sure?" the pilot of the C-130 asked.

"Yep. I saw a number of them looking us over when we came aboard. Recognized those dumpy fatigues and the sloppy, dark blue-green Sandinista berets. The insignia of rank was right, too. Wherever we're going, there's gonna be a fucking war."

"TWX in from Caracas, Colonel," Legion Sergeant Major Pops Henderson announced as he entered Colonel Norman Stand Watie's office at Corsair Cay.

"Bad news, no doubt," Watie answered. "But I've been expecting that. Let me have it." He unfolded the pulp-paper message slip and read aloud. "'Due to worsening weather conditions and fuel requirements, the Venezuelan governments regrets to inform you that we are suspending search and rescue operations for your downed C-130D aircraft.' Dammit! I know they're out there somewhere. I can feel it in my bones. Those damned South Americans were searching in the wrong place." Watie surged his huge frame from the overlarge swivel chair. He started to turn away from his desk, then swung back and swallowed the telephone handset in one big hand.

"Get me Air-Sea Rescue headquarters," he commanded of the switchboard operator. When the connection had been made, he barked into the mouthpiece, "This is Colonel Watie, AFL. Let me speak to your commander."

"Yes, Colonel. But he's busy on another line right now. Can you hold?"

"I can hold nothing, dammit. This is an emergency. I want Dave Cheney *at once!*"

A meek "Yes, sir" answered him.

In a second, Rear Admiral David Cheney came on the line. "What is it, Norm, as if I didn't know?"

"The Venezuelans are pulling out of the search for my boys, Dave. I want your word you won't knock off quite yet, eh? They're out there, I know it. I'd direct the search farther to the west. They must have drifted that way, from the last reports of anyone seeing them. Say, off the coast of Central America. Can you do it?"

A long pause followed. "Norm . . . we're spread rather thin down there. Between Castro and those other assholes in Nicaragua, they claim damn near all the airspace in the area. A slight miscalculation and we could trigger an international incident."

"Piss on your international incidents. This is an emergency, a life-saving operation in international waters. If you want, I'll try to get you some F-18s and 111s for top cover."

"Good God, no," Cheney came back. "That would only provoke those hotheads into launching a few SAMs. Nothing they'd like better. I'll, ah, recommend the search area be extended and the time allotted for at least another two or three days. Beyond that, there's little I can do, Norm."

"Thanks at least for that, Dave," Watie replied.

While he had been speaking, Lieutenant Colonel Stan McDade entered the office. He listened carefully and now raised a finger to indicate he had something to add.

"I want to have the coverage extended to include the coastal waters and somewhat inland along the Panamanian coast."

Watie relayed the request. "They'll do what they can," he informed his G-2 and acting station commander. He added a few words of small talk and hung up the phone.

"Then we'd better prepare some sort of search of our own," McDade pressed. "Something's got me going on this.

A gut feeling that we'll learn more in Panama than out in the Caribbean."

"I'll give you what I can," Watie agreed.

All of the grizzled combat veterans of the American Foreign Legion snapped to attention as the customized Lear jet taxied to a halt in front of them. The door opened to reveal the inventor of Second Chance Body Armor. "It's him," someone gasped, as ten thousand men fell to their knees in reverence. Even Ursula, the incredibly beautiful blond Amazon warrior, whom the men called the "Lesbian Goddess" because she had spurned all advances by them. She began breathing heavily, her large golden mounds heaving in the constraint of the skintight pink Spandex suit she had made and worn for this historic occasion. He approached; she ran forward and threw herself at his feet. "Take me, my stallion," she cried, her voice husky with emotion as her trembling fingers groped at his belt buckle. . . .

. . . Fingers groping at Rick Davis's seat-belt buckle brought him *whoofing* out of the wild dream he had been having. Close to his own face, he saw the lovely features of Nadine Richards, the cute, comely, blond and desirable young thing who had served as stewardess—and to hell with this libber neuter term "cabin attendant," Rick thought—on the flight to Corsair Cay. Outside, the blades of the twin turboprops hummed normally. He smiled and she answered his implied question.

"Sorry to awaken you, Mr. Davis. I wanted to make sure your seat belt was buckled. We're due to land in fifteen minutes."

"Oh, ah, thanks, Nadine," Rick grinned up at her. "And, ah, could you bring me another of those terrific dark beers?" He shook his head and pushed up on the center bow of his horn-rimmed glasses. "Jeez, how anyone could get away with naming it the SS Brewery."

Nadine returned with frosted steinkrug and a foam-topped bottle. "Because it's the *quaffin'* SS, not the *Waffen* SS," she managed through a suppressed giggle. "You asked me that two hours ago when we were over Tennessee."

"I know." Rick winked. "Maybe it's just because I like your company. Sit down here beside me."

Nadine thought it over. Why not? her mind prodded. She had been recruited into the Legion by Lieutenant Mark McDade, who was personally flying the Legion's King Air on this trip. Nadine had graduated from one of the nation's top airline training schools and taken a job with TWA. On a routine flight, she had encountered Mark McDade. They'd clicked together like the poles of two magnets. He had a raw, vigorous male-animal aura that captivated her. She had the long, lean good looks that Mark doted on. Their brief affair turned into a suggestion that she join the Legion.

Lured by Mark's six-foot-one, broad-shouldered frame, his clear blue eyes and boyish grin, Nadine considered, then accepted. She'd undergone Legion Basic during the Venezuelan campaign, and her first full-time assignment had been the trip to Michigan to bring Richard Davis to the Cay. In the interim, she'd learned of Mark's flamboyant style, his philandering and outright infidelities. She knew he had a Casinova-like inability to remain long with one woman. But, what the hell, he was one damned fine lover while it lasted. She could even forgive him the incredible scene she'd heard of at the marina back in San Diego. So long, at least, as she could use these amorous adventures to allow her a certain modicum of freedom in that category.

Seating herself and snapping the buckle in place, she laid a soft, slim-fingered hand on Rick's arm. "Have you been a contractor to the Legion for long, Mr. Davis?"

"Yeah, for a little over a year. And, ah, Nadine, call me Rick."

"What all have you provided?" Her question came in a tone that implied more than material goods.

"The ballistic vests, of course. Hardcorps and Softcorps. Also the helmets and the bucklers. Are you familiar with those?"

"You bet. I had to use them in Basic, Rick."

Davis blinked, making a reevaluation of this gorgeous bird. "*You* took Legion Basic, Nadine?"

"Of course. Everyone has to. It was fun. Hard, but fun."

"That's what she said last night," Rick quipped.

Nadine only blinked, then riposted, "Which one, Rick?"

"*Touché*. Anyway, what I'm down here for is a demonstration of the ballistic fairings I designed for the Hondas. That and a meeting with the brass on some other ideas."

Nadine pushed out a lip in a slight pout. "That won't leave you a lot of free time."

"That remains open to negotiation. Provided we don't get into a hell of a mess with the test runs."

"What happens if you do?" Nadine inquired.

"Then I might be here for a long damned time."

"*That* I just might learn to like," Nadine responded with more than a little promise.

CHAPTER TWO

Seen from the air, the upside-down parrot shape of Corsair Cay had a sort of aesthetic appeal. Greens, yellow, tan, and blue blended into a convincing image. At least it did until the King Air began to descend. The works of man, ugly and straight-edged compared to nature, began to emerge. Oddly, Rick Davis saw only roadways, the airstrip, and a large area that could be a parade ground. Everything else had long ago been placed under clever, high-quality camouflage. Not even a color-blind analyst could ferret this out, Davis speculated. Mark McDade set the Beechcraft down smoothly and taxied off onto the first ramp. Davis glanced out the window while the turboprop turned and braked. Undoing his seat belt, he began to grin.

Some dream. Right out of one of those lurid adventure novels of the seventies, Rick reflected. Only two persons made up his reception committee. One, tall, lean, and mean, the typical career soldier. The other a veritable giant. Taller even than the blond super-soldier, looking like he'd been poured into his uniform, with a little left in the crucible. Black hair, shaggy even in a crew cut, eyes of glittering obsidian, wide-set in a broad, high cheekboned face. Thick, handsomely shaped lips and a jutting jaw. Rick Davis read "Indian" all over him. Both wore the spread-winged silver birds of full colonels.

"We're here, Rick," Nadine said sweetly and unnecessarily.

"So I see. Well, I'd better get out and meet the brass."

Davis stepped down the built-in loading stairs of the King Air, the grin still plastered on his round, comfortable face. Had he been watching too much TV? So far in dealings with the Legion he had worked mostly with a major—uh, no, make that lieutenant colonel now—named Seagraves, and a Major Orenda. Now he extended his hand to the recruiting-poster officer and arranged his vocal cords into cordial tones.

"Colonel Watie, I presume?" Rick asked.

"No, he's Watie, I'm Cutler," Lew answered back, beginning to enjoy their guest's reaction.

"Oh . . . God . . . he's a big one, ain't he?" Rick quipped.

"White man speak with forked tongue," Watie rumbled in an exaggerated bass.

Then they were laughing and slapping each other on the shoulder. A Legionnaire went to the cargo compartment of the King Air to retrieve Rick's luggage and departed with it. Mark McDade and Nadine Richards went their own way, leaving the trio alone on the tarmac.

"Good to have you here, Mr. Davis," Stand Watie said at last.

"Make it Rick, Colonel, and I'm glad to be here."

"We, ah, have to get out to the range," Lew Cutler interrupted politely, glancing at his watch.

"What? So soon?" Rick queried. "No obligatory trip to the O club first?"

"Heaven forbid!" Watie boomed. "We'll take you to the Hoffbrau for bratts and fried potatoes after the test run, but the officers' club is used only for parties and to entertain outsiders like the Pentagon brass, visiting congressmen, and the press."

Colonel Cutler led the way to the most outlandish staff car Rick Davis had ever seen. Rick found himself staring at a wicked-looking variation of the Gatling gun. He slapped the multibarreled weapon and spoke to Stand Watie.

"Quite a staff car you have here."

Watie produced a boyish grin. "Yeah. I fell in love with them. Once you see what these bastards can do, you will, too. Rick, did you ever consider shooting down incoming missiles with a shotgun?"

"Huh? Is that what this is?"

"You bet. Twenty-mike-mike, fully open casing shotgun," Watie proudly told him. "Comes out roughly a 30mm and holds one hundred and twenty steel balls for each of six thousand rounds per minute."

"Should bring scalding pee on infantry in the assault," Rick speculated.

"It does. We made pussycats out of a Colombian outfit called the Tiger Brigade with them." Huge teeth sparkled whitely. "Poor bastards aim and fire the things at themselves every time they fire a rocket at us."

Rick wisely decided not to ask for details. They climbed aboard the Panhard, and the diesel engine rumbled throatily. At Range Six, Major Mick Orenda waited for them. He greeted Rick warmly and ushered the trio to an advantageous observation spot. On the way he outlined the demonstration.

"We've set up a charging, armored motorcycle target, and a live-fire charge on dug-in targets. The dummy rider on the motorcycle is dressed in a Second Chance Hardcorps vest, as well as the new ballistic fairing. A squad of couriers will charge the fixed positions with Hardcorps, also with Jack-hammer shotguns mounted in the new fairings. Everything is about set, whenever you're ready."

"Colonel, any news about the downed bird?" Lieutenant Colonel Tachikawa asked gravely.

"Nothing good," Watie answered him. "Venezuela's called off their search teams. Dave Cheney's going to give us all the time he can." He saw the expression on Rick Davis's face and explained about the missing C-130.

"Damned shame," Rick responded. "A guy walks through the hellish sort of fighting I heard about in Venezuela, only to go down at sea. I'm sorry it happened and I sure hope you find them."

"Oh, we will, if Stan McDade has anything to say about it," Watie assured him. "Now let's get on with this demonstration, Mick."

"Yes, sir," the hawk-nosed Cherokee major responded. "The target will run straight down this concrete track with the rain gutter buried in the center. It will be supported by outriggers on each side, and we expect it to really be moving by the time it reaches us. The rider will work it into third gear at low speed, lock the throttle wide open, and bail off before she tops that rise."

Crisp commands went out over the radio and a motorcycle fired up in the distance. The engine changed tempo twice, then bellowed throatily as it lugged its way toward the power curve and the dummy's head appeared. The bike sped directly toward the observers, rods screaming agony as the tach needle swept past red-line and pegged. It closed to about one hundred meters and the marksman in a low bunker opened up with an AK-47. Through binoculars provided, Watie, Cutler, and Davis saw the fairing scarring but no penetrations. At fifty meters, the first AP rounds stuck in the Lexan windshield. Still none penetrated. At ten meters, the first burst of three missed the hardened steel plates in the fairing and stopped in the dummy's Hardcorps. Wise to the program, Rick Davis drew a .357 Magnum from under his light jacket and shot the front tire of the bike.

Disappointment and chagrin registered on his face when he discovered what the others already knew. The bike had run-flat tires. By that time the dummy flashed past steel posts, embedded for the purpose, and broke away the outriggers as Mick Orenda hit a remote kill switch. The bike ran off the concrete ramp, bogged its front wheel in soft sand, and flipped.

"Son of a bitch! Now, that was impressive," Davis enthused. "And I'm the guy who used to go around shooting myself with .44 mangle-'ems and such. What now?"

In answer, the air filled with a fluttering roar of incoming 60mm mortar bombs that lifted huge gouts of earth on a nearby hill and covered the engine noises as a squad of couriers charged the prepared target area from somewhere behind the viewing stand. As the barrage lifted, riders began laying down final covering fire from their Sidewinders and Jackhammers mounted in the fairings. The riders wore Hardcorps vests and leaped the positions by running up firing parapets when not able to dodge them. Once on the other side of the dummy enemies, they slid their Hondas into tight, right-hand one-eighties and laid them down.

Arms swinging in rhythm over the supine bikes, the couriers chucked grenades into the enemy holes. Dull crumps followed. When the dust settled, the couriers could be seen standing by their bikes with cleared weapons held aloft in the signal for victory.

"Range master forward," Mick Orenda commanded over the PA system.

The designated range master moved quickly among them, verifying the condition of weapons, and then signaled that the spectators could come forward and inspect each position. Rather than casual joshing, the awed onlookers kept a contemplative silence as they viewed the result.

"It's apparent that all couriers are in position to fire on the enemy's rear from the barricade of their bulletproof fairings," Stand Watie pronounced. "And that their fire during the short time span of the assault would have been accurate and dense enough to keep all but the most dauntless enemy heads down. I think we can safely say we have a successful piece of equipment here."

"I'm . . . impressed. And I designed that fairing," Rick Davis responded. "The thing is, I wonder how I could adapt those exercises into our next pin shoot?"

Modern electric lighting—not added until 1964—made pools of brightness in the high-ceilinged, Spanish colonial-style office in the presidential palace in Panama City. President of the Republic of Panama, Arturo Moldinado, sat at his desk, an expression of deep concentration lining his face. His soft black hair had been styled into a Jack Kennedy sweep over a broad, clear forehead. Across the desk from him, Colonel Jaime Ortega, chief of intelligence, stood at rigid attention.

His reason for this was not the strictness of his commander in chief; rather, it was from the gravity of the information he had delivered only minutes before. Moldinado glanced up and observed this, dismissing it with a wave.

"Take a seat, Jaime. I don't like this any more than you, but there's no need for that parade ground formality."

Ortega relaxed slightly, sighed out the breath he'd been holding, and complied with his superior's request. No sooner had he seated himself than President Moldinado began questioning him. With each word, the tension escalated.

"You're sure of this, Jaime?"

"*Sí, Presidente*. Absolutely," Jaime returned.

"Jaime, we were at school together, swam together in the ocean as boys. Inside this office, or anywhere that others who might not understand are not around, I am still Arturo to you. Damn the strictures of high office. Is Dalton Hunter also plagued with petty plots and craven conspirators?"

For the first time, Jaime Ortega allowed a smile to form. "I'm certain he is, Arturo. Any man who achieves prominence has done so by making enemies. For example, in your case, *Coronel* Enrique Gonzales Gorman. He grew up with us, as you remember I'm sure. We used to call him 'Sauerkraut' and tease him about his blond hair. His hair grew darker as he got older, or else he uses dye, something my agents haven't uncovered so far, but so did his moods. In secondary school, you used to beat him out for all the prettiest girls. From what I've uncovered, I don't think he ever forgave you for that."

"And what have you uncovered, Jaime? Oh, I've known for months there's some unrest and discontent in several *Fuerza Defensora* units. The officer corps is not what it used to be. At least there we can't fault Enrique. While we went to schools in the United States and Argentina, he went to Saint-Cyr."

"Yes, and afterward threw in his lot with Manuel Noriega. Which, need I remind you, has been the reason he's been passed over three times for promotion to general? My information has it that he has Napoleonic ambitions of becoming generalissimo or field marshal, something of that sort. I'm afraid," Jaime added, "your rumors of discontent are more than substantial. And it's not an enlisted revolt, or mutiny if you prefer, against certain unpopular officers. Rather, it's a full-scale coup d'etat in the making, with the objective of bringing back Manuel Noriega and his communist friends."

"*¡Condenación!* Noriega and his drug-dealing cabal, the communists, all that over again? Noriega was a butcher, an animal, a pig! I'd see Panama back in the hands of the Americans before I'd have him in power."

"*Y yo igualmente*, Arturo. But back to the revolt. Unfortunately, more officers, it seems, are involved than enlisted men."

"Who? I need names to act, Jaime."

"Arturo, I don't have names beyond those I gave you. Not

as yet, anyway. Only that it's to happen soon. Too damned soon for us to do much about it, I'm afraid."

"You want me to leave the country, Jaime? Go into exile?"

Jaime Ortega looked sadly into the face of his friend. "At least you would be alive that way, *amigo viejo*."

"Is it . . . that imminent?" President Moldinado asked haltingly, suddenly aware of the gravity of his friend's disclosure.

"It could be . . . tomorrow. It could be next month. *¿Quién sabe?*" Jaime sighed. *"Ya lo creo se nos acabo del tiempo."*

"We may have run out of time, Jaime, but remember what they say: *'En politica hay que simular buena cara aunque se pierda,'*" Arturo responded.

Ortega sighed again. "If you'll pardon my being crude, I think we'll have a hard enough time saving our asses in this political situation, let alone saving face, Arturo."

Starlight and the image of a sliver of moon sparkled on the placid water. The Soviet freighter had passed through the Gatún Locks and through the narrow neck into the lake of the same name. Cypress knees, shrouded in lianas and Spanish moss, made sharp black silhouettes against the velvet background. The forty-three Legionnaires and their air crew saw none of this natural beauty. They remained in the sweltering hold, which now smelled like a steel-lined locker room full of sweaty gym socks and jockstraps. Fortunately, Legionnaires had been conditioned out of smoking by the exigencies of the modern electronic battlefield or someone would have suffocated. Through this miasma, Legionnaire Andros Kalamantiano came to Captain Bob Fuller.

"I told you earlier we were passing through the Gatún Locks, Captain. We're at anchor now somewhere in Gatún Lake."

"Any idea where?" Bob asked.

"We didn't steam for long," Andros speculated aloud. "I would say near one of the horns of the mainland, peninsulas, or around the southwest end of Barro Colorado."

"What's that?" Fuller inquired.

"A large island. One of the biggest in the lake, which is huge. There's a game preserve there and a research observation station of your Smithsonian Institution across the southern channel at Gigante."

"Ummm," Bob responded noncommittally. He had his own opinion of the zany scientists usually employed by the government to work for the Smithsonian. Lint-brains, most of them, in his book. Andros was continuing and Bob leaped ahead mentally to catch the meaning.

"—licate ecology, according to the Institution annual report I read on the Cay," Andros advised.

"I don't think our Nicaraguan friends give much of a fuck about the ecology," Bob suggested. "From the sound of all that shit they're unloading, I'd guess they're getting ready for some major construction work. Heavy objects don't get moved easily in thick jungle or swampland."

Mike Logan, the pilot, approached with a frown. "They've been at that for hours. What could they be up to?"

"I don't know, Mike. They've got troops, probably at least seven hundred aboard this vessel. And they're unloading heavy stuff. This is primarily an equipment transport, to judge from the big hatches in her sides. There could be quite a cargo of earth-moving stuff or even armor. It could be an invasion or it could be some sort of secret base the Panamanians want set up now that they're cut loose from the U. S. of A.," Bob theorized.

"Neither alternative sounds too good," Logan observed. "When do we eat? It's been a good twelve hours, my stomach tells me. And damn those fucking Ivans stealing our watches."

"We're prisoners, remember?" Fuller answered laconically.

Kalamantiano ran stubby fingers through his curly black hair, then groomed his short jet beard with the oily accumulation. "What the captain says about eating, I can say, too. They are late feeding us."

"Probably the work on deck," another Legionnaire put in.

Ten minutes passed and the off-loading noises ceased. A few seconds later the hatch flew open. A Soviet sailor stood there holding a large battery-powered lantern. Beside him the familiar slight figure of Lieutenant Chapenko edged forward.

"You may open the portholes, but show no lights. The

evening meal will come in fifteen minutes," the Soviet officer informed them.

"You're so kind to announce it," Fuller wisecracked. "Will dinner be a formal affair?"

Although lighter by sixty pounds, Chapenko backhanded Fuller. "Save your insolence for the natives."

Tasting the salt flavor of his blood, Bob Fuller wanted to lift the arrogant Russian off his feet and wring his neck like a chicken. Only the greatest of will, and the training of his escape-and-evasion classes prevented him. He glowered while Chapenko stalked to the hatch and went out. Fuller had what he'd been after.

To judge from the casual brutality, the lieutenant belonged to one of Moscow's "organs," probably the SK, the Soviet Kolonial, the animals who terrorized the military into compliance. If so, this was no simple freighter, but an adjunct to a military mission. From the mandatory Soviet intelligence classes G-2 sponsored, Bob knew that all the 'organs' reported directly to KGB Central.

The Red sailor set down his lamp, and keeping them under the baleful eye of his AK-47, left the hatch open. Fuller motioned to the portholes and Paul Challenger and another tall man set to opening them. Even the slight breeze that entered seemed a springtime zephyr in the fetid atmosphere of the hold.

Everyone breathed deeply and tingled with the refreshment of it. Pots and pans clanging, a mess steward approached with a large, tiered roller cart. Behind him came another. Their guard rose from his crouched position in the companionway and stood ready while they positioned the servers. The prisoners shuffled into a semblance of a line and began receiving their evening meal.

"Bean soup," a voice grumbled. "Or should I say *water*? This place is gonna smell like a sewage plant."

"What'd ya expect? Caviar?" Gun Sergeant Simmons snapped.

"Fuck those fish eggs. But I'd settle for a T-bone and french fries."

A chorus of groans answered him.

During the meal they heard the distant, popping sound of

rifle shots and some shrill cries. By the time the first trays were being turned in, the voices grew louder. Fuller leaned toward his sergeant.

"Paul, I want you and Janos to cooperate," he whispered, "after an initial show of resistance. You know the drill."

Before the last of the trays had been surrendered, the chatter had grown considerably louder and carried a hysterical note. Bob addressed the Legionnaires.

"Sounds like this is it, boys. That must be the Smithsonian crew," Fuller advised "Only civilians would be so foolish as to antagonize a captor with all that sniveling. So now they're prisoners, too. It looks worse all the time," he mused in conclusion.

The second of their two daily meals had been completed when more visitors tromped down the companionway and brought the guard to his feet. Two Nicaraguan officers entered the crowded hold, leaving a dozen men in the passage, weapons at the ready.

"You will come with us," the senior of the officers commanded.

"What for?" Bob Fuller demanded.

"It is not your place to question, imperialist pirate. But, since you have already asked, I'll tell you." A big, simpering grin spread on his face. "You are to serve the liberation of Panama as compulsory laborers here on Barro Colorado." His companion glowered at him as though he had revealed some great state secret.

"Like hell we will!" Fuller exploded. "That 'compulsory' shit is slavery."

"You will come with me," the pockmarked senior ordered.

"Where to?" Bob asked ungrammatically.

"To see *Primer Comandante* Corrales," came the simple answer.

"Hey, we're prisoners of the Soviets. You fucking Sandinistas have nothing to say in the matter," Fuller countered.

"Come with me or be shot here on the spot," the icy voice compelled.

"Well, if you put it that way," Fuller said with a shrug. He adjusted his boonie hat to a rakish angle and sauntered out of the hold in his green slingshot undershirt.

"Mr. Fuller, or should I say, Captain Fuller?" Corrales began without formalities. He produced a sneering smile at Bob's reaction. "Oh, through the courtesies of the *Komitet Gosudarstvennoi Bezopasnosti*, we have been provided with the proper rank for each of you. Captain Fuller, as a mercenary, you must realize better than most that soldiers of any nationality need enormous labor forces behind them to succeed. You and your men shall provide part of that workers' second front for the liberation of Panama."

"No, we shall not. Besides, as I told your flunkies, we're prisoners of the Soviets," Bob countered.

"Not anymore. Moscow advised the captain of the *Pohl'yeh-z'yehml'yah* that you and your men are to be turned over to us for temporary use and permanent confinement."

"What about a trial? Even the Soviets go through some mockery of one before imprisoning a person."

The sneer turned to a grimace of evil. "You are mercenaries, and as such, not subject to humanitarian considerations, let alone the protection of the Geneva convention. You will work or you will die. It is as simple as that. You . . . you arrogant *gringo cabrón*, what are you to the destiny of the brown peoples of the world? To the oppressed of the Third World? I would take great personal pleasure in blowing out your brains right here, only Captain Vorshavski would be upset over the mess in his stateroom. Now go down there and tell your men they will work or else."

"I'll not do that."

"We don't have one constructed yet, but I shall see it is the first thing prepared ashore. Then I'm going to have you put in it. The hole. You've heard of it, haven't you?"

Grim visions of Vietnam and horrible, inhuman suffering flickered in Bob Fuller's mind.

CHAPTER THREE

Night lay heavy over Barro Colorado. Mosquitoes hummed thickly in the humid air and other night insects kept up a steady background susurration. Here and there night birds cried and other creatures of the darkness emerged to seek their prey. Iron pole stanchions on weighted bases held temporary lights, their actinic brightness dimmed by undulating clouds of winged insects seeking nirvana in the immolating heat of the carbon-arc elements. Bulb lights didn't escape attention, either. Into this weird world of black-and-white cinema, prodded by the bayonets of Nicaraguan soldiers, marched the captured American Foreign Legionnaires. In the absence of Captain Bob Fuller, Lieutenant Robert Pruitt, now senior combat officer, led the column.

At once they were set to work opening crates. Among those laboring beside them, Bobby Pruitt recognized the short-sleeved shirts and knee-length trousers of French Foreign Legion uniforms. He stored the information for future usefulness. A round, solid Nicaraguan sergeant approached and rapped out in a command voice: *"Quiero tres hombres para una grande abertura de excavación."*

"Dig your own fuckin' hole," Janos Vajdar growled back.

It earned him an AK butt in the small of his back. "Do you wish to join your *Capitán* Fuller in the hole, *¿hombre?* That smart mouth will dig you one just like his."

Three big Nicaraguan noncoms stalked the line of Legionnaires, two armed with short, heavy whips. The other, a bayoneted AK slung over his shoulder, cradled three shovels. Identifying his prey, the senior stopped in front of Charlie Cunningham, and the man with the shovels dropped them and unslung his weapon. Pruitt groaned.

Cunningham was the least likely Legionnaire in his command. He'd made it through training on sheer guts and Pruitt's tolerance. Scrawny, his hips wider than his shoulders and with a receding chin, Cunningham had a body that trembled and quaked at the least threat to its well-being and, despite good food and a heavy exercise regimen, refused to fill out and provide him with even minimal stamina.

Something about Charlie's stubborn refusal to be dominated by fear or hardship had struck a responsive chord in Pruitt. He'd watched the little fellow wage his internal war, first with curiosity, then a sort of awe, and finally a grudging, horrified respect. No matter how terrified the little misfit appeared, he could always force his trembling limbs to perform a given task, whether it be stepping out of a perfectly good airplane, rappelling off a six-story tower, or futilely battering at a barracks bully. Pruitt knew what was coming.

"Peek op de shovel, peeg."

Cunningham stared six inches over the bastard's shoulder, face suddenly white and trembling fingers clutching the seams of his cammie trousers.

Pruitt glanced around at the guards with AKs shouldered at the ready. No chance to help, none at all. The only thing he could do was get himself and perhaps all of his command blown away.

Swiftly, with no warning, the deadpan commie slammed the weighted haft of his whip into Cunningham's balls. The gutsy little Legionnaire doubled over with a soul-wrenching groan and landed face first in a fetal position, hands clutching his savaged groin. The Nicaraguans alternated whipping him until he passed out and was bayoneted.

The paragon of socialist virtue stepped up to the man who stood trembling and outraged beside Cunningham's position in the line.

"Peek op de shovel, peeg."

"Pick up the goddamn shovel, Challenger." Pruitt's voice

held resignation for the present and a promise of retribution. "Our day's coming."

With deliberate reluctance, Sergeant First Class Paul Challenger stepped out of line and bent to retrieve the tool.

"Move eet, peeg." The whip wielding Red waited until the Legionnaire's hand closed on the wooden handle, then brought the lash down on Challenger's buttocks with his weight behind it.

"Yaaagh!" Shovel still in his hand, Paul spun to face his tormentor and caught the eyes of the AK-armed guard, simultaneously recalling the loud click of the weapon's selector being switched to full auto, which had frozen his guts a moment before the lash struck. Paul had the presence of mind to drop the shovel and throw his hands up. He was too terrified to take much pleasure in seeing disappointment wash over the man's face. Awareness of a small victory would come to Paul later, with the rage.

Paul and two other men went to work to construct one of the infamous torture chambers so popular with communist cadres throughout the world. When completed, they were promised, it would contain Captain Bob Fuller. During a short break, while tepid, dusty-surfaced water was brought around by complaining members of the Smithsonian contingent, Robert Pruitt took the opportunity to work his way over by the French Foreign Legionnaires.

"*Vous êtes avec la Légion étrangère?*" he asked a soldier with the shoulder tabs of an officer, using terribly accented high school French.

"*Mais oui,*" came the quick, low reply. The officer studied Bobby's camo trousers and reached his conclusion quickly. "*Vous étes avec la Légion americaine, n'est-ce pas?*"

"*Oui.* And, ah, can we speak English by any chance? I'm about to run out of French," Bobby added, a boyish grin on his face accented by dark, curly locks that hung over his forehead.

"Of course, if you wish. Did you come with this latest group of Nicaraguans?"

"Sort of. Our plane went down in the Caribbean, and the

Ivans pulled us out of the water. Somehow we got turned over to the greasers for slave labor."

"That is a shame, to be made so vulnerable and then captured. We were working for the Panamanian government. Training for their *Fuerza Defensora*. The units we dealt with revolted, I suppose you could say. Early one morning Nicaraguan soldiers came out of the jungle and we were taken in custody. They trucked us here and we came over to the island on boats this morning. Perhaps . . . now that you are here, we might plan for some sort of, ah, escape?"

Bobby let his grin spread to a relieved smile. "Exactly what I had in mind. They're gonna put our CO in the hole for refusing to allow us to work. Once he's out, we can get to work on it."

"Until then, *mon ami*."

What a vision! Lew Cutler looked across the green desk pad at the most lovely corporal he had ever seen. Nadine Richards, in her Legion uniform, stood at attention, saluting and offering a sheaf of papers.

"Corporal Richards, Legion Juliet reporting, sir."

Lew returned her salute and managed to control his voice. "Oh, yes. You're the one TDY to the King Air, right, Corporal?"

"Yes, sir. I have the service and maintenance log here, sir."

"At ease, Corporal. Better yet, take a chair," Lew said, reaching for the bound papers. "Ah, thank you."

Nadine perched on the edge of a chair close by the desk. Cutler glanced over the logged hours of flight, fueling and lubrication reports and initialed a signature block, then carefully read the crew chief's report on down time and needed maintenance. He looked up at Nadine and produced a winning smile.

"The crew chief says the starboard engine is due for a complete tear-down and overhaul." He'd said it conversationally, but it came out a question.

" I couldn't say, sir. Mark, er ah, Lieutenant McDade did mention it was running rough on warm-up lately."

"In matters like this, I've learned to trust the crew chief

over a pilot anytime. Looks like you're going to be out of a job for a while."

"We have to fly Mr. Davis back first, sir."

"Of course. Well then, after that. Ah, by the way, after you've returned these to Stinson Field, do you have any pressing duties to perform?" Lew's intense gaze filled in the unspoken part of the question.

"No, sir. That is to say, not any official duties. I'll be off," Nadine evaded.

"Colonel Watie's giving quite a bash for Rick Davis at the Hoffbrau. Perhaps you'd like to attend?" A shark couldn't have exhibited more teeth.

"I'm afraid I can't, sir. That is, I've already made a commitment." Conscious of, and sensitive about, employer-employee relations, Nadine didn't know how to react to this situation.

"Well then, perhaps next time?" Lew eased off.

One could easily interpret Nadine's obvious relief as expectation. "Oh, yes, yes, sir. That might be possible."

Lew flashed another world-class smile. "I'll hold you to that, ah . . . Nadine." The next instant he became all business. "One more signature to authorize the King Air to go to Pope AFB for major overhaul and we're in order."

Hospitals, military or otherwise, all smell the same. Disinfectant, ether, and misery are tops on the list of odors. That's how Richard Davis saw things as he entered the convalescent wing of the Legion hospital on the Cay. Inside the door he caught the faint odor of orange blossoms. Farther on, he swore he detected the scent of fresh strawberries. His puzzled look conveyed itself to his host.

"Ultrasonics," Colonel Stand Watie explained. "You're not really smelling what you think you smell. Your nerve centers are being stimulated to provide pleasing substitutes. Same with these brightly colored walls. We have a computer whiz who likes to experiment in the realm of syberitics and a chief medical officer—whom you'll meet in a moment—who doesn't believe in pus-green walls for a hospital."

This cheerful response served not to greatly enlighten

Rick, but to puzzle him more. Why all this for a military hospital? Norman Watie answered his unspoken question.

"Our recovery rate is phenomenal. Hours per man per bed on our wards are half that of any similar facility. I don't understand the hocus-pocus behind what they're doing, either, but it seems to work. Ah! Here's the recovery ward for our boys who were in Venezuela. Doc Tortora will meet us here," Colonel Watie concluded.

Someone had rigged a bedtop table tennis layout, and two patients batted the ball back and forth with vigor. Three men sat methodically squeezing handballs while they watched an old John Wayne film on television. No one called the room to attention, Rick noticed. Watie walked to the center of the ward and raised his arms above his head to attract their notice.

"Hey, guys, here's the fella who's responsible for you being here instead of out on Hero's Hill. This is Rick Davis from Second Chance."

Ragged applause and a few hearty cheers followed. Rick suddenly found his throat tight. It was like those first letters he got from cops who had their lives saved by Second Chance vests. Grinning a bit lopsidedly, he walked to where he could be seen by all.

"I, ah, well, I guess all I can say is that you are the reason I made Second Chance vests and body armor. To, ah, have you here, I mean, able to talk and get around and maybe even answer some questions. Will you do that for me?"

"Yeah." "Anytime, Rick," came the enthusiastic replies.

"Okay, okay. Some of these questions might sound dumb. They're not. First off, what did your body armor do best for you?"

Answers came quickly, with nearly all in agreement. "Shrapnel protection," one heavy infantryman summed up. "The Columbians were big on grenading and artillery. We had more shit flying around than a beehive at honey time."

"You hardly even feel the impact of an AK-47 round," another added. "A lot of the enemy had FN/FALs. They stung like a bastard, but didn't penetrate. I caught it in the shoulder when I turned sideways to reload."

"A lot of guys ragged me," a heavy machine gunner from

Bravo of the Second spoke up, "when I went down with a hit during the landing in the Orinoco campaign. Hell, you guys ought to know a bullet can't knock you down unless it dumps the guy who fired it. Simple physics. Reflexes caused me to go down, not hurt. I was simply surprised by the impact and *expected* to go down. Without that Hardcorps, I'd of been a goner, Mr. Davis."

Dr. Mike Tortora arrived then and introductions were made. He nodded in approval while his patients talked about their wounds.

"I lost an eye to a grenade fragment," one young Legionnaire spoke up. "But I didn't get a scratch on my body, and I only had a vest on."

"You wouldn't have been hurt at all, Jake, if you had a buckler," a buddy chided him.

"Look who's talkin'," Jake came back. "You got your big toe blown off by an old son of a bitch with a shotgun."

Eventually the talk wore down and the procession moved on to another ward. At the far end of the room, eyeing them balefully, Carmine Brown sat in his wheelchair. The visitors paused briefly to talk to the other inmates, then gathered around Carmine.

"How's it going today, Carmine?" Lew Cutler inquired.

"How's it go any day, Colonel?" Carmine came back from his well of self-pity.

"I have something special for you today, Carmine," Lew went on, ignoring the plea to join in his bitterness. "The Legion's very own floating pleasure palace is about to come off the ways. The job of cruise director is still being held for you."

"What good does that do? They got ramps between decks for this wheelchair?"

"There are elevators on a luxury liner," Doc Tortora put in. "Besides, what's to worry? By the time the ship's ready, you'll be walking again. Your prosthesis has been fitted, hasn't it?"

"Yeah . . . but, Doc. I—I can't use that thing. I—I'm all thumbs," Carmine concluded with a malaprop metaphor.

With a consoling farewell to Carmine, the brass departed. Lunch at the Hoffbrau was to be special. Stan McDade, Legion G-2 on TDY as base commander, had prepared sauer-braten. After they left, Carmine sourly ruminated over the proposition offered to him. Despite his determination to feel sorry for himself, ideas began to take root.

Silly damned brass, he ruminated. They think all their crummy Legionnaires care about is a tumble in the hay. What do they know? Oh, true enough for some, Carmine acknowledged. The cruds and men like himself, whose deformities make real romance a joke. Driven by the certainty of his loss, Carmine found himself speaking aloud.

"I know, an' they damn well ought to, that men need women on a romantic, noncommercial basis. This can't be no floating whorehouse. If it's gonna work, it's gotta have class."

A warm glow began to spread from his brain through his atrophying body. Yeah, after all those years with the Family, he had more than an idea or two on how to approach *that* problem. Damn betcha. It would require a little ingenuity and a lot of moxie. Sure, piece of cake, though. By God, he'd show them. He *would* take the job.

Lunch had taken a long, casual hour and a half, with generous servings of sauerbraten, red cabbage and potato pancakes, and an ocean of the best brew the SS Brewery had to offer. Back in his office, Colonel Watie patted his stretched stomach, belched comfortably, and longed for his pipe, which he'd given up as an example to troops whose lives depended on low infrared signatures on the battlefield. Watie had considered snuff or chewing, then decided he had enough bad habits. He seated himself and looked up at the light rap of the Legion sergeant major.

"What is it, Pops?"

"Admiral Cheney on the line for you, Colonel."

"Shit. You wouldn't look so glum if it was good news. I'll take it." Watie reached for the telephone as Henderson departed. "Watie. What is it, Dave?"

"We've had to call off the search, Norm. By now they would have been spotted by us or the Venezuelans, or picked up by someone. That or..."

"They're shark bait," Watie finished for him. "Dammit,

Dave. Forty-three good men. I can't . . . I *won't* write them off just yet. You can't stretch this another twenty-four hours?"

"There's a small coastal trader and two sport boats missing somewhere between Galveston and Veracruz. I haven't the manpower to search for them *and* keep this up. Besides, the budget watchers are screaming at me as it is."

"All right—all right!" Watie tried to calm his rising anger and sense of helplessness "I . . . I'll do what I can without you. Thanks, Dave. I know you've done your best.'

"Sure, Norm. But maybe not quite enough, eh? I don't blame you for thinking that. Hang in there. Maybe you'll get lucky."

"Good-bye, Dave." Watie hung up and pushed the intercom. "Pops, I want a meeting set up for Colonel Cutler and McDade."

CHAPTER FOUR

Two days following the tense meeting in which additional levels of inquiry were laid out to search for the missing Legionnaires, Lieutenant Colonel Stan McDade hurried to Colonel Stand Watie's office. While he waited in the orderly room, Colonel Watie sorted through the papers on his desk, choosing a thick report from Colonel Taylor at the Venezuelan Legion Academy in Punta de Piedras. He flipped through the pages, paused to smile glowingly at various passages, then reached the financial section and slid his calculator over. He began to punch in figures when the intercom buzzed.

"Colonel McDade to see you, sir," Pops Henderson announced.

"Send him in, Sergeant Major." Watie returned to the report, glanced up when the door opened. "Ah, Stan. Be with you in a moment."

Watie waved vaguely toward a chair. Then he continued his happy perambulations with the calculator. At last he totaled, uttered a low, happy whistle, and turned his attention to his visitor.

"We'll get to why you came here in a moment. First, you've heard the Venezuelans made an offer for the Colombian equipment we captured?' His right eyebrow crawled toward the small silver spot at the edge of his bristly hairline.

Stan stroked his white Vandyke. "Ridiculously low, from the latrine grapevine."

"Yes. Well, it was open to negotiation. Chuck called Colonel Seagraves in to head a negotiating team and got them to commit to itemized flat rates. So much per M-48, so much per FAL, ad nauseam." Watie's grin gave him the look of a huge, well-fed cat.

"Good Lord!" McDade's green eyes lit at the thought.

"From what I can see here, Stan, the Legion's financial woes are over." Watie leaned back, his expression going suddenly flat. "Lieutenant Colonel Taylor requests reassignment. He has the Academy on its feet and a good second in Major Campbell."

"Great!" Stan's reaction was suddenly tempered by his commander's pose.

Immediately relieved, Watie grinned. "I was afraid you might be reluctant to give up command."

"Hurrmph! Too damned routine and restrictive for me, thanks."

"That's what I'd hoped your reaction would be. Anxious to get back into intelligence?"

"Whatever," Stan deprecated, then shrugged massive shoulders eloquently. "That brings me to why I'm here." He waited until Watie's inquiring look gave permission to change the subject.

"Carib fishermen saw a plane go down and the survivors picked up by a freighter," Stan announced.

"How solid?" Wariness in the commander's tone indicated this was not the first false lead.

"They told their story in a Chiriqui Indian village and it filtered through. My men are searching for the fishermen now."

"Jesus! After all this time . . . Why wouldn't the freighter have reported?" Watie studied his G-2 for a moment, as though he held the answer. Then: "Stan, I have a project I'd like for you to head up. We'll discuss it later. Right now I want you to give full attention to this lead."

"Yes, sir." Stan smiled. "I've taken the liberty of having Mark file a flight plan to Great Corn Island. The U.S. still has it leased from Nicaragua and the strip will handle the King Air. From there we'll contact the Caribs."

"Lew Cutler tells me the King Air is down for an engine

overhaul, but we'll get you there. By the way, how's your number-one son taking to life as a Legionnaire, Stan?"

"Hurrmph! If you call flying that winged cathouse and chasing skirts the life of a Legionnaire, he's doing just fine." Stan grinned impishly. "Wait till I get him to sailing a canoe around the Caribbean again."

"Oops, sorry, Stan. I'm going to need him around here. I'll start a boat down to exfiltrate your party in case you run into trouble, or send a Helio Stallion if air will help."

"The boat will be fine. We shouldn't get in too much trouble before it can arrive, and it will supplement the charter job I've arranged for."

"Find those boys for me, Stan. And don't forget to look for a jeep carrier, will you?" Watie concluded with an enigmatic wink.

Lew Cutler had been rather surprised by the identity of the visitor to his office. A new Carmine Brown sat across the desk from him earnestly laying out his ideas.

"Look, Colonel, we can't have just a place for the Legionnaires to screw and gamble away their pay. The tables have to be honest. Odds alone are enough to make the house a fortune. So the casino has to be straight, no exceptions. And believe me, I know. After all those years . . . aw, never mind. Now the ladies. We can't have a bunch of bimbos on board. Good-lookin' dolls preferably, but not pros."

"How do we manage that, Carmine?" Cutler asked dryly.

"I've got a couple of ideas I'm workin' on. Like I was sayin, Colonel, the ladies have got to be world-class fluff. Oh, and we should have a few hard-core hookers along for those guys who are too dumb or shy or ugly to make out with the quality birds. Now, a good casino has a good floor show. We'll need the best. Top-name bands, soloists, headliner star performers, real socko acts."

"Who pays for all this?" Lew prompted.

"From the casino take, the markup on booze, the fares paid by ladies and the Legion guys," Carmine explained.

"You propose to *charge* the ladies for coming aboard?"

"Sure. Why not? I'll go into that later, Colonel. Next thing, the food. We'll have to have only the best quality, cooked by a top chef and well-trained kitchen staff, and served properly, with all the fancy trimmin's. Here's the big one, Colonel. The ship ought to *go* somewhere. Not just cruise in a circle outside territorial waters, but really go to, oh, say the Virgin Islands—hah! that's a kick, ain't it?—or the Bahamas. Maybe to New Orleans for Mardi Gras, that sort of thing. An' it's because of this that the good-looking broads will pay for the privilege. We make the price so low they can't resist."

"I don't know, Carmine," Lew said doubtfully, playing the devil's advocate. "It seems like quite a risk. An expensive proposition that depends on finding the right sort of women, as you outlined a minute ago." Cutler sighed heavily and rubbed his palms together. "I'll have to think on it, discuss it with Colonel Watie and the staff. One thing for certain. If we went your route, it would take a knowledgeable, dedicated, and persistent man to make it all spin."

"No worry on that account, Colonel," Carmine assured him as he rubbed vigorously at where the socket of his prosthetic leg rubbed against his stump, while he tried to puff out his chest and indicate his qualifications.

Bird noises had diminished remarkably, given over to the din of heavy construction. Two more Soviet ships had offloaded Nicaraguan troops and their equipment, including T-72 tanks and Soviet 130mm self-propelled artillery. They departed in the night. Barro Colorado began to take on the aspect of a major military installation. *Comandante de División* Juan Bautista Corrales, now reduced to assuming the lowly rank of *primer comandante* in deference to their Panamanian rebel hosts, sat at his desk. The quonset hut had gone up in astonishing time, partitions installed and individual offices furnished. Corrales harbored no grand illusions over the reason for being here.

No one was liberating anyone from anything. The power grab could be seen as only one more step toward a predetermined goal, decided upon in Moscow and acted upon as a calculated gamble. If it failed, if the United States asserted the authority granted them under the 1979 treaty, Noriega's "revolutionary government" of Panama would be deposed, he and his troops pushed out, and the canal would be in decadent Western hands again. If not, it would become a Soviet concession, to operate as they wished. Neither Panama nor Nicaragua would benefit. Yet, as President Ortega said before their departure, it did constitute a means for paying back some of the enormous sums advanced them by the Soviets. Corrales fancied himself an intellectual. And a cynic. So the whole scheme suited him. The field phone on his desk whispered insistently and a knock sounded on the door. Damn, everything seemed to happen at once since they arrived in this pest-ridden country.

"Come in," he commanded as he reached for the telephone. "¿Bueno? Primer Comandante, er, Coronel..." Whichever way he answered it he was sure as hell to have the opposite sort of party on the other end. "... Corrales. Sí. You never cease to astonish me, Ramón. Ah, momentito." To the fatigue-uniformed men who entered, he waved to chairs. "Sit down. I'll be with you in a minute." He continued on the phone. "I'm glad to hear that, Ramón. How soon will you be able to pour the footings for the long-range SAM pads? Ay, qué bueno. Keep me in touch. Adiós." He faced the trio of Panamanians.

"What can I do for you gentlemen?"

"Coronel," the most junior began. "It is my honor to introduce to you Coroneles Obrigón and Gorman of the Fuerza Defensora. That is Coronel Enrique Gonzales Gorman, senior colonel of the Fuerza, soon to be general," he added as an afterthought.

"It's my pleasure, gentlemen. As you could see coming over here, we are hard at work preparing this central control facility. I hope it's good news you bring to me?"

"That it is, Coronel Corrales," Gorman began. "We are to inform you that all is in readiness. Following your final briefing, we are in position to make the initial moves in la capital and at Colón. Then, as soon as you start waylaying ships passing through the canal, the defection of entire units of the Fuerza will be assured. Our rebel forces will control the interior within two hours, according to plan. By the time word gets out about the ships missing from the canal, Panamá and Colón will be in our hands. Pressure from outside will cause the government to fall."

Obsidian eyes glittering, Corrales fixed Gorman with a cynical smile. "And, of course, your military junta will be obliging us by picking up the pieces, *¿verdad?* My congratulations. By tomorrow, the first of our forces will be sent across to Darien and make ready to proceed in both directions on the Trans-Panama Highway toward the two entrances to the canal. Within seven days, all of our combat units will be marshaled on the highway and ready to be set in motion. You can base your plans on that timetable. Now, *señores*, will you join me in a drink? It's good Russian vodka," he added with a slight tone of derision.

"Colonel Watie," Lew Cutler announced with a perfectly straight face, "may I present General, *le Duc de Burgundy*, Reynard Touchard and Colonel Monfort d'Oumvrille of the *Légion etrangère*. Colonel d'Oumvrille commands the Second Foreign Parachute Regiment at Calvi, Corsica."

Watie's shaggy brows raised in surprise as he came to his feet and exchanged salutes. "Gentlemen, I am honored. The successors to d'Anjou have always held a special place in my interest and admiration. Please be seated. What is it brings you to the Cay?"

"We have come on a confidential matter, Monsieur Colonel," General Touchard began. "It is because of the distressing news we have received regarding the disappearance of an aircraft and a number of your men. That is the correct reading of the situation, *mais non?*"

"Right on the button," Colonel Watie responded.

"Well then," Touchard expanded, "for once it is advantageous that your American penchant for total candor has again made this unfortunate event public. For, you see . . . and I will get to the point at once, we, too, have missing men. They likewise have disappeared from contact in the area of Central America." The general shrugged.

"To be specific," Colonel Monfort took over, "a detachment of twenty-eight officers and men of the Foreign Legion were assigned on contract to the Panamanian government to help modernize their *Guardia Nacional* now that the American presence has departed. They have not made contact for the past five days with their Panamanian counterparts, nor with French or Legion liaison in Panama City. Naturally, when we learned of your loss, we became, ah, curious."

A stricken look crossed Stand Watie's face, then he brightened with enthusiasm. In three bounding strides he crossed to a large navigation chart on one wall. A long, thick finger stabbed into the Isthmus of Panama.

"There!" he declared in a booming shout. "That's where our Legionnaires have disappeared. I'll stake my life on it, by God. Only why? What in hell's going on in Panama that would account for our forty-three and your twenty-eight being all but spirited off the earth?"

Big, round Gallic shrugs answered him. "That is something we may not learn until we manage to find them," Colonel d'Oumvrille said elaborately. "Ah, that is, er, I assume that you of the American *Légion etrangère* are going to prepare and mount a search."

"You damn bet we are," a thoroughly aroused Stand Watie responded.

"Rest assured that we of the French Legion will provide any and all assistance we are able to put forth," a beaming General Touchard offered.

"Including a double manifest of my paras," Colonel d'Oumvrille promised.

"We, ah . . . ah, that is, er . . ." Watie floundered and Cutler glowered at him. "Why, sure. That's a great idea. Most generous of you. It will be an honor to serve alongside you."

General Touchard smiled and nodded his agreement.

"If you gentlemen would like, we can seal this bond with champagne," Lew Cutler offered. "Not French, I'm afraid, but guaranteed purely Legion."

After the Legion winery champagne had been consumed and arrangements were made for quarters for the visiting officers, Stand Watie looked nonplussed at his liaison man. Events had moved swiftly and his earlier elation still kept him buzzing.

"You mean . . . you mean we're gonna . . . gonna have to work with those Frogs?"

"From the way it looks, we are, if we want our men back."

"How do you mean that?"

"For starters, they're the only ones with a legit entreé to Panama, in the event we need one." Cutler grimaced. "For another, the press will crucify you and the Legion, should you refuse. For that matter, who supplies Panhards and Giats and MARS turrets . . . ?"

CHAPTER FIVE

Two hoots of the steam whistle on the *Islandia Queen* announced it was under way and ready to clear the lock gates. With regal dignity, the glittering cruise ship slid into Gatún Lake. Passengers lined the rail on all three open decks. They marveled at the riot of color presented by the myriad parrots, cockatoos, and macaws. Thick, iridescent clouds of parakeets performed an aerial ballet, which drew oohs and ahs from the women aboard. Behind their gorgeous performance lay the drab green monotony of the jungle. On the bridge, oblivious to this splendor, First Officer Jurgen stood to the right of the canal pilot, who had the con. Captain Olive had gone to his cabin to refresh himself for the morning ahead.

"Steady as she goes," Carlos Aguilar, the pilot, commanded the man at the wheel. "Stand by to make three points to starboard. There's a new sandbar developed over the other side that needs watching."

Aguilar continued to gaze intently ahead. Was it *expectantly*? Jurgen wondered. The pilot had seemed unduly agitated since they had taken him on at Colón. Jurgen hadn't known what to make of it. He was due to be relieved by the captain in twenty minutes. He'd let Captain Olive worry about the pilot, Jurgen decided. Any speculations Jurgen might have had as to cause would have fallen far short of the terrible actuality.

Today the rich *gringos* pay, Aguilar thought with heat. It couldn't be long now. He had better get ready. No, he reconsidered, it would be wiser not to show his hand too soon.

Wait until his comrades arrived. Less chance of something going wrong. In the distance he noticed some tiny specks streaking across the water. Had they put out from Barro Colorado?

First Officer Jurgen noticed a small craft also. "Who could that be, Aguilar? I thought Barro Colorado was closed because it was being used as a game preserve."

"It is," Aguilar answered curtly, displeased with the distraction.

"Could it be the scientists there had some sort of trouble?" Jurgen persisted.

"No!" The single syllable was sharp. "They would go to Gigante."

"Well then . . ."

Through the tall windows of the bridge, Carlos Aguilar could clearly see that the revolutionary flag of Nicaragua flew from a short staff above the flying bridge of the lead craft. A nasty smile creased his lips as he bent to his chart case and extracted a tiny, deadly Skorpion machine pistol. Before anyone on the bridge realized what he was about, he had inserted the magazine and racked back the bolt.

"Everyone do exactly as I say and you won't be hurt." Aguilar's English came out harsh, more accented than usual.

"What is this?" Jurgen demanded, startled out of his previous thought. He wasn't disoriented enough that he couldn't surreptitiously reach over and press the emergency signal that connected to the captain's cabin.

"It is the liberation of my fatherland," Aguilar replied in a raised voice, vibrant with fervor. "Today we strike down the puppets of the imperialistic *yanquis* and free our people from their oppression."

"What utter nonsense," Jurgen blurted. "We're a neutral ship, under Liberian registry. Put that damn thing away before someone is hurt."

Aguilar answered with a five-round burst into the overhead. An unfortunate gesture, in that it set slugs to ricocheting wildly around the bridge. A seaman manning the depth finder cried out and slumped into his seat.

"You're mad!" Jurgen shouted.

"If you mean insane, not in the least," Aguilar countered

through a wicked smirk. "I am a soldier of the New People's Panamanian Defense Order. I am a patriot."

"You're a bloody damned pirate," Captain Olive snapped from the entrance to the bridge.

"Ah! Captain. Welcome to the liberation of your ship. Pardon me. Helmsman, order all stop. Now, Captain, as I was saying. Those small craft contain soldiers of our comrades in Nicaragua. They will board and take control. Any show of resistance will meet with instant retaliation." Aguilar paused while he felt the dying vibrations on the deck plates as the mighty shafts slowed and stopped. He nodded satisfaction. "Back one-third."

"Back one-third, aye," came the reply. The engine room telegraph clanged its bells.

Aguilar counted ten. "All stop."

"All stop, aye," the helmsman repeated.

"Now, Mr. Jurgen, be so kind as to order a gangway lowered to receive boarders," Aguilar commanded coolly.

"Like hell I will!" Jurgen, angered by this little shrimp's arrogance, bellowed.

He made a grab for the open drawer of his duty desk, where a Smith & Wesson .357 Magnum lay. His fingers closed over the grip and he nearly had it out in the open when Aguilar triggered the Skorpion again. Hot little 7.62mm slugs stitched Jurgen from navel to nose. He reflexed with each impact, then slowly leaned back against the seat stanchion and folded onto the floor. A spreading pool of blood marked his passing from this world.

"I said to do as told and no one would be harmed. This *estúpido* did not obey me. Now, Captain, if you please? Lower the gangway."

In ten minutes the detachment of Nicaraguan troops had filed aboard. They went about securing the passengers, confining them to their cabins while the *Islandia Queen* got under way again. Aguilar issued orders for a course that totally differed from any Captain Olive had ever experienced in canal passages.

Skirting dangerous sandbars and treacherous narrows, the cruise ship went around the south end of Barro Colorado and turned toward the island beyond a hooked peninsula. Olive

stood helplessly by while the vicious Panamanian pilot doubled back to ram the spit of land on which men and equipment swarmed like insects. A grating, rending sound came
from the bow and everyone not secured for the jolting stop
got yanked about in a wild tangle of arms, torsos, and legs.
When the tremors ended, Aguilar picked up the public-
address microphone.

"Attention. Listen carefully. All officers and crew, except
for minimum-maintenance personnel, will line up on the
festival deck and prepare to disembark. All male passengers
will do likewise. Women passengers to remain aboard.
There will be no exceptions. The soldiers among you are
prepared to shoot to kill any who resist. The forward, port
gangway will be lowered now and disembarcation will
begin. *¡Viva la revolución!*"

Glumly, in fear of the weapons brandished by the hard-
faced, wild-eyed Nicaraguan troops, the officers and crew
assembled and left the ship. Grumbling and threatening dip-
lomatic reprisals, the male passengers followed. As they
marched along the shore, Captain Olive looked at the large
concrete structures close at hand. So new they had barely
cured, they showed dark, damp spots along the milky ex-
panse of walls and abutments. The captain suddenly recognized them as SAM missile sites. What in God's name was
happening here? Then, with a mounting dread, he realized
that their captors intended to callously use the women hostages' lives as an umbrella of safety over these monsters of
war.

Carmine Brown looked resplendent in a white dinner
jacket, snowy waist front, black satin-striped trousers and
bow tie. Seated to the right of the captain of the *L.S.S.
Poseidon,* he seemed to be enjoying himself immensely.
Carmine still used a cane to get around with his prosthetic
leg. It pained him from time to time. At least that's the way
he described it to his therapist. Actually, it pained him all the
time. He had met Captain Student, the crew, and casino staff
earlier. They had pleased him quite well.

Captain Student, with his farseeing, light blue eyes and
slight German accent, reminded Carmine of a man in a

wooly white turtle-neck sweater, dark blue trousers, and soft felt slippers, standing in the conning tower of a U-boat. Student's balding dome, fringed by a graying tonsure, suggested nearly enough age to have done so. Carmine wondered how Student would sound saying, *"Torpedos los."* His mild manner and cultured, considered way of speaking belied all that. The rest of Carmine's junior officers had been equally acceptable.

The ship's doctor had an urbane, lighthearted attitude and the twinkling, roving eyes of a letch. The purser was so obsessed with his ledgers and order forms that he might as well have been a mole. His assistant, a young, boyish, and bumbling American with an air of Dartmouth about him, was a dedicated extrovert. Well-meaning, Carmine considered, but a klutz. The assistant cruise director was a pert, perky blond little beauty who had her mind riveted upon being a success at her career, yet managed to exude so much femininity that there was no doubt as to her disdain for the more strident of her sisters, those who *demanded* acceptance without any effort at performance. The head bartender and director of food services turned out to be a witty, laid-back young black man who had been a former Air Force mess sergeant. Another plus for the staff. Yet, not all was copacetic for Carmine.

He considered the maître d' and club manager to be a San Francisco faggot with a phony French accent. He'd have to be replaced if Carmine had anything to do with hiring. Yet, he had not as yet committed to taking the position as cruise director. Even after Lew Cutler explained to him that his relationship with captain and crew would be somewhat like that of owner, rather than a subordinate to the captain. Through all this preamble to dinner, Colonels Watie and Cutler lost more patience with Carmine and his attitude than they thought they had. Now, with the remnants of rich desserts removed and demitasse and brandy in place, Lew Cutler got down to hard terms.

"I'm . . . still not sure I can . . . handle it, Colonel," Carmine told Cutler, a martyred expression on his face. "You take a ship rolling in heavy seas with this . . . this Mattel leg of mine . . ."

"Horse dung!" Lew Cutler exploded. "Are you sure you didn't lose more than a part of one leg? Something a little higher?"

Carmine colored, but refused to explode in rage. Calmly he gained control of his breathing and heart rate, then launched into a detailed explanation of what he had in mind. Colonel Watie took immediate interest and clearly showed how intrigued he'd become by the time Carmine wound down.

Discussion of the cruises went around the table. In the end, Carmine received his way. "It's agreed then," Lew Cutler said gruffly, reluctant to concede a single point. "There will be one trial cruise to the Bahamas. An ad will be placed in the D.C. papers to attract women passengers."

"Why the Washington papers?" Captain Student inquired.

"Because of the ratio of men to women in the capital," Cutler explained. "The next thing, I suppose, is to contact an advertising agency, or maybe Mark Kelly, to come up with a cleverly worded ad."

Carmine grinned in victory and handed over a folded slip of paper. "You think that ad might read like this?"

Lew Cutler opened it and read aloud from the boldface printed inscription.

SWEETHEART CRUISE!
Departing Wilmington, Delaware, Sept. 1, the *L.S.S. Poseidon* will make a two-week Cruise of the Bahamas. Single young ladies of good character are offered an all-expense passage for the remarkable bargain rate of only $650, including meals, hotel accommodations, ground transport in the islands, baggage handling, port fees, and gratuities. Lavish dining and dancing are featured aboard, along with skin diving, sailing, and glass-bottom boat tours of the reefs available at slight extra cost. For reservations, write SWEETHEART, Box 643, Old Battery Station, Charleston, South Carolina 29423.

"That, I think, will do nicely," Carmine summed up.

* * *

Primer Teniente Gabriel Ramón María Morgan liked the life he made for himself in the *Fuerza Defensora*. He was happily married now and the father of an infant girl. His father's family proudly traced its origins back to the *inglés* pirate Henry Morgan, who had boldly crossed the isthmus and sacked Panama City. There had been *Coronel* Morgans in Panama for more than a century. With a new rank structure since the days of Trujillo, he even had a chance of becoming the first General Morgan. Little had ever occurred to cause Gabriel to doubt the wisdom of pursuing a military career. Until recently, at least.

Of late, First Lieutenant Morgan had become uneasy over rumors of some sort of uprising among the senior officer corps and numbers of the troops. Such a thing could not affect his small outpost at Darién along the shore of Gatún Lake, Gabriel Morgan believed. His sergeant and the men had come from several different units. They had moved here only recently, after the American withdrawal. Gabriel Morgan liked the Americans and missed their presence.

Many times as a child he had received *propinas* from them in the form of cold soft drinks, ice cream or even *yanqui* money. Not that he had been a beggar. His family position precluded that. Simply that many socially prominent *norteños* had treated him like one of their own. Some had taken him along as a guide and companion for their children and let him go swimming in the ocean and live for weeks with their family. Gabriel didn't care much for the new attitude of his country.

"Why hate the Americans?" he had asked his superior, Captain Fiero. "They gave up the canal, didn't they?"

"Because they are . . . they are . . . *gringos*," came the captain's weak, unreasoned reply.

Secretly, Gabriel thought things much better when the Americans ran the canal. Since his boyhood in the early eighties, under Panamanian control, much of the fine equipment in docking and repair facilities had sat unused and rusting. No one knew how to repair it, and the principals of the government-owned organization that had taken over believed the monies allotted for maintenance to be more beneficial in their private Swiss accounts, rather than tied up in unpleasant reinvestment. Since then it had become worse. Or had he only grown older and more perceptive?

A knock sounded on his office door. "*¿Bueno? Entrarse.*"

Lieutenant Morgan's sergeant entered, along with a strange *Fuerza* officer, a captain. Gabriel Morgan pushed back his chair and rose to salute his superior. While still raising his hand to the side of his head, Gabriel got a startled glimpse of the captain drawing his sidearm. Before Gabriel could react, the officer shot him twice between the eyes.

Muscles already responding to the command to rise flexed and propelled Gabriel Morgan over his swivel chair and slammed him against the wall. Smiling wickedly, the captain holstered his pistol and turned to the sergeant.

"*¿Sargento?*"

"*Estoy listo, capitán.*"

"*Prosigas, por favor,*" the officer commanded.

With a growing smile of satisfaction, the sergeant ran out onto the small parade ground, shouting, "*¡Viva la revolución!*"

Monkeys made haunting, mocking sounds in the trees that surrounded the Nicaraguan army compound on Barro Colorado. Their vocal exercises seemed to goad the big, powerful-shouldered man behind the desk. *Coronel*, actually *comandante de división* in the Nicaraguan Army, Corrales had become increasingly unhappy over his enforced position, so inferior to his rightful place. As commander of a motorized rifle division, one of three in Nicaragua's crack Sovietized army, Juan Bautista Corrales enjoyed considerable influence and admiration in his homeland. Here, in this stinking jungle, forced by the unspoken rule of *machismo* to accept the pretense of lesser rank, so as not to offend . . . bah! He'd been through that far too often. Corrales looked down over the brush of his Joe Stalin mustache at the construction progress reports.

Not bad, all considering, he acknowledged. The last of the SAM sites would be ready to receive its complement of V970VK surface-to-air missiles by the next morning. If the

Panamanians he commanded in his mixed force would work as efficiently . . . Ah, well, another impossibility he could foresee not reaching fruition. What was it his KGB instructor had told the class about working with underdeveloped nations?

"Ask everything, expect nothing," that was it. At the time, Juan Corrales was not aware his classmates considered his own Nicaragua to be "underdeveloped" and laughed behind his back. Now, on the verge of being promoted to general in the *Komitet Gosudarstvennoi Bezopasnosti*, his hard shell of cynicism would prevent any hurt from such a revelation. It didn't keep him from chafing at the irony of being shackled with a Panamanian counterpart who dreamed of whole galaxies of stars on his collar tabs. Juan Bautista Corrales considered Enrique Gonzales Gorman to be a buffoon. His attention returned to the report.

They had lost seven prisoners so far. One had been bayoneted the first night the American Legionnaires came ashore. Two had been shot as examples, and the other four had died from overwork and heat prostration. Far above average, Corrales noted. He'd have that arrogant *yanqui* Fuller taken out of the hole today. Perhaps his resolve would not be so stiff. Corrales looked up as an aide rapped sharply, entered, and saluted.

"Comrade *Comandante*, the rebel radio has announced a call for a general uprising in the cities. They also inform us on the secure channel that the first of the defecting units has reported in. A First Lieutenant Morgan has been eliminated and Captain García is in charge. The troops have saluted the liberation and support the revolution."

"Good. Stripped of all the dialectic dogma, it means the usurpers are shooting the loyal officers and taking charge. Better progress than I had expected. Send for Major Chavasos."

"*Sí, Comandante*. Right away, sir."

When Umberto Chavasos arrived, Corrales wasted no time on formalities. "Umberto, send word to our reliable associates in Colón and Panama City. Tell them to have all ships seized during the next forty-eight hours. It is critical, because before long the two openings for the canal will be closed and under command of the rebel forces."

"*Inmediatamente, Jefe.*" Umberto paused, then grinned. "This is good news. Soon this *gusano* of a country will fall and we can go home.'

"Not before we do a lot of fighting, Umberto. I feel it in my bones."

CHAPTER SIX

Fresh out of the hole, Captain Bob Fuller took over his duties as head of the escape committee. During the short midday break, while their guards ate their noon meal and took a short siesta, Fuller caught up on events. His plan of resistance had been defeated by the simple expedient of the Nicaraguans beating the men until they submitted to work. The food, though of dubious origin and terrible quality, was surprisingly ample.

"Mostly beans and rice," Paul Challenger informed him. "With some occasional monkey meat or fish thrown in. Not five-star cuisine, but we manage."

"How are you doing?" Fuller asked him in an altered tone. "You and the others I designated to play along with our captors."

"Okay, I suppose. We have access to nearly every part of the base. They even used us on setting up a big radar installation on the only high spot on the island. Those who aren't in on it, and that means all of the civilians and most of the French, think we're assholes. I talked with that officer, Major Fouchet, and he said he'd done the same."

"Good thinking, Paul," Captain Fuller responded. "We'll have a meeting of the committee tonight after lights out. Pass the word, and see that Fouchet and his escape people are there."

"I'll do that, yes, sir. What are you going to do now?"

"Get in trouble again, Paul. I'm going to protest officers being forced to work, at least. It's expected, if nothing else.

No reason to let them suspect it's any different in the Legion, eh?"

When the whistles blew to resume work, Bob Fuller walked over to a Nicaraguan sergeant and demanded to see the commanding officer. He refused to do any work until he had spoken to the man in charge. It earned him a roughing up, but other officers saw it and, with Paul Challenger passing the word, likewise dropped their tools and refused to work. The Managua commies didn't have enough holes to put all of them away, that much they knew.

Confronted with this, the sergeant pushed and prodded Bob Fuller to Corrales's office. Inside, Bob's insolent and slothful manner disappeared and he reported quite properly, with a snappy salute.

Corrales laid down a thick document and scowled. "I do not take salutes from mercenary scum. What is this I hear, that you did not learn your lesson in our little confinement cell?"

Bob held the salute. "Oh, I learned my lesson, sir. The men are all working, sir. There'll be no trouble with them."

"Then what is this latest insolence?" Corrales snapped.

"No insolence, Colonel. It's only a matter of regulations, sir. According to all international agreements, officers cannot be compelled to work at forced labor. All I ask is that you see to it that the few officers among us, the pilot and co-pilot of our plane, the navigator, the French officers, Bob Pruitt, and myself, be exempted from the work force."

A soft smile of remembering the achievements of his allies changed to one of harsh cynicism. "I expected as much. It doesn't take long for the false superiority you decadent Westerners feel toward your men to exert itself. I expected you to come to this . . . though not quite so soon. Either way, your request is denied. All will labor for the 'glorious revolution,' even if it takes a whip to accomplish it."

"But, sir, that violates . . ."

"That is final. If you don't want to go into the hole again, leave it alone and forget all this nonsense. You are dismissed, Captain Fuller."

* * *

Savannah, Georgia, sweltered under palpable humidity and the late August sun. A tall, handsome man, meticulously attired in a powder-blue blazer and thin white flannel slacks, with comfortable if old-fashioned Airflight shoes, walked along the waterfront in the opposite direction to the flow of traffic. Ahead, a number of small shops that catered to the tourist trade had established themselves on a short pier. The blond, broad-shouldered gentleman turned in there and went directly to a tobacco shop that tried to capture the flavor of New England through rough-hewn cedar planks fronting its single display window and low doorway. Without pausing, he entered.

"That's it for a while," one of two men in a plain sedan at the curb declared. "He's gone to ground at the Dutchman's."

His nod indicated the large, English tavern-style sign outside the store. *Klaus Bluetermann*, it read. *Tobacconist to Gentlemen of Discrimination*.

"I don't know why we waste so much tape and our time like this," his companion complained.

"Why's that?"

"The case will never come to trial," the cynic explained. "At most we'll wind up exposing him, the CIA will take him from us, then wind up exchanging him for one of ours. Odds are it'll be two or three of ours, since he's such a big fish."

"What about all the evidence connecting him to those agents caught out on the island?"

"The Bureau didn't develop the evidence, so we won't use it. It might be contaminated, and that would embarrass the Bureau."

Inside the shop, the handsome fashion plate greeted the proprietor warmly. "Klaus, it is good to see you again. It's been too long."

"Comrade Gulyakin, how are you?" Klaus Bluetermann said enthusiastically.

"Please, Klaus, it's Albert Thurgood now," Ardaky Gulyakin, bon vivant and major in the *Komitet Gosudarstvennoi Bezopasnosti*, corrected gently.

Gulyakin had occasionally worked with the intelligence

specialist from the DDR and come to like him. Klaus was a competent professional. Perhaps now he could get somewhere against the cursed American Foreign Legion. East Germany's interest in the Legion had come to Arkady's attention only a month ago. When he learned that Klaus had been assigned as control for the DDR apparat, he decided to pool resources. So far it had proved a wise course.

"What do you have for me?" Gulyakin inquired.

"The Legion is going to operate a sin boat. They have purchased and renovated a small liner. It will have a casino, restaurants, and plenty of women to slake the lust of their mercenary killers. First sailing is September fifteenth," Klaus informed his superior.

Gulyakin's smile, white and even, flashed warmly. "That is good news. I suppose there might be some way to put it to our advantage. I'll pass it along to the Department Four people and see what use they might find for it."

"Do you have anything to send?" Klaus inquired.

"No. I put out a rather lengthy report this morning for my own station. You'll hear about it soon enough. It appears the Legion has learned how to make a profit out of their dirty little wars. It shouldn't take long to find some means of putting an end to that. The reply is to come back here," Arkady added.

"I'll be watching for it. Have you been bothered anymore by the FBI?" Bluetermann asked, changing the subject.

"Not in the least. I've detected occasional light surveillance, but nothing threatening. Two of their clowns are outside, as usual, watching me take my morning constitutional. Central informs me that the Bureau has decided to keep quiet about the whole affair on Corsair Cay."

"Good, then. Would you join me in a little drop of schnapps?" Klaus invited.

"Ah, not before noontime, thank you, Klaus. Perhaps next contact we can arrange to go to lunch?"

"That would be nice. *Auf wiedersehen.*"

"Good-bye, Klaus. If you have that schnapps, drink a toast to the early demise of the American Foreign Legion."

* * *

While Captain Bob Fuller waited for the escape committee to arrive, he took time to review his present situation. He figured he had three solid assets. Most important was Chiquili, an Indian who had formerly been an instructor at Fort Gulick's School of the Americas. Chiquili had to be the ugliest Indian anywhere, Bob reflected. Which was saying something for the natives of Central America. No denying, though, he was good.

Second to Chiquili, Bob felt he had a gold mine in an ONC K-26-2 navigational map. It might be outdated, but the terrain features remained the same. The committee had come by it from one of the civilians working at the game preserve. That brought to mind the status of the rest of the civilian prisoners.

The crews of the freighters and "love boat" might be counted upon in a pinch, he reckoned. As to the male passengers, he lumped them with the Smithsonian employees. Those he didn't trust on general principles. However, Dr. Abbott seemed a large cut above the normal knee-jerk liberals who filled such jobs, so he became the only nonmilitary member on the committee. Third of his assets, Bob rated the French Foreign Legionnaires.

Several had recently completed assignments in Chad and other hot spots and retained their keen edge, thus making them prime escape material. The remainder had been trained, had iron discipline in the face of their captors' harsh treatment, and could fight when and if the time came. And fighting might be every bit as important as an escape plan.

With five freighters and the sex ship grounded on the island, Bob had become sure that something big was under way. When it broke, he figured to get a piece of the action. That it would no doubt happen soon made it even more important to delay no longer before initiating an escape. Toward that, too, his training had conditioned him to see seven days as max for making a break before deterioration through work, malnutrition, and/or health reasons made it impossible. Whatever the case, he would have to do with what he had.

* * *

Heavy, soaking, chill rain drummed on Bob Fuller's camo canvas boonie hat. Adopted from the white hunters, who had called them Cape Horners after the turn of the century, the hat's crown could be unfolded to form a one-and-a-half-gallon bucket. Bob worked his way closer to where Sergeant Paul Challenger plied his shovel in sullen resentment. Keeping his head down, he spoke quietly, watching the guard from under his hat brim.

"How's your ass?"

"Sore, dammit."

"Skin broke?"

"Nah."

"Then pass the word to Janos: meeting at the latrine area at eighteen hundred."

Fuller didn't wait for the mandatory "Yes, sir." He was already concentrating on easing close to the next key man on his list. The captain felt the fates were smiling upon him. Had the whip lacerated his sergeant's flesh, Fuller would immediately have replaced him with second best, due to slow, erratic healing in the heat and humidity.

Bob estimated breakfast no more than an hour past. Already he was hungry. By noon, he'd satisfied himself that all the prime players would be in the game. Water cascaded into the canteen cup as he slurped noisily at his cold bean soup and ran the plan through his mind one more time, searching for loose ends.

"Over here." Paul Challenger stopped so suddenly that Corporal Janos Vajdar bumped into him when the voice hissed out of the stygian blackness of the tropical night and driving rain.

The nine shadowy figures huddled under a forest patriarch the Nicaraguans had chosen to leave as partial camouflage and to support netting that shielded from satellite observation. Circumstance made it hard to believe such things as satellites could coexist with the beasts of the evil empire.

Bob Fuller outlined the plan while the French commander translated for the benefit of his men. Dr. Tucker Abbott, sole representative of the civilian contingent, held his peace.

Two of the other men, one French and one American, represented two twelve-man diversion teams.

To Paul Challenger, the most telling point was that he had been chosen to lead the breakout. His enthusiasm for the project went downhill from there as the woefully short and primitive list of assets was read off. Jesus, he thought reverently, I'm sure going to need Your help with this.

Paul Challenger did not consider himself a religious man, nor was he a coward. The awesome responsibility of leading others into such a project with so little to work with, and so many who would pay the price of failure was intimidating.

"You've laid out the how, Captain." Paul hesitated. When?"

"This goes down on the next rainy night."

"Tomorrow?"

"If it is still raining, yes."

"If you'll be seated, Colonel Watie, I'll tell the President you're here."

"Thank you, ma'am." Watie's ears darkened, and he fumbled his briefcase in hitching up his trouser seams.

The lord and master of thirteen thousand men scattered from Corsair Cay to Zalambia to the Legion Academy in Venezuela suffered agonies of embarrassment because he couldn't recall the name of President Hunter's lovely private secretary.

Within the Legion, his ability to address the most obscure Legionnaire by name was legendary. Yet since the death of his beloved Eula, women had been so small a part of his life that even when he made an effort, there was difficulty in separating or identifying them. By God, he must be getting a phobia or something.

While the girl spoke quietly into the intercom, Watie decided he'd pay more attention to Honey . . . Honey what's-her-name. Damn, even there . . .

"The President will see you now, sir." The smile was lovely, and a little knowing, even forgiving.

"Hrumph! Yes . . . er, hrumph!" Damn, he sounded like a belligerent walrus. Definitely time to make a change, thought Watie as he admired the slim waist and flaring hips that swayed ahead of him into Hunter's office. He felt more nostalgia than actual lust.

"Colonel Norman Stand . . ."

"Norm, come in," Dalton Hunter greeted.

". . . Watie, Mr. President." Again the smile flashed as she finished her announcement and closed the door.

"Have a seat. Can I get you a drink?"

The President's effusiveness began to blink red warning lights in Watie's brain. Somewhere the fecal matter had contacted the agitator blades. He could smell it already.

CHAPTER SEVEN

As usual, Hunter poured from a decanter, which drew a knowing grin from Watie. The reason Hunter chose to use decanters was rooted in the integrity of his character, and the lack of same in the media.

Like Watie, Hunter was convinced that no one could tell a good expensive Scotch from a good *in*expensive Scotch. By decanting the stuff, he could save the taxpayers' money and at the same time ease out of the catch-22 a hostile press would make of it. Ergo, by "unbiased analysis" he was either a pretentious snob or a cheapskate that offended visitors with inferior booze.

"To fallen comrades," Hunter proposed, offering the glass. Then, hesitating at the expression on the big Indian's face, he matched the grin and they took a sip.

"I know it's anathema to you, Norm, but have you ever considered politics?" Again reading features, Hunter opted not to pursue the matter.

"Forget I asked. I . . . we have a problem, Colonel." Title as well as tone conveyed business.

"The canal, Mr. President?"

Hunter's eyebrows shot up.

"What the hell do you know about the canal?" Hunter held up a cautioning hand, then continued.

"Ships have been disappearing in the Panama Canal. In fact, every ship that entered over a two-day period failed to exit. An official inquiry of the Panamanian government resulted in an immediate coup."

Hunter hesitated, then took a deep breath.

"A flight of F-18s took heavy losses to SAM missiles, and we even lost a Big Black Bird." The last confession appeared to hurt. The CIA's fantastic snooper had been in operation since the sixties and this marked the first loss in action.

"What about the legitimate government?" Neither noticed the lack of a "sir."

"For all we know they are dead; held incommunicado at the very least. This has been very cleverly handled, Norm. The best scenario McDonald's people over at the Agency came up with indicates this is a move by Moscow to put ousted General Manuel Noriega back in power. To keep the preliminary moves secret, ship's captains at both ends of the canal were told the exit locks malfunctioned and were under repair. That prevented two-way travel until pilots sympathetic to the revolt could be put aboard to pave the way for what must have been armed boarding parties. Ship's chandleries and agents at both ends had been arrested and replaced during university-student riots that broke out at the same time, probably staged for the purpose. There are now thirty-some ships, on Gatún Lake.

"Three hours ago, I gave a partial briefing to Congress on the situation. I doubt anything coherent will come of it in the immediate future. When I left, they were talking seriously of forming an investigating committee, and already fighting over how many seats each party would get. Need I remind you which is the majority party."

Watie told him of the visiting French Legionnaires and their mutual speculations.

"We're three days into an op plan, sir."

"Better make that an operations order, Colonel Watie, with the earliest possible date."

Hunter hit a button on his desk.

"Send in Mr. McDonald please."

"Mac has the details, including satellite pictures of what appears to be a Soviet-supported invasion by Nicaragua." Hunter hesitated as the door swung open.

"Director Mr. Stanley McDonald." Again she flashed Watie the knowing smile.

There was barely time to reflect that she was making fun of him before the presence of the CIA director chased the thought from Watie's mind. A mere six feet, two hundred thirty some pounds, and with intense blue eyes set in a face like old leather under a bushy head of salt-and-pepper hair, McDonald commanded full attention in any company. It was not until the director found his own powerful hand engulfed in Watie's mighty paw that his aura began to fade.

An assistant had followed and set up the familiar easel for a briefing.

"That will be all, Chambers." Stan's voice was reminiscent of a skipper speaking over the howl of wind and wave.

"Where are we, Mr. President?"

"He's fairly well up to date, Stan. I mentioned Noriega and the satellite pictures, not their content."

"Excellent starting point, sir." Stan popped open his briefcase and spread its contents on the President's desk. "This peninsula on the southern end of Barro Colorado appears to be the focal point."

An hour later, Watie knew as much as the CIA about activities in Panama, including not only the hostage-protected SAM base, but also that the canal had been taking ships in for two days. None left. Panama City and Colón were in the hands of rebels, and it looked for all the world like the takeover of the entire Canal Zone was complete.

"We have troop ships, including the attack carriers, either standing in or already off the shores of Panama," Hunter said. "In one hour, I must present the entire situation to Congress."

"Fat lot of good that will do," Watie rumbled.

"That is precisely why you may include any resource of the combined arms of the United States into your operations order . . . short of nuclear weapons, of course."

The ancient twenty-four-foot Chris Craft trembled uncertainly when it crashed into heavy seas. Saltwater and torrential rain drenched the bridge as skipper Stan McDade wrestled the antique into the lee of Great Corn Island, then began to ride the high chop toward the pier. Damn, he was getting too old for this kind of bullshit.

Despite his own mental reservations, his crew performed sharply, and they were soon fast to the heaving pier. Stan jumped for the floating dock and barked his shin, nearly tumbling into the trough between the boat and old rubber tires that served as fenders.

"Goddamn it!" the portly skipper roared, and sailed his sodden boonie hat out over the angry waves. "Ah, shit. Stupid."

The anger was self-directed, first for renting an antique out of sheer nostalgia, second because it turned out to be another fruitless cruise, and finally because he would now have to purchase another boonie hat.

He turned and stomped toward operations while the crew tried to remain inconspicuous. Slamming through the door of the rusty quonset hut, he stopped in momentary surprise.

"Atten-hut!" bawled his first sergeant.

"At ease!" Stan bellowed back with a degree of satisfaction at the violence of the ritual, and the way it matched his present mood.

By the time the office returned to routine, Stan could dredge up a genuinely mellow smile. Lieutenant Carlyle Boyd put a serious dent in it.

"We have a scrambled ears-only on hold from Cherokee Zero-zero." Boyd rubbed the jagged blue scar on his right cheek. "Tried to reach you for the last hour."

"Ah, shit, like nearly everything else on that tub, the radio went out." He turned to the radio operator. "Patch me through, Sparks. I'll be in the office."

Fifteen minutes later, Lieutenant Colonel McDade stuck his head out the door.

"Lieutenant Boyd, if you'd join me, I have new orders for us both.

"Our guys are prisoners in Panama," Stan began as soon as the door closed behind the husky black officer. "The commander has dispatched an OV-10 to pick me up. You'll be in charge here. Watie expects our people will stage an escape, and he wants someone here to get on the horn as soon as you have our personnel in hand. He's assigned you a whole squadron of Helio Stallions to help in the search of the coast."

"Wheeooo!" whistled Boyd. "De boss am serious dis time." He dropped the Gullah act when Stan glared at him, then unfolded a chart and pointed to a spot on the coast fifty miles north of Colón.

"Do not get any closer than here with either air or sea craft. The zone is crawling with missiles. If you make a rescue, notify base by radio, get them on a Helio and to the nearest jet-capable strip. The Navy will do the rest and someone will tell you where to go from there, probably me."

Stan heaved a deep breath, then got up to pour them both a tot of Barbados.

"If, when we finish this, you'd be good enough to have someone pack the gear in my quarters and bring it to headquarters, I plan to sleep on that cot until my chariot arrives."

Static fuzzed, the tinny voice drifted in and out on the shortwave set. Lieutenant Colonel Chuck Taylor listened with an intensity that characterized his every act. This time it had more meaning than usual. If what he heard proved to be true, the world was in a deep pile of feces.

"—dicates that there is no resistance in Colón at all. Representatives of the legitimate government of Panama in that city have barricaded themselves in the Hilton Hotel. There's belie——a number of American businessmen and tourists have been caught there also. In Panama City, fighting continues in the streets, with elements of the *Fuerza Defensora de Panamá* attacking each other. Foreign tro——sently unidentified, are participating on the side of the rebels. We'll bring——ate when we can."

"Goddammit!" Chuck swore. "And here I am sitting in Punta de Piedras wet-nursing a military academy."

"Not for long," Chuck's S-2, Major Jay Solice, informed him as he entered the office. "We've got orders. You're to return to the Cay and take command of Fourth Cohort. Your assignment is to whip them into shape for an immediate operation."

"*Panama!*" Chuck responded with enthusiasm.

"More 'n likely, Chuck," Jay agreed. "I'm transferred also. I'm to be assigned to Legion G-2. So I guess it's goodbye Venezuela, hello Panama."

"You don't sound too happy, Jay."

"Happy I'm not, Chuck. Eager, I am."

Chuck Taylor eyed the short, stocky Apache Indian and let a grin spread on his face. Jay usually had a warm, friendly smile and a quick wit. Angry, he could use his hard muscles and years of skill to bring scalding pee on any aggressor. That Jay looked forward to a scrap in Panama Chuck had no doubt. And, by damn, so did he.

Music of the balalaika drifted through the room. The haunting instrument had long been favored throughout the Balkan countries, even northward to Hungary and in European Russia. It had its roots, though, in Bulgaria. Like himself, Arkady Gulyakin considered as he listened and sipped vodka. Arkady had been born Arlos Borkanin in the mountain town of Stara Zargora, and spent his childhood there. A promising boy with a quick mind and the ability to handle abstractions, he had been sent off to school in the Soviet Union and ultimately joined the KGB.

His assignment to Wet Affairs had been anticipated. Since long before Andropov, *Mokkryee Della* agents had all been Bulgarians. At the time of his appointment he had assumed a great Russian name, as did many of his colleagues. None used their own identities. Most, like himself, had used a wide variety of cover aliases to fit their assignments. It suited their Soviet masters as well. In the event of compromise or capture, Bulgarian intelligence received the blame, not the KGB, and for the simple reason that the world press never bothered to point out that *all* organs of Soviet intelligence answered to Central. Now Arkady listened to his native music and fretted.

Increased activity around Corsair Cay greatly disturbed him. Damn the cursed Legion. They couldn't be getting ready for another mission so soon, he reasoned. It could mean only one thing: the situation in Panama.

The ever-present racial and political paranoia among Soviet leadership had prevented him from knowing about the revolt in Panama until it became public. Particularly after his years of loyal service, this inherent distrust rankled. Worse, he had only just been informed by Central of the report of the KGB control aboard the Soviet freighter regarding the Legion prisoners turned over to the Nicaraguans at Barro Colorado.

Worst of all, his superiors had ordered him to stay out of Panama until the fighting ended. He badly needed a few of the Legionnaires for his own operation against the Legion. It left him in a tenuous position. With one tapered, well-manicured finger he scratched behind the ears of the large ginger cat that filled his lap.

"Ah, well, Viktor," he addressed his feline companion. "We'll have to continue on more roundabout approaches for destroying the Americans' Legion," Arkady concluded unhappily.

For the first time since losing his leg, Carmine Brown counted himself a happy man. Having submerged his self-pity, Carmine made rapid progress in his recovery. He'd become quite proficient with his prosthetic leg and responded well to physical and, of late, emotional therapy. He had also undertaken the task of interviewing hookers who answered his ad in an underground newspaper. The purpose had been to recruit thirty sisters in sin, half serving as rotating staff on his ship while the other fifteen underwent Legion Basic training. They would alternate their duty aboard the floating bordello with that of regular Legionnaires. In particular, two of the multitalented tarts had struck his fancy. Twenty-year-old twins, with whom he found great pleasure in conversing.

"You two have really made my day," Carmine told them at last. "I know we've gone over a great deal, but I'd like to sum up what you've been told so far. First off, you will be enlisted for a period of six years, like any other Legionnaires. You'll undergo combat training. Also, any clerical or administrative skills will be tested and exploited. Because of the nature of your, ah, assignment here, you will be allowed a change of duty on request, without prejudice. That includes combat service, if you so desire, though the Legion is not too hot for women on the front lines."

"Why's that?" Penny, or Patty, inquired.

"It's not some vestigial chauvinism," Carmine promptly replied, impressed at his improved vocabulary since joining the Legion. "Let me assure you of that. If you were a couple of Brunhildes, there'd be no problem. The simple fact is, most women do not train themselves from childhood to be able to hump some seventy pounds of body armor, another seventy of gear, ammo, and weapons around the battlefield. Your muscles aren't developed the same way as a man's."

"What about airplanes or those armored cars?" Patty, or Penny, asked sweetly. "We could work them, couldn't we?"

"And you might. Provided you get trained in them. The Legion puts everyone to his best use. To get back to the subject, you must pass Legion Basic and will be given specialized small-arms training. Additional branch training will depend on ability. While assigned to the *Poseidon*, you will receive daily checks for VD and weekly for drugs. Please recall that booze is *not* a drug in the Legion's book. Before you sign up, you'll have an opportunity to read the Legion Articles and learn the penalty for infractions of either rule. Now, that's all the official stuff. I, ah, have a few personal questions.

"You're twenty and twins, that's obvious. Is it true that one twin can often feel, or sense, what the other is experiencing?"

"Oh, yes," Patty and Penny chorused.

"That's what got us started in, ah, being working girls," one twin added.

Alert and suddenly aroused by the direction their conversation had taken, Carmine leaned forward and spoke through a wolfish grin. "How's that? I mean, you can tell me. As cruise director, I'm sort of your father confessor," he urged.

"Well, ah, when we were, ah, very young. Oh, eight or nine," Penny or Patty began. "We always got a, ah, tingling sensation when the other one was, ah, scratching her itch. If you know what I mean."

"I, ah, think I do," Carmine responded, a powerful erection surging in his trousers.

"Well, then, one time we got to talking about it. That led to experimenting. We found it was double the fun when we did it together. We could really have a ball when we had a friend stay over for the night. Then, along about sixth grade . . . that's right, isn't it, Penny?"

"Uh-huh," the other blond, blue-eyed lovely responded. "We were eleven."

Carmine felt more at ease now that he had cataloged the girls. Penny on his left, Patty on the right. Penny continued the story, to Carmine's erotic delight.

"I had a boyfriend who was in the seventh grade. One summer afternoon he invited me to his folks' home for a swim. We got to fooling around in the water and decided to skinny-dip. There wasn't anyone else at home, so we were safe enough. Bobby took his surfers off and I slipped out of my bikini. He was already hard as a rock and I couldn't take my eyes off it. We swam for a little while, then started wrestling in the shallow end. The next thing, we decided to get it on together."

"By then I had the hot sweats," Patty put in. "I knew something super was happening to my twin. The ol' itch like to have driven me wild."

"We got out of the pool and picked a chaise lounge for the big moment. Neither one of us had done it before, and it must have been funny to anyone else. To us it was almost a tragedy. It took the longest time before Bobby could get it in just right. When he did, it hurt like fire for a moment, then the world went crazy. We managed for about two minutes, then Bobby just let go. After a while we decided there must be more to it than that and tried again."

"It was better, I can tell you that," Patty advised. "I was on fire. I got an old E.T. doll we both used for that purpose —it had a big knob of a head and a neck a lot longer than our fingers—and set to work with it. I wasn't completely sure what Penny was into, only that it had to be fantastic. When she came home and told me, I couldn't wait to get some for myself. First chance I had, I pretended to be her and came on strong to Bobby. In no time he had me on his bed with my shorts and panties off and his cutoffs around his ankles. I guess I'd used ol' E.T. a bit more, or deeper, than Penny, 'cause there was no pain at all. It was *heaven*. Pure pleasure from the start. We really worked at it and learned how to make it last."

"Patty told me all about it and we decided to share. Bobby was ours for the next two years. After that..." Penny shrugged eloquently. "Well, we couldn't get enough. At fourteen we started taking money for what we liked and did best. Seemed sort of funny, but then . . ."

"That's, ah, that's quite a story, girls," Carmine responded in a sweat. "Tell me, which one of you gives the best head?"

"We both do," the twins said as one. "Do you want to judge for yourself?" Patty added.

"Er . . . ah, well, ah, that is . . . sure," Carmine concluded in a weak, anticipatory voice.

Interviewing, Carmine decided, could be one of his most delightful duties.

CHAPTER EIGHT

Even the poorest of calm-water sailors found himself in the small-boat program at the Cay. Every unit had suddenly been ordered to participate. Arizona Jim considered it amusing. His own platoon had been through the training already and served as instructors, along with Bravo of the Second. New consignments of Folbots, some brightly painted, though quickly redone in Legion OG, arrived weekly from the factory in Charleston.

"Looks like we're gonna fuckin' paddle our way to our next operation," Bill Kane grumbled.

"Which won't be long, from what the latrine gazette says," Jim advanced.

"Yeah. You can always tell, Jim. Staff officers are nowhere to be seen. That's a sure sign. 'Cause, what the hell, there can't be any more training they can heap on us. So we've got a go to somewhere."

"My bet's Panama," Jim confided. "We're gonna go find our missing guys."

"Could be, Jim," Bill allowed. "We've got that Basic graduation parade this afternoon. You figure any way we can duck it?"

"Hey, drill and cermonies are the backbone of the Army, Bill," Jim made mock protest.

"Not this army. Killin' the enemy's our hallmark," Bill countered.

Jim pondered on it a moment. "You're right, of course.

Even so, remember how good it felt when we reached that point? It seems like a hundred years ago now."

"You're an incurable romanticist," Bill chided.

"I also want to get our guys back," Jim told him.

"What says they didn't get lost at sea?"

"I, ah, don't feel it in my gut, that's what," the young lieutenant responded. Despite his promotion, Jim still felt closer to the enlisted men than his brother officers.

The trumpets wailed. The flat sound of kettledrums rolled across the parade ground at Corsair Cay, marking the rhythm as the graduating class passed in review. Out ahead, with their leopard skins and tall Legion eagles, the lictors marched proudly, kilts swaying. Behind the band came the graduates and their cadre. After the parade, the speeches, the announcement of the honor graduates and listing of pro-pay points earned, Colonel Stand Watie addressed them in a stern manner.

"This is a day of celebration in a time of uncertainty. Forty-three of our men are missing. It seems likely now that they are somewhere in Panama. Conditions there, considering they have not contacted us, indicate that they may be prisoners of the revolutionary junta. We intend to exercise every option open to us to get our men out. Our French brothers also have Legionnaires unaccounted for, and have offered any assistance they can provide. Together we're going to get those troops out. And we're going to do it in record time." Watie paused while the entire Legion cheered.

"Now that you have graduated from Basic, you have your second eight to look forward to. Until then, you have three days' leave, though you will not be able to leave the Cay. Following that, you will receive assignment to vacancies in the five Cohorts or to Legion support units. The time may come not long after when you may have to go to the relief of your brothers, or they to yours. When it happens, I know you will deport yourselves as true Legionnaires. That's all . . . and congratulations."

"When are we gonna kick ass in Panama, Colonel?" a voice called out from the rear of the formation.

Watie glowered, then broke into a smile. "Soon, Legionnaire, I can tell you that. Damned soon."

* * *

With a hiss like a piñon-log fire, the solid gray downpour blotted out visibility beyond a few feet on Barro Colorado. The escape committee had specified a night of heavy rain for the attempt, and only two days passed before they had their optimum conditions. Work had ended at 5:20 that afternoon because of darkness. The six escapees gathered early, along with Chiquili, in the corrugated-iron-sided latrine.

"Here are your machetes, knives, and dry rations," Bob Fuller informed them in the dark. "Check each item and store them carefully. Paul, you have the map. Guard it well. That, and Chiquili, are all you have. Chiquili has also made gourd canteens for all of you. Anything else I could say would just be bullshit." Bob took a deep breath, sighed it out. "Good luck. And get the Legion down here to kick ass."

"*Monsieur*," Captain Marcel Laroquelle spoke up in an impassioned whisper. "On the honor of d'Anjou's arm, I pledge to all of you that the *Légion étrangère* shall be in the forefront of the rescue mission."

"Thanks, Captain Laroquelle, though if it's all the same with you, I'll settle for that crazy Cherokee bastard and his wildmen from the Cay," Fuller responded, his throat tight. The Frog, by God, meant it, he knew. "Twenty minutes to the first diversion. Next time I see you, I'll buy you all a beer."

Hearts racing, the escapees waited through the next twenty minutes, ears straining for the first sounds of the disturbance. They came in a rush of excited Spanish.

"*¡Incendio! ¡Incendio! ¡Alarma! ¡Traigan aquí las bombas!*"

Fire indeed spread rapidly among barrels of hydraulic fluid, lubricating oil, and heavier grease. More shouts rose from the guards for the fire trucks and several grabbed up CO_2 extinguishers in a futile attempt to retard the flames. Nicaraguan soldiers, awakened by the shouting, ran from their barracks area, most only half dressed. Few had weapons along. The dread blaze could not be fought with bullets. Several dull explosions sounded as the more volatile of the liquids let go. Unseen in the excitement, the seven escapees slipped out of the latrine and sped through the shadowy area of the camp toward the north edge of the island.

"Allons, mes amis," Laroquelle declared as they topped a low rise and the camp disappeared from sight. "We are, as you Americans say, on our own."

Actinic white joined the orange-red glow at their backs. Lights began to come on inside the Nicaraguan compound. Fire alarms jangled at the SAM sites, and dutiful men tightly closed the heavy doors of the hastily constructed magazines. Paul halted a moment and gathered the others. When he was certain they could see his direction, he pointed.

"Over that way. There's where we'll find the native canoes. Maybe three hundred meters from here."

Rain made a gray shroud that cloaked the fleeing men in invisibility. Back at the camp, whistles shrilled and crisp orders barked on the PA system. The prisoners were being lined up even as the deluge, coupled with expert fire-fighting techniques began to get control over the blaze.

"They're going to have a roll call," Paul announced.

"Oui," Private Alexis Koropopous agreed. "They will soon discover we are gone."

"No" Paul assured him. "That's what the second diversion is all about."

Before he could elaborate, they located a string of canoes along the muddy shore and selected one. This Janos and Alexis pushed out into the lake. Everyone boarded except Paul, who set about removing any sign of their presence with a smooth board. Then he, too, climbed in. Paddles bit deeply and the canoes glided away over the rain-dimpled surface. Far behind now came the command for a roll call.

At once men began to shout and point toward the sky, running about in confusion. Several hid among the buildings and set to work with the limited materials at hand. A carefully aimed rock, hurled by a former minor-league pitcher who worked as athletic director on the cruise ship, took out a large floodlight. Another became victim of a crude slingshot. Angry orders, yelled in Spanish and English, went ignored for a long while.

After an hour of prodding and pummeling, with frequent

threats to shoot the lot, the prisoners began to assemble. Less than half stood in rigid formation while the tropical rain continued to sift through the trees. Their ranks split into wild confusion when a loud blast ripped the corner of one of the Nicaraguan barracks buildings.

"That ought to do it," Captain Bob Fuller informed Major Gaston Fouchet, the commander of the French contingent. "With this much confusion, the guys who got away should have at least twelve hours' lead over their pursuers."

"It is a good thing, *non*? My men are accustomed to jungles and to hardships. Yet, given another few days none could have chanced it. Now, in three, four days, they should reach a friendly village and get word to our headquarters."

Bob's scenario didn't contain quite so much optimism. "Depends on how soon the Beaners discover they're gone and how much importance they attach to getting them back. Could be they send a platoon out after them. Or the whole countryside could be alerted. We'll have to wait and see."

Tired after a hard day at the Pentagon, Lew Cutler returned to his hotel room at the Mayflower Hotel in Washington, D.C. He'd chosen the old establishment because of its proximity to the White House, where he was due the next morning. With meticulous care he stripped to his undershorts and hung up his uniform. He snagged the handset of the telephone and called room service.

"This is four-oh-seven. Send up a bottle of Glenlivet, ice, and soda. Make it in half an hour. Thank you."

A shower sounded even better than a good stiff drink. His chores attended to, Lew went to the bathroom and adjusted the water. He slid out of his shorts and examined the fortunately small number of scars that marked his sun-browned body. He'd picked up a couple in football at the Point. The two puckered bullet wounds came from Grenada. The rest he'd obtained courtesy of the KGB since that day he'd been assigned liaison to Hunter's Legion.

Christ! If only he'd kept his hands off Angie Willowby, he'd not have become a target for those flat-faced Slavic hit men. Too late to cry over that, he thought, resigning himself to the past. Besides, though a part of him hated to admit it, he'd come to like the Legion. Admire it, really. A finely honed fighting force he'd not mind commanding himself. So thinking, Lew stepped into the shower and let the hot water cascade over his body. His mind drifted to the day's encounter.

Even with the President's assurance of no stops, it had been like pulling teeth to get the Pentagon wizards to approve purchase of even more Folbots, or issue the quantity of anti-PAM he had requested. Napalm still had a bad name from the days of Vietnam, General Collingwood had cautioned.

"Use it judiciously," Collingwood had urged him.

"How does one 'judiciously' apply a thousand two-hundred-fifty-pound canisters of sticky, flaming death, General?" Lew had asked facetiously.

"By not using it at all," Collingwood had growled. "If we had our way, you wouldn't receive it. But . . . the President has ordered that you get what you ask for, so we've no choice."

With the tone set by that encounter, they went on to the other items on the "shopping list." By the time it ended, Lew felt like the interviewee at a session of the *Santa Hermandad*. Yep, he reflected, the Inquisition had nothing on Collingwood and Willowby. Oh, shit! That name again. Lew lathered up and settled for a solid, therapeutic sting of water on his hide. Eyes closed, the muscles began to relax and the tension lines left his face. Lew luxuriated in the pounding spray as he exposed front, back, and profiles to the pulsations. Gradually he changed the temperature until the water ran icy cold. Satisfied, he shut off the flow and toweled briskly.

Lew stepped out on the bath mat when he heard a knock at the door to his room. Room service, right on the tick, he conceded as he wrapped the large, fluffy white towel around his waist and padded barefoot to the door. He opened it to discover a little surprise bundle on his figurative doorstep in the lovely form of Angie Willowby, wife of Lieutenant General Eugene Willowby, one of his antagonists of earlier in the day.

"UH! . . ."

"Lew, honey, aren't you going to invite me in?"

"Er, ah, Angie, ah, what are you doing here? How'd you find me?"

"Later. I look like an idiot standing in this hall talking to a wet man in a towel." She pushed on past Lew and poised herself in the center of the room. "There. That's better. Close the door."

"*Angie!*" The name came out strangled. "Do you know . . . do you have any idea . . . Did you give any thought to what coming here could do to me?"

Angie pouted. "Eugene and I had a fight," she said simply. "A real knock-down, drag-out, piss bringer of a fight. He called me a whore and threw me out."

"Over *us*?" Lew demanded, his words still ripped from an occluded voice box.

"No, silly. That was a long time ago. This was, ah, some other, ah . . ."

"Some other guy?"

"Guys," Angie said in a low, contrite voice.

"Oh, shit."

"Yes, Lew, 'oh, shit.'"

"Why did you come here? How'd you know I was here at all?"

Angie moved in close, placed a small, warm hand on Lew's bare chest. "I, ah, knew you would be at the Pentagon today. I sort of called around and found out at which hotel you'd registered. Our fight was last night and, ah, well, Eugene did sort of mention your name."

Lew groaned. "In what context?" he inquired.

"He was cursing something awful over finding out about my, ah . . . and throwing things around the room. Then he said it only made matters worse that he had to face one of my former lovers the next day, so you see I knew you'd be somewhere in town."

What made you so sure it would be me? Lew wanted to prod her with the question, make her feel his own momentary sense of betrayal. Then, looking at her smooth complexion, heart-shaped face, and little-girl innocence, he relented. Her blond hair glistened in the lowering light from outside and her blue eyes became soft pools of desire. In spite of his reaction to Angie's revelation, Lew felt a tingling from the contact of her hand on his skin. A swelling movement at his groin betrayed long-suppressed emotions. Angie stepped even closer.

"Oh, Lew, baby, what can we do?"

"*We?* Where do you get that 'we' stuff?" Lew demanded, his gray eyes turned to ice.

"I don't even have a place to stay."

"Where'd you stay last night?" Lew demanded, fighting his growing sensation of raw lust.

"With my sister in Arlington," Angie's tiny voice replied.

"Can't you go there now?" Lew inquired, the long, powerful fingers of one hand combing the thick tangle of his curly, light brown hair.

"Lew . . . well . . . ah, she's on Eugene's side," Angie wailed.

An agitated motion of her slender, well-formed body dislodged the towel and it fell from Lew's waist. Angie glanced down at the rising evidence of Lew's inner mood, and she put her arms around his neck. They kissed. Cool and dispassionate at first, at least on Lew's part. Then the floodgates of memory opened and their long, torrid affair cascaded over Lew's meager defenses.

Washed away on sizzling remembrances, buoyant with an upsurge of new desire, Lew felt his resolve spin away like a fleck of foamy flotsam. Behind Angie's neck, his fingers worked away at the zipper of her dress. It parted easily and the skintight garment peeled away from creamy flesh.

Their embrace ended and Lew stepped back a pace. "My God, you haven't changed, Angie. Not one bit."

With the seductive grace of an accomplished ecdysiast, Angela Willowby shed the remainder of her clothing. For a long moment, the nude couple stood in silence and examined each other. Lew sighed heavily.

"You're as lovely as I remember, Angie. You know I could never resist that fantastic body of yours."

"Ummm. Nor I yours. Am I going to stay here tonight, my handsome stud horse?"

"I'd gladly kill regiments to keep you here," Lew responded, all the heat of their past involvement burning in his hard-muscled body.

"Then ... make love to me, Lew. Right here, right now. On the rug, on the couch, in the middle of that table. In bed and in the shower and oh, God, *everywhere!*"

Grinning, Lew wrapped strong arms around Angie and carried her to the soft white rug before the imitation fireplace at one corner of the living room of his suite. Her legs parted eagerly, and he felt the combined heat of their aroused flesh as he sought to penetrate once more the magical portal that had given so much pleasure in the past. Then a peremptory knock sounded.

"Oh, hell, room service," Lew blurted, shaking with the intensity of his arousal.

"Tell them to come back later," Angie pleaded.

"Only be a minute," Lew assured her as he rose and crossed the room.

He retrieved his towel, undid the latch, and accepted the cart, while he cleverly kept the service boy from looking beyond his broad, suntanned shoulder. He signed the tab, added an excessive tip, and hustled the teenaged attendant away with voluble thanks. Then Lew secured the door and bounded back to a panting, aching Angie.

"Oh, now, Lew honey, hurry!"

With utter abandon, Lew plunged to the depths, drawing a prolonged wail of rapture from Angie as he sank into the silken confines of her magnificent passage. Such shenanigans wouldn't do ol' Lew any good, but he couldn't stop enjoying it, he acknowledged in a whirl of euphoria.

CHAPTER NINE

Firelight flickered in reflection off the floor-to-ceiling picture window of the large, tightly built log structure. Nestled in among the pines and fir trees of the western slopes of the Adirondack Mountains in upstate New York, the two-story structure blended into the surroundings with a natural ease that belied the efforts to achieve that effect. Inside, Oriental rugs had been scattered over the smooth, highly polished hardwood floors. Before the fieldstone hearth lay a large brown bearskin. White teeth and little red eyes created a fierce mien. Soft light fell from muted lamps on the figure of a man seated comfortably in a Victorian velvet wing-back chair before the low fire.

Jason Aldridge, aka Jason Cook, John Templeton, Jacob Gold, Andrei Alandorov, and a long string of other names, wore expensive flannel trousers, a soft silk shirt, and tweed jacket with leather patches and saddle-stitch seams. He took his ease alone, as was his custom. A small rosewood spinet table beside him held a decanter of twenty-year-old brandy and a single cut-crystal glass. Soft strains of Haydn came from the concealed stereo, the laser-disc reproduction flawless. The *Requiem* provided ideal counterpoint to the mournful moan of the pines outside, barely audible within.

"Excellent," Aldridge judged aloud, addressing the large, soft-eyed hound that lay at his feet. "Now we shall have a look at the mail."

Preparatory to this small duty, a long, sensitive artist's finger pressed a flush-mounted button on the table and an electric motor hummed softly to close the heavy drapes. In even greater solitude, Aldridge selected a thin, solid silver letter opener and slit the end of a thick cream-colored envelope. From its interior he extracted a single sheet of paper of the same impeccable quality.

" 'Jason,' " Aldridge read aloud. " 'The time has come for us to again solicit your remarkably excellent services. You are well aware that our organization does not often seek outside assistance, even of such outstanding quality as yours.' "

A lie, Jason Aldridge thought cynically. They used outsiders more often than their own, particularly in this part of the world. Silently now, he read on to the conclusion. His wide, thin-lipped mouth spread in a satisfied smile as he lay the missive aside. He'd waited for this one for a long time. The money was more than adequate. The employer familiar and quite acceptable, if not his favorite. The target a considerable challenge.

Jason sipped from his Châteaux Saint Martin and smacked his lips in appreciation while he considered the commission a moment. Yes, he would do it. For this, Jason decided, he would use his marvelous new custom Sako rifle. A true masterpiece of the Finnish gunsmith's art, that one. It would do . . . nicely.

Soft and eternal, the susurration of the surf permeated even to the staff conference room. The faint, complaining shriek of the Cay's perennial gull population failed to impinge on the quiet, meaning-laden words Colonel Norman Stand Watie delivered to his staff officers.

"All stops are out this time. Lew Cutler verified that over the past two days at the Pentagon and the White House. The Legion can ask for anything in the line of support, short of nuclear weapons, and receive it. I say again, gentlemen, *anything*. Hell, before we get through with this Panamanian affair, we're gonna have us an aircraft carrier."

His electrifying statement brought murmurs from all save Sam Seagraves. Sam had been the one to plant the idea with Watie of requesting an old jeep carrier from World War II, ideal for the OV-10s, choppers, and the new Moller Merlin

200X Aerobot VTOLs Seagraves had been looking over. "God, what a plane," he had enthused to the Legion commander.

Top speed of 403 mph, with a range in excess of 1,000 miles, a 4,900 fpm rate of climb, quiet operation, computer stabilized, powered by five rotary engines, and run on automotive fuel. The little two-place mothers could take off and land vertically and had near-Stealth characteristics. Hughes Aircraft had already developed several military configurations whose performance figures were still in the top secret category. But before they got any of them, or the carrier for that matter, a lot more would need to be known. Meanwhile, much to his satisfaction, the Old Man was carrying his ideas forward.

"The drawback is that the ass-sitters in the Pentagon have finally kicked through when we have a situation where the big, fancy equipment can't be used. The SAM installation on Barro Colorado, and those at strategic military bases inside Panama, cannot be hit without considerable loss in aircraft. Further," Watie went on to explain, "those hard stands on Barro Colorado are impossible to attack from the air, due to the presence of the cruise ship and its female-passenger hostages. A flight of F-18s got blasted to hell and gone, then informed by ground control at Barro Colorado that female civilian hostages remained aboard the vessel. Nicaraguan MiGs now occupy Panamanian air bases along with the *Fuerza*'s old F-4 Phantoms. Quite sensibly from their point of view, they refuse to operate away from the antiaircraft umbrella on Barro Colorado and at the ends of the canal. Both ends of the canal are now closed to all but Soviet or Soviet-client shipping. The facilities are commanded by artillery and rebel elements of the *Fuerza Defensora*, backed by Nicaraguan troops. More are pouring in daily off the Trans-Panama Highway, including heavy armor."

"What about the *Fuerza*?" Lieutenant Colonel Andrews inquired. "Did they all go over?"

"No, Andy," Watie responded. "There're reports of fierce fighting in the interior between loyal units of the *Fuerza* and the rebel forces. That's all moot, considering that the government has dissolved, fled, and its members are in exile, either in foreign countries or trapped in the Hilton Hotel in Colón. The rebels have hoisted a red flag over the capital. Worse, the Soviet bloc nations have recognized the revolutionary government, the so-called People's Reform Movement, and have moved for a UN referendum against any aggression directed toward reinstatement of the ousted government of President Arturo Moldinado."

"Where does the U.S. government stand?" Major Rounding, the Legion armor commander inquired.

"Stan? I'll let you handle that," Watie offered.

Stan McDade rose with ponderous dignity. He tugged at his snowy Vandyke and wiggled the waxed ends of his mustache before responding. "Somewhere between a wish and a wash, I'd call it, Gordon. Half of Congress is so busy making the proper knee-jerk response and babbling about 'agrarian reform movements' they haven't bothered to learn what country they're talking about. The Senate is wavering in indecision and subjected to tremendous internal and international pressure to reopen the canal under any circumstances. Intelligence estimates indicate, and mine agree, that the Soviet Union will be handed possession of the canal as a fait accompli within thirty days unless something is done to stop it. The American media, as usual, is well established on its mental trampoline. On one hand the press is criticizing the administration for not taking decisive action in the Panama 'muddle,' as they term it, to reopen the Canal. On the other, they are also praising the 'reasonable' approach of the Soviets in putting Panama's future, and that of the Canal, in UN hands."

"That's sort of having your cake and eating it, eh?" Major Gordon Rounding observed dryly.

"Exactly, Gordon," McDade agreed. "Mobilization of large conventional military forces takes a long time and, so far, no country seems willing to take the lead in that direction. Which leaves the Foreign Legion as the only organization ready and able to take action on short notice."

"We wouldn't stand a snowball's chance alone," Lieutenant Colonel Don Beisel, the air liaison, blurted.

"True," Watie took up the briefing. "However, several nations, including the British Commonwealth, West Germany,

Chile, Brazil, and Argentina, have rushed strike-force troops to the general area. It's expected that they will follow the Legion's lead, whatever the hell that's going to be, once we commit our forces. Also, the French Foreign Legion is insisting on a piece of the action. They're sending a couple of manifests of paras, all they can spare from other area ops." Watie paused at another raised hand. "Yes, Mick? What do you have?"

Major Orenda rose and adjusted his Franklin half-glasses, then addressed the gathered officers without reference to the thick sheaf of papers in his hand. "The alternate ops plans are worked out, and I want to run them past the staff before we settle on the final scenario to go with."

Quickly Mick Orenda summarized three unworkable sea and air approaches to Barro Colorado, careful to give all strengths and weaknesses of each. Then he presented an outline which had obviously had a lot of time spent on it.

"We land at Nombre de Dios on the Caribbean coast. It's lightly defended and intelligence indicates it's outside the AA umbrella. After an air and sea assault on the town and the airport, we bring in the requisite number of those big Japanese seaplanes, and using nap of the earth and the radar shadow of Mount Salud, transport crews to clear an airstrip on the shores of Lake Madden. Next we airlift in the Legion with enough small boats for transport down the Chagres River to Lake Gatún."

"You'll never get enough equipment down that way," Major Fenner of transportation protested. "That river goes near to dry parts of the year."

"Right you are, Hank," Orenda answered the challenge, then calmed his audience with a confident smile as he pointed to the large area map. "But this is the rainy season. If we can take and hold the Madden dam, then open the spillways at the right time, there'll be enough water to handle shallow-draft boats."

"How do we get equipment from the top of the dam to river level?" demanded the transport major.

"Initially with captured trucks. Later on we'll be able to use the breakdown barges developed for the Navy SEALS to bring in enough rolling stock. We will be facing severe transport problems over the short stretch of road, since the barges are limited to deuce-and-a-halfs."

"I suppose the jet skis would be in on this?" Fenner demanded.

"Of course. They'll be our cavalry."

"I don't like the least bit of it," Fenner declared flatly. One of the staff who least liked Orenda, Fenner saw himself as the supreme tactician, though his position in transportation and the fact he'd never had a combat command might have indicated to a more sensitive man that his superior officers had yet to recognize his talent. Nevertheless Fenner knew that inventive genius did not take the place of sound tactical knowledge. He fashioned the rest of his response accordingly.

"Don't try to James Bond it, Orenda. No matter what, the rebels and the Nicaraguans are bound to have the dam heavily guarded. This way there would be considerable fighting. That would alert the main force to our intentions. It might also cause the dam to be blown, either by overzealous prosecution of the attack or by the enemy forces. That could ruin the whole canal, unseat the locks, cut new, strange channels. The Chagres, even with the floodgates open, is still a narrow river, a bottleneck where an alerted enemy would trap and annihilate us. It's entirely too risky. We have to restrict ourselves to some sort of frontal attack on Barro Colorado."

"And get the hostages killed, including our men?" Orenda snapped.

"Hostages are expendable. That's a part of Legion doctrine of battle," Fenner snarled.

"Thank you for the reminder," Orenda answered coldly. "Particularly since I'm the one who wrote that part into it. Only this time the circumstances are different. There're a lot of innocent women, some children, and a number of male cruise ship passengers involved. The Legionnaires, even the French, know what to expect. The others don't. We have to come up with something that at least offers a fifty-fifty chance. Otherwise the press will crucify us."

Watie let the debate run for another fifteen minutes, then called the meeting back to order. "Gentlemen, I've listened closely to all proponents and their solutions. To my way of thinking, there's only one sensible way in. We'll take the risk it represents, but we *will* take the Madden dam and strike directly into the enemy's vitals. What's the term? The soft underbelly. God grant us no Monte Casino. . . . We have the general plan; I want the details completed by fifteen hundred tomorrow. That's all. You are dismissed."

Excitement rustled through the barracks area of each Cohort. Bravo Century of the Second reached a particular state of nervous agitation. The word had gone out only the previous day. Like all five Cohorts, theirs had received sixty allotments for two-week berths on the casino ship for a cruise to the Bahamas. The lucky three hundred would be drawn from Zalambian vets only. Bravo Deuce had the most of these, so competition became fierce despite the fact the ten lucky ones would be drawn by lot.

"Look, everybody has a fair chance," as Bill Kane put it. "An' the guys whose numbers come up might be willing to use them for stakes in a crap game or at poker. If so, that increases the chances for some of the others. Nothin's final until someone steps up the gangplank."

"Aw, don't be stupid, Sergeant," one of his squad complained back. "Word is there's two hundred eighty-five career broads from D.C. gonna be on board, along with fifteen female Legionnaires—volunteers working the cruise to see what it's like. You think anybody in his right mind would risk losin' a chance at something like that?"

"Would anyone in his right mind join the Legion?" Bill quipped back. "Every one of us is a gambler of sorts, right? Even Carmine Brown, the cruise director—used to be in my squad back in Zalambia, by the way—has set up a sort of game of chance on this cruise, outside the casino I mean. Every Legionnaire on board puts up ten bucks. That's three thousand large, you get me? The winner of the pool is the one who can identify the Legionnaires from the career girls, with smaller cash payoffs to second- and third-place winners, too. Now, if that ain't a gamble, you tell me what is?"

"What are we sittin' around here arguin' about?" another Legionnaire inquired in a tired tone. "The quaffin' SS is holdin' the drawing at the Hoffbrau in half an hour. Let's go."

From Captain Harshman to the lowliest replacement, Private Leonard Goldman, the entire Second streamed from the barracks and walked to the area around the Beyerisher Hoffbrau. There the eager troopers met with their brothers from the other Cohorts, all of whom awaited the results. Only representatives of each Century were allowed inside. The Second had chosen Lieutenant Jim Levin as the man most trusted. Amid shouts of encouragement, he started for the building.

Captain Jason Black of Alpha First joined him at the door. "Jim, you're looking great," he said sincerely.

"Thanks, Jase. I'm getting settled in, for sure," Jim answered.

Despite combat in two stiff campaigns, to most people Arizona Jim still looked like a skinny Jewish kid from Scottsdale, Arizona, which he freely acknowledged he had been when he joined up. His experiences had told, though, Jason Black observed, and a few white hairs had begun to make a regular appearance at his temples. Jim walked with a confident swagger and had learned how to command both obedience and respect. He wished Stony Black good luck and conveyed the faith the men had in his ability to draw the names of the most deserving. Black and Jim entered and found a table. Almost at once, two brown bottles appeared beside their hands, with frosty mugs to follow. Sam Seagraves cut the music and stepped to a spotlighted corner of the bar. An uneasy quiet held sway over those inside.

By contrast, out on the grounds surrounding the popular beer hall, a party atmosphere prevailed. Service carts made the rounds, dispensing Stan and Sam's famous beverage at the bargain price of a dollar for a half-liter bottle. Business was noticeably brisk. At last the awaited moment arrived and a hush descended. None could hear, in spite of strained ears, the names called off inside. All could speculate. Then a loud whoop sounded through the open door.

Lieutenant Jim Levin appeared there, gesturing wildly. "Hey, Charlie! Charlie Smith, where are you?"

Grinning broadly, Charlie Smith, now platoon sergeant of

fourth platoon, Bravo Second, stepped forward. "Hot damn! You mean I got one?"

"Right, you lucky dog. If only. . ." Arizona Jim let it hang, and walked back inside.

Time went tensely on while more names came from the huge wire basket. Only five remained at last, and the odds became incredible. *If only.* The words haunted Jim Levin. A few seconds later, Arizona Jim needed no prompting to cut loose with a horrendous Apache war cry. "I got one!" he shouted on the end of his bellow. "I don't believe it, but *I got one!*"

CHAPTER TEN

Far from being a group one would choose to argue with, the President's cabinet presented a formidable phalanx in the Oval Office. Outside birds sang, a dog barked in hysterical joy, and little Tommy Hunter, the President's son, climbed a tree on the White House lawn, to the horror of the Secret Service agent assigned to the boy. Inside, Tommy's father faced a far more serious challenge on the dark blue-green sea-swirl of carpet. With a snort of impatience, Dalton Hunter rose from his desk, the big rosewood one Franklin Roosevelt had favored, and stalked to a collection of maps on a fold-up stand. He threw back the dark red cover with its white letters that spelled TOP SECRET in large, bold characters.

"Gentlemen, I fail to see your point," the President challenged.

"It's really quite simple," Harlan Balfore, the secretary of state, said in his uncomfortably familiar voice that flirted on the edge of a simper. "All you have to do is look."

"I'm aware of your disapproval, Harlan. What I'm asking for is an opinion from the remainder of my cabinet, particularly you, Josh."

Admiral Josh Colton, chairman of the joint chiefs of staff, left his chair also and took a careful look at the exposed map. "This is Lake Madden? And the dam we are concerned with?"

"Right, Admiral," Harlan Balfore interrupted before the President could make any response. "That dam was built and paid for with American money. Taxpayer money. It's in the best interests of the United States to see that nothing, not any sort of damage, happens to Madden dam."

Josh Colton cut Harlan Balfore a disgusted look. "Don't you think it is of even greater importance to get the canal out of the hands of communist invaders from Nicaragua and the homegrown Reds in Panama?"

"There's no evidence of foreign intervention in the Panamanian upheaval. It's certainly not communist inspired or controlled." Balfore's snippy voice casually dismissed the admiral's remarks.

Admiral Colton glanced apprehensively at the President. "Bull—shit, Mr. Secretary. If you believe that, then you must still have a thing for the tooth fairy and the Easter bunny. Where do you get such astonishing news?"

Harlan Balfore pursed primrose lips into a show of distaste before deigning to reply. "From the most reliable of sources, I guarantee you. Foreign Secretary Sakharovsky has assured me that there is no Soviet involvement in the overthrow in Panama. It is the work of an agrarian reform movement among the peasants and sympathizing elements of the *Fuerza Defensora*. Any reports of foreign intervention, Sakharovsky informed me, are sensationalist inventions of the ratings-hungry media, or of bored espionage agents seeking a little attention."

Josh Colton produced a thin line of frigid smile. Frost coated the edges of his words. "I presume you mean good old Alexandr Mikhailovich Sakharovsky?"

"Why, of course. The man who replaced Litvanov as foreign secretary. I spoke with him in Moscow via satellite only an hour ago."

"The *same* Alexandr Mikhailovich Sakharovsky," Josh bored in, noting an approving grin forming on Dalton Hunter's lips, "who has, since 'sixty-five been a member of the First Chief Directorate of the *Komitet Gosudarstvennoi Bezopasnosti*? The former foreign department of the KGB? Who, since Andropov, has been first chief of Department Five, including *dezinformatsaya*? That Sakharovsky?"

Balfore spluttered. "Th-That's a—a cheap shot, sensationalist move, Admiral. You're making something out of nothing. The man's former bureaucratic achievements, of which I was of course aware, have nothing to do with his present position in government."

"Sure. Like there's no connection between sheep disappearing from the flock when there're coyotes around," Admiral Colton scornfully answered him. "When are you going to awaken to the fact the Soviets are our *enemy*? We wouldn't need to consider risky plans like this if the pinko politicians would face that and remember it's the people of this country they're supposed to represent, not some amorphous Marxist 'whole.' Hell, we wouldn't even need a Foreign Legion if you striped-pants schmucks would start telling the Russians to fuck off now and then instead of falling on your knees to kiss their asses." A stricken look suddenly crossed the admiral's face, and he turned to the President, mindful of Hunter's feelings about profanity. "I'm sorry, Mr. President, I'm afraid I let my personal feelings intrude. Forgive my language if you will, please, and my unwarranted attack on a fellow cabinet member."

Instead of the thunderous scowl Josh Colton expected, the President still grinned broadly. "No apologies needed, Josh. You spoke your mind. Well and good. I want everyone here to do the same. Then we'll call in Colonel Watie and inform him of our thinking. That way he can plan effectively, and hopefully, without dissension."

"I've stated the Soviet position," Balfore said with finality. "In light of the critical condition in Panama, I feel it is a foolhardy and even dangerous proposition to allow the Foreign Legion to go muddling around in there for no purpose but to rescue an insignificant number of their personnel."

That brought immediate ire from the entire cabinet. For twenty minutes the discussion ranged over the possibilities and alternatives relating to the operations plan put forward by Colonel Watie. Often sharp, the comments struck home as the President listened. At last a consensus was achieved. As a group, the cabinet expressed the same objections as the Legion staff. Dalton Hunter listened quietly, then summoned Colonel Watie.

"Sit down, Norm. We've been going over your op plan. What it comes down to is one uncertainty. I'll warn you, it's a big one. It has to do with the Madden dam. There are some in the cabinet who still vehemently oppose any direction of attack that could bring possible harm to the canal and to that dam. The majority, though, agree with me. All the same, Norm, if you fail in any particular and cause the Madden dam to be blown, with the resultant damage to the locks or canal in general, there's nothing that I can do to save the Legion from a vengeful world."

"I understand that, Mr. President. I thought it was the Legion's job to take the heat off the nation and its government, which makes us the logical choice to do something about securing the canal and getting back our own boys. We intend to do it in the best way possible, with the least damage to the man-made objects in our path."

"Well then, it goes without saying that this is to remain under the strictest security. Nothing, absolutely nothing, is to be said about the proposed strike into Panama. No leaks, no advance whispers, no friendly words of advice to good friends like A. M. Sakharovsky." The President paused a moment, his eyes shifting gaze to again take in Harlan Balfore. "I'm, ah, tempted to have certain people placed under house arrest and held incommunicado until the operation is completed in order to prevent any leaks," Hunter said speculatively.

Stand Watie saw the direction of the President's gaze. The secretary of state, eh? He'd been listening with an intensity unusual in the striped-britches bunch. Colonel Watie rose and motioned the President to follow him. They stopped, facing Harlan Balfore.

"I quite agree with the highest security classification for this operation, Mr. President," Watie began, showing a bland smile to Balfore. "And I sympathize with you regarding internal leaks. I think I can save you some trouble on that account." Watie's gaze shifted, to bore directly into the gimlet eyes of Secretary Balfore.

"Oh? How's that?"

"If anyone does provide a leak . . . and it costs the life of one single Legionnaire more than anticipated, I'll come back here, take the leaking bastard by the throat, cut off his balls, and feed them to him. Then I'll personally skin him alive, a square inch at a time, making certain it takes a long, long time. Then I'll feed what's left to the ants."

To no one's surprise, Harlan Balfore broke out in a sweat and asked to be excused. Before he departed, he turned back to the room and addressed everyone in general.

"I've decided to take advantage of an offer Dalton made me some time back, to make use of one of the communications-blacked-out executive retreats. I feel that a few weeks there will rejuvenate my outlook and improve the quality of State Department decisions in the future. I'd like to ask, Dalton, if you will, to provide me with a suitable Secret Service guard detail to insure my privacy."

"I'm delighted you've decided to take advantage of one of the retreats, Harlan. I know you'll benefit greatly from the experience. Although, at such a critical time," Dalton Hunter went on, without any trace of sarcasm, "we'll be hard-pressed to make do without your advice. Ah, well, I suppose your assistant will have access to anything you might consider critical. We can call on him. So, off you go. Have a nice trip."

Stand Watie shook his head after Balfore's departure. "If *I* ran the camp he chooses, he wouldn't come back at all."

"They're operated by the National Park Service, Norm," the President chided, "not the CIA."

"Yeah," Stan McDonald inserted with a heavy sigh as he walked up to them. "More's a pity."

Paul Challenger sweated bucketfuls. It might as well be blood, he considered light-headedly. The sickly sweet growth-within-rot smell of the low-canopied, oppressively humid jungle drew heavily upon him, sapped his strength and reason. He knew Captain Bob Fuller had chosen him to lead the escape because of his time in the Navy, confident Paul would be able to put his maritime knowledge to use when the escapees reached the coast. The captain should have picked someone who thrived on jungles, Paul reasoned, because the program called for them to first *get* to the coast before his expertise could be employed. Without Chi-quili, Paul acknowledged, they'd have been up a well-

known creek without a paddle on more than one occasion so
far.

Their route from Barro Colorado to the fishing village of
Cocel del Norte, where there was also an airstrip, could not
be traversed in a straight line. Left to their own devices,
Paul surmised, they would have fallen into the hands of the
Panamanian rebels long before now. The reason for this
course was simple. Paul and his group would purchase or
steal a boat, then sail due north until they ran into one of the
Colombian-held islands off the coast of Nicaragua. There
they could find a radio and contact the Cay. As a secondary
means of spreading the word fast, Captain Laroquelle of the
French Foreign Legion, a rated pilot in addition to being the
executive officer of the advisory group, would make a separate attempt by taking a plane from Cocel del Norte. That
was the grand plan and so far they'd been lucky.

Paul estimated they had made better than twenty-five
klicks, with only one brief brush with search parties. At that
rate, they should cover the remaining thirty to thirty-five
kilometers in a day and a half. If their luck held, Paul
thought hopefully. With Chiquili on point, Paul felt confident they had avoided all pursuit. Relaxed, Paul munched on
the contents of a sardine can, which he dropped when the
silent Indian point man faded into the jungle an instant before the sharp rattle of FN/FAL fire.

"Ambush!" Paul sang out, the splatter of sardines and to-
mato sauce drawing a division of ants to a spot near his feet.

Before he or any of the others could react to the hidden
attack, Paul saw Heinrich Shemmel, one of the French Foreign Legionnaires, stumble, then twist grotesquely and fall
to the thick humus mat of the jungle floor. In the next moment all of the remaining escapees disappeared into the un-
dergrowth.

"Oye, Sargento, aca hay un gringo muerto."

"¡Callarse! I don't care if you have a dead *gringo* there,
keep quiet or we'll have a dead *soldado* over there," the
rebel *Fuerza* sergeant advised.

"Where have they gone?" another ill-trained *Fuerza* soldier inquired aloud, giving away his position.

"*¿Quién sabe?*" his friend, the light machine gunner replied from close by.

A compressed puff of air sounded from nearby. Almost instantly, the machine gunner felt a sharp sting in his throat and slapped at the expected mosquito to find instead the long, thin shaft of a blowgun dart. His eyes bulged in horror and he made an attempt to rise and run from this terror of his childhood dreams. Already his legs would not cooperate and he made only three steps before he dropped to his knees.

"*¡Dios mio!* I've been poisoned! *¡Una flecha de veneno!*" he wailed in a sobbing voice. Then, looking about as though to pinpoint his killer, he fell face first into eternity.

Eyes wide, the frightened soldier watched his friend die, then began to quake when he heard the solid chunk of a machete blade, a common sound from his childhood. Only this time, he knew, it was the neck of a man, not a chicken, being severed. A plethora of blood droplets pattered like rain off to the rookie's left.

In a rush, at sight of a huge black man with a machete running straight at him, his nerve gave. "*¡Salva me, mi Dios!*" he shrieked and ran out onto the trail.

There a tall, blond *gringo* looked at him a brief instant before cleaving his head from crown to neck with a powerful stroke of an axe. Paul Challenger grunted as he extricated the wide, razor-edged blade from the corpse's skull, then faded back into the jungle. From across the trail, a tearing crackle of full-auto fire shredded leaves and twigs above Paul's head. Back in the direction they had come from came the tromping of feet which should have been the closing of the ambush trap. Paul held the FN/FAL NATO rifle comfortably and brought it to his shoulder as the first of the *Fuerza* pair stumbled into the open, mouth agape at the sight of their assistant squad leader lying on the trail with his head split lengthwise.

Paul shot him before he could convey his surprise to his companion. The second of the *Fuerza* ambushers had his head go sailing backward when he encountered a masterful machete stroke from Janos Vajdar. A shrill scream followed from the forward semicircle of the ambush and then silence.

"Looks like we got 'em all," Paul observed as he checked the immediate area. "Must have been only a squad."

"The sergeant has some papers on him," Private Alexis Koropopous announced in French.

"Bring them here," Paul requested when Captain Laroquelle translated. Paul read the Spanish easily. "Ummmm. It seems there's some sort of all-points bulletin out on us. We're big time to the rebels and the Nicaraguan Beaners. From here on it's gonna get tight. At least we're all nicely armed with these FN/FALs, courtesy of the revolt. We'd better make tracks. Those shots might bring more little brown men with a big hate for us."

Carmine Brown thought of himself as one happy man. Based on applications already processed, he wound up with more gals trying to book the cruise than he had berths. In fact, he had already started a waiting list for the next cruise opportunity. The Legionnaire volunteers could wait for another run. The first and most important to Carmine would be all paying ladies. How could the brass object to that? Best yet, he'd discovered his handicap to be an asset with many of the young applicants. Witness the nude lovely who presently kissed his stump while doing delightful things with her hand farther up.

Carmine and his present love occupied the bed in his spacious cabin aboard the *L.S.S. Poseidon*, which rose and fell with a slight rolling wallow in the troughs of the Atlantic some sixty-five miles out to sea. Remarkable tingling sensations came from his missing leg while Luanna's soft, warm, moist hand encircled his rigid maleness and stroked it with an excellence unrivaled by all save Theresa Maria LoCarlo back in seventh grade. Wow! Had she been good. Ten smooth, hard strokes and Theresa had had Carmine coming all over the place.

It had been in the front row of the balcony of the Rialto Theater in Brooklyn, and some of the dumb little kids down below must have thought it was raining through the roof. Terri had giggled and Carmine joined in, her nimble fingers making sure he never even went soft. Then she started giving him fantastic head.

No, that was Luanna giving him head. "Oh, wow, and double wow! Step aside Miss Terri Maria LoCarlo," Carmine declared with solemn sincerity, unaware he spoke aloud. "You were good, but nowhere like this."

"Mummmph—unggg?" Luana inquired.

"Wha—?"

"Whoof Tar-Mar?" Luanna asked around the bulging red tip of Carmine's maleness.

"A little girl who gave good head . . . fifteen years ago in Brooklyn."

Luanna came up for air, her golden hair swaying in sweet waves around her pixie face. "Fifteen years ago, I was a little girl in Wichita, Kansas, and *I* gave good head."

"You still do," Carmine complimented her sincerely. "But fifteen years ago, you couldn't have been a day over eight."

"So? I still gave good head. My older brother taught me."

"Unnng!" It was Carmine's turn to be shocked. "Uh, less talk and more action, baby, or I'll toss you to the sharks," he quipped to cover his embarrassment.

"Okay, sweetie-pie. I'm all yours," Luanna answered enthusiastically as she bent low over Carmine's upthrust organ.

This could be terribly nervous-making, Carmine considered, with plenty of moral and philosophical questions he'd have to work out before things went much farther. Like the relationship of this to his wife of record, daughter of Don Fazzio Carpella. Also whether or not it could be considered "normal" for women to be attracted to a handicap. As it stood, he believed lovely little Luanna would give his stump a blow job if he asked for it.

Assuming that such behavior was not normal and healthy, could he consider himself the proper person to become his, er, sister's keeper? Would he be morally strong enough to cut them off?

Right now, Carmine found himself determined to lie back and enjoy, writhing under the magical lips of fair, unfreckled Luanna, while steaming for the Cay to pick up his lucky Legionnaires for the cruise.

CHAPTER ELEVEN

From the dark blue of its broad stretches, the Atlantic splintered into a dozen subtle shades of pastel azure to near Kelly green, then into white-churned chartreuse as its waves broke on rocks and ran over sandy shallows around the pair of islands some thirty miles off the coast of North America. Corsair and Cat cays far from represented a barrier to the mighty ocean, yet managed to disrupt its serene cobalt sameness. Seen from the air, the effect was remarkable, steadying, a promise of land to come.

When the big transports swung parallel with the islands for a downwind leg, similar impressions filled the mind of Captain Antoine Redoux of the *Légion étrangère*. The French rondels on the wings and fuselages of the two aircraft looked like red-white-and-blue bull's-eye targets. They'd come nearly half a world away from Corsica to fight for their own and the American Legionnaires, with still farther to go. Yet, how nice it would be to settle on this attractive island, lean back, relax, and let the rest of the world go by. It seemed so uniformly green, brown, and shadowy, where were the Americans' training areas? An indicator light on the forward bulkhead flashed red and Captain Redoux took his seat and strapped in for the landing. Idly he wondered what he would find below.

Colonel Stand Watie and his staff stood in a roughly rectangular formation to welcome their French counterparts. Beyond the far end of Stinson Field they heard the drone of powerful engines, and the small specks resolved into fat-bellied aircraft. The cruciform objects lowered in the air, landing gear extended like the questing talons of predatory birds. They touched down with graceful ease and lost speed rapidly. Under direction from the tower, they turned left onto a crossway and taxied toward the northwest ramp. There they halted and disgorged their passengers.

"Staff . . . at-ten–tion!" Gordon Rounding, acting XO called out as the first French officer's foot touched ground.

While the rank and file formed into cohesive units, the block of five officers advanced to where the Legion staff stood rigidly at attention. There the senior, Captain Redoux, produced a sharp, parade ground salute. Stand Watie returned it.

"Three Company, Second Foreign Parachute Regiment, *la Légion étrangère* has arrived as ordered, sir," Redoux rapped out in Gallic-accented English. "I am Captain Antoine Redoux, commanding."

"Welcome to Corsair Cay, Captain Redoux," Colonel Watie responded, extending his huge paw, which entirely engulfed the smaller man's hand.

Redoux looked up at the broad, dark face of the American commander and pumped his hand firmly, wondering if he'd ever get his back. "I suppose I should say that like Lafayette, we are here."

Watie chuckled, a sound Redoux compared to the grinding of gravel. "I'm hardly a George Washington, but the sentiment is apt. We've had quarters prepared. Unfortunately it's a tent city. All barracks space is taken by our own men. It'll be comfortable enough. There's even a cantina of sorts for as long as you'll be here. We're loading transport ships in the morning. 'Operation Waterway' is on. You'll be leaving right away also for Cartagena to prepare for an assault landing. The destination will be given later. Meanwhile, make yourselves at home."

Two hundred ninety-nine tense, eager faces waited outside the headquarters building on Corsair Cay. The three hundredth unhappy Legionnaire, Arizona Jim, stood at ease in front of Colonel Stand Watie's desk. He had presented himself as a spokesman for the three hundred Zalambian

veterans chosen by lot to take the test cruise on the *L.S.S.
Poseidon* to the Bahamas. Now that they had received alert
orders and were expected to be packing their gear, their disappointment had turned to bitter resentment. Not until Jim,
one of only two commissioned officers among the lucky
winners, volunteered to act as spokesman did they cool off
and stop making dark threats. He spoke passionately and
with logic and waited for the final result.

"You spoke most eloquently, Lieutenant Levin. There was
fire and conviction in your words," Stand Watie informed
him sincerely. "I was moved by them. Unfortunately, I
wasn't moved enough. There're forty-three of our comrades
out there somewhere, we believe on Barro Colorado in the
Canal Zone, and we're by God going to their rescue. To do
it we need every man with combat experience, everyone familiar with their faces and used to moving around in jungle.
Which means precisely the sort that constitute the three
hundred lucky participants in the cruise." Watie assumed a
momentary hangdog attitude. "Allowing the drawing to be
held at all was an unforgivable oversight on my part."

"Yes, but, sir, Carmine is off the Cay, ready to load the
vacationers. And we're supposed to be packing field gear.
Instead of a Labor Day cruise, we're getting ready for a
Labor Day assault. The men are a little more than disap-
pointed over it."

"I know, and I'm sorry. That's all I can say," Watie responded as he reached for a paper on his desk, a gesture of
polite dismissal.

"Think about the women, too, sir," Jim began on a new
tack. "They took that cruise to meet men and have a good
time. They're going to feel mighty let down. Perhaps even
cheated. They didn't expect a cruise to the Isle of Lesbos."

Watie scowled, then his expression brightened and he
reached for the telephone handset. "You've a point there,
Levin. A most valid one. If we want this to work in the
future, we've got to make sure the girls are happy now and
always. Ah," Watie said into the receiver when it squawked.
"Get me the President, please." His finger traced down one
of the pages of a red leather-bound volume. "This is Mule

". . . Lantern," he announced, giving the scrambler code for the day and hour.

That would do it, Jim thought excitedly. The President would authorize leaving behind the three hundred so that the first cruise could be a success. So long as the girls went away talking about how good their trip had been, future cruises would be assured. Also, the horny three hundred winners would be more than ready to satisfy their needs. Remembering the girls had been a good idea.

"Mr. President, this is Norm Watie. We've a little problem that's developed here in regard to the operation in Panama." Quickly Watie explained, ending with a summary of Arizona Jim's observations about disappointing the girls.

"So you see, Mr. President, we have to rectify that somehow."

"You absolutely must have these men for the operation? Well then, how about substitutes? Get someone else to go along and keep the girls happy."

"Such as, sir?" He listened as Hunter told him. "I'll be damned. Whatever you say, sir. We'll do it, sir. Good-bye, Mr. President." Watie turned to Jim. "The problem's solved. Carmine and his floating bordello will get under way at once and head for Virginia. The President's authorizing the use of three hundred Marines from Quantico. Not to take your places in combat, but on that ship."

Jim paled and his mouth gaped. For a moment he tried to form words, then took a deep breath and gulped against a dry throat. "But, sir!" he blurted. Ah, well, he sighed, finis to any sympathy-for-the-girls ploy. Hell, Jim suddenly laughed at himself. He hadn't known it *was* a ploy until the jealousy hit him over the Marines taking their places.

"Yes, sir. Very good, sir. I'm glad the problem was taken care of satisfactorily, sir. By your leave, sir, I'll . . . return to . . . my quarters and . . . finish packing."

"Look at all those sons of bitches," Legionnaire Private Norbert Settles whispered to Paul Challenger. "How do we get past them?"

"We take the long way around," Paul informed him.

When they returned to the others, a quiet council was

held. Paul outlined the platoon-strength roadblock and two large patrols that stood between them and Cocel del Norte. He concluded with the really bad news.

"That means we're in for at least a fifteen-klick detour. I know we're out of food, and all the fresh water is in a single canteen. We can't shoot game or it will attract someone to where we are. Any delay could be a disaster. Yet, what choice have we? It's that or try to shoot it out with a force ten times our size."

Alexis Koropopous smiled thinly. "I am no John Wayne. Let us use judgment and caution here."

"I'm of like mind," Marcel Laroquelle agreed.

"Then we shove off to the west, into deeper jungle, where the patrols won't expect to find us," Paul announced with finality. His stomach chose then to growl with hunger, as though possessed of a separate understanding.

Arkady Gulyakin sat at his desk in the Savannah safe house, despondently shuffling papers like a fourth-year cadet assigned to Central for the summer. He had put in motion the three stratagems he felt would stand some chance of completion. Although aimed at individuals rather than the organization as a whole, the success of any two of the three should spell an end to the Legion as a cohesive fighting unit. Only time would tell. Although nominally head of each of the missions, Arkady had to content himself with keeping hands off and waiting for reports. Distractedly he lighted another cigarette.

"Stoy tot! Vee brosseel kooreet'!" Arkady snapped aloud, smashing out the burning coal.

"Stop what, Comrade Gulyakin?" Feodor Dobredyn inquired, entering in a rush. "What have you given up?"

Was that a smug smirk on Feodor's lips? Arkady coldly studied his second in command for a moment. Then he nodded toward the ashtray. "You know perfectly well, Comrade Dobredyn. I have . . . ah, *I am trying* to give up smoking."

"Oh, quite right. Does it cause you to be so formal you forgo calling me by my given name? Am I no longer Feodor to you?"

"What difference does that make?" Arkady grumbled.

"Nothing. Only . . . that you are getting terribly irritable over this noble sacrifice for the socialist order, Comrade."

Gulyakin suppressed a flash of anger. "Are you making fun of me, Feodor?"

"*I*, make fun of you, comrade? Why, never."

"You know I am suffering the torments of the damned? You realize my temper is on its thinnest edge?"

"Oh, yes, comrade, and I sympathize. It is truly a monumental undertaking and we are all proud of your dedication to Marxist-Leninist principles. Smoking and excessive drinking are costly and counterproductive. As such, they are both enemies of the well-ordered socialist state. They do harm to a person's body, which is to do harm to the property of the state, which is a crime. They are also offensive to others who do not indulge in such rude and disgusting habits. Therefore smoking and drinking are enemies of the perfect Soviet socialist state and must be abolished."

Gulyakin forced a small smile. "You've learned that well and say it almost as though you believe it. Why is it I think you're mocking me?"

"Perhaps because we are alone and I think I might get away with it?" Dobredyn suggested.

"Oh, to hell with it, Feodor. Get the peppered vodka from the freezer and open a foil packet of Bluetermann's fine cigars. Such stoic suffering is for doctrinaire fanatics, not pragmatic men like ourselves, eh?"

CHAPTER TWELVE

Thirty-seven Frog 9 surface-to-surface missiles slammed into the predawn sky from launch sites protected by Quarry Heights on the outskirts of Panama City. They were immediately followed by slightly less thunderous roars as flights of SA-2 Guidelines leaped to engage Navy and Marine pilots flying from the carrier *Lexington*.

Thirty seconds later, batteries at Colón on the Caribbean coast also launched. The allied assault on the Canal Zone began. The six-thousand-pound Frog 9's sorted out their targets at apogee just as their idiot brains began to receive conflicting information from Naval ECM operators who'd picked them up within instants of launch, through the warning of an AWACS, the giant bird with its dinner-plate antenna, safely out of range.

At the tail of the big rockets, the powered speed brakes popped out and 111 tons of sudden death dove into the ocean three miles short of the first target.

High above the sea battle, another kind of duel took place as the SA-2's locked on to individual aircraft. For most of the mechanical idiot savants, the act was fatal. Each, as its radar identified a target, gave the on-board electronic countermeasures officer its location and trajectory. A beamed signal from the target overrode instructions and created a ghost image for it to home on. The missiles detonated far from the jets their masters intended should die in the blast. Old F-4 Phantoms, armed with ship-killing missiles, aimed them at the points of bright green on their radar screens and fired, while MiG 21s screamed in and released a cloud of air-to-air missiles.

Most were evaded by ECM or dodged by use of flares and careful maneuvering. Six found their targets and the two-man crews of the allied jets died in fiery orange balls tinged with greasy black smoke. Sixteen-inch naval rifles on the battleships *New Jersey* and *Missouri* spouted dense curtains of flame-tinged smoke as their huge projectiles winged shoreward, and surface-to-surface missiles opened up from cruisers and frigates off both coasts. Under their hissing, roaring bombardment, destroyers edged in closer to shore and delivered their salvos of five-inch naval rifle fire. The ground erupted.

Quaking violently all the way to its substructure, the earth spewed skyward, great clots of it. Dust, smoke, and the acrid odor of high-explosives detonation choked the throats within a thousand meters of the barrage area. Roads lurched out from under motorcycles and bicycles, automobiles skidded precariously. The shriek of incoming shells and the whirring moan of flying fragments of shrapnel turned the countryside into a prolonged sort of hell. In the midst of all this madness, landing craft huddled around transport ships like frenzied pups around a nursing bitch. Like so many ants, camo-clad figures swarmed down the cargo nets.

While they did, laser beams laced the air above the gently heaving sea, directing more lethal packages of ordnance to their targets. Radios crackled and klaxons blared. Landing officers shouted themselves red-faced and sweaty. The barrage increased in ferocity to the point of a single, horrendous bellow of mind-destroying noise. Then the first landing craft departed.

They came in three waves. The United States Marines, doing what they did best, what they did better than anyone else in the world. Thousands of steady, well-trained, and blooded Nicaraguan troops and their shell-shocked Panamanian counterparts in the *Fuerza*, waited for them. At two thousand meters, smooth-bore 60mm tubes on the landing craft began to belch "smart" projectiles at the laser-designated targets. At a thousand meters, few of the remaining 12.7mm Soviet machine guns dared to reply. While the fearsome devastation descended on the rebel defenders at each end of the canal, a third landing opened on another front.

From the flight deck of the *U.S.S. Belleu Wood*, a squadron of OV-10D's winged their way through the pink-tinged dawn. Below them, additional cruisers and destroyers lobbed shells and missiles at two coastal towns below the Canal Zone on the Caribbean side. Frightful damage resulted, as huts, mud-block business establishments, and a brick schoolhouse, all previously taken over by revolutionary forces, flew into the air, rent into small bits. Removed physically and emotionally from the horror below, the pilots of the OV-10s lined up on the airstrips that caused the villages to become objectives. Their night-fighting equipment made easy work of their designated targets.

Flames from the antiaircraft installations and battered villages leaped high in the air behind the tails of Legion Foxtrot, as Lieutenant Colonel Don Beisel's OV-10s pulled off and assumed an orbit at eight thousand feet some five klicks from their target areas. Each flight held there, ready to give further assistance if needed, and waiting to land. Time had not permitted Legion pilots to be trained in carrier landings, and success of the airborne operation that followed them would determine if they survived or not.

Right on time, lumbering C-130s lined up to deliver their sticks of Foreign Legionnaires, American and French, onto the airstrips at Nombre de Dios and Palanque. Only pitifully light, sporadic ground fire greeted the blossoming canopies. Palanque had a dirt strip, not the least significant to the rebels' strategic overview, but sufficient to handle the OV-10s. This would be their temporary home. The large, hard-surface runways at Nombre de Dios would accommodate all of the Legion's heavy air. Before the first troopers landed, they saw flashes of white fluttering in the breeze.

Bravo of the Third, who spearheaded the jump, encountered immediate, stiff resistance from the direction of Nombre de Dios. "Hey, I thought this was supposed to be a cakewalk," an agitated voice crackled over the command net. "Those little fuckers are shooting at us."

"You expected bread, cheese, and wine? Make a proper report or clear the net. Over."

"Roger, Choctaw. This is Tandem Three," Bill Kane responded, somewhat subdued. "We have a concentration of fire from Sector Three, mortar, light and heavy MGs, some AKs from infantry. Over."

"Roger, Tandem. Agency and Pulsar, move along flanking lines to Sector Three. When you are in position and have visual contact with Tandem, suppress hostile action in that area. Choctaw One, out."

Elsewhere at Nombre de Dios, the Naval guns and air strike had so badly mauled the hapless rebel contingent of the Panamanian Defense Force that the confused and groggy defenders stumbled into the open and welcomed their captors with open arms and shaking knees. One blank-eyed young lieutenant summed it up when he spoke with Charlie Century's commander.

"At last there is esooomeeone to surrender to and estop the awful esh-ah-shelling. We are at your essservice, *señor*."

At Palanque, the French met no resistance at all. Within ten minutes of their forming up on the ground, the airstrip had been cleared and the first thirsty OV-10s touched down. Fortunately, the omnivorous turbo engines of the Broncos would eat anything combustible for a while. Refueling from local gasoline supplies commenced at once. After the last of Foxtrot's craft taxied to the ramp and cut the master switch, a fat-bellied C-130 lined up on the runway and deposited nine parachute-supported pads of six fifty-five-gallon drums each, filled with JP-1. More would follow, the pilot assured ground control over the command net at 134.6. After their next mission, the mixed diet would insure clean running. Back in Nombre de Dios, the cleanup continued.

"Chickasaw One, this is Kiowa One-seven. We have a mission for you at Lima-lima three-zero-one-three-seven-two, bearing two-niner-five to target. Target is a brick factory building and woods adjacent. Friendlies have panel markers at one-eight-zero to two-four-zero from your approach position. Over," the FAC attached to Charlie of the Second called off.

"Roger, Kiowa One-seven. Bearing two-niner-five at Lima-lima three-zero-one-three-seven-two. What do you need? Over."

"We need a mixed load, with GP bombs on the factory, AP and anti-PAM on the woods, over."

"You got it, over."

In less than three minutes, four of the OV-10D's of Legion Foxtrot streaked in, lined up on the correct heading, and began their run on the designated targets. The lead aircraft dropped down from four thousand feet and released its package of two 500-pound general-purpose bombs on the factory. As it began its pullout, the most vulnerable moment, the second Bronco began a strafing run at two thousand feet, as it descended into a shallow dive that delivered two 250-pound anti-PAM bombs into the woods. An instant later, the familiar crackling ripple and whooshing roar of igniting napalm tore at the air. Roiling black smoke rose from the edges of the glowing orange streak of death.

Totally unfamiliar with this flaming messenger of doom, the Panamanians of the PDF and their Nicaraguan comrades gaped in scrotum-shrinking horror. Several involuntarily blurted oaths or fragments of prayer as the sticky, burning matter surged closer to them.

"*¡Madre de Dios!*" gulped a numbed PDF private a moment before the terrible concoction splashed over him.

"*¡Chingen a sus madres, gringo cabrones!*" a burly Nicaraguan sergeant bellowed, his last word turning into a shriek of agony.

"*Hay Dios mio, me pesa ofenderle a Usted . . .*" a young rebel prayed fervently, then wept unashamedly when he was spared from the fiery immolation.

More GP bombs struck the factory from the third aircraft, and the walls bulged outward on the second and third floors. Bricks rained down in a confusion of red dust and smoke. Behind it, the fourth OV-10 spread more anti-PAM on the jungle. Screaming, writhing figures did grotesque dances before falling as blackened clumps in the smoldering foliage. Another pass by the deadly quartet and they winged their way back to rearm at Palanque. From everywhere in sight of the grimly awesome display of might, the remaining defenders began to show white flags and hastily surrender. On the command net word came that another wave of Marines, held in reserve for the purpose, was on its way.

"Seahawk, this is Cherokee Zero-zero. Thanks for the offer, but we don't need the Marines. All opposition is eliminated and we have things in hand."

A cranky complaint answered him, ending with, ". . . but we've got a job to do and we're anxious to get on with it. Over."

"Granted, Seahawk. The way I see it, we have one job and you've got another," Watie informed the sputtering Marine commander. "Colón needs you far more than we do. Thanks again, but no thanks. Cherokee Zero-zero, out."

Watie turned to his staff, who had taken over one of the remaining intact buildings at the airfield. "Now we can get down to the task of unloading supplies and equipment. Then bring in those borrowed Japanese seaplanes and fill 'em up."

Within an hour of the cease-fire in Nombre de Dios, carrier-based planes headed inland to knock out the radar site on Mount Salud. They encountered the first notable force of rebel fighters and accomplished the mission with light casualties. The giant seaplanes, the only ones of their kind in the world, had been reluctantly loaned by Japan for the Legion's operation. They sat, squat and ungainly in the water, their cargo doors open, receiving equipment for the airstrip construction at Madden Lake. Jump manifests had been published and the briefing went on while Colonel Watie, with nothing else to do, paced the floor of his command post.

"So far it's been easy," Major Orenda observed to the commander.

"Too damned easy, if you ask me," Colonel Watie snapped back. "I don't want to be a doomsayer, but the Nicaraguans have had a week to strengthen all the weak points, yet we waltzed in here like a Boy Scout troop on an Overnight hike. Somewhere along the line, we're sure to fall in the shit. "They've got their hands full at each end of the canal," Orenda provided in an attempt to ease Watie's foreboding.

"Sure, and only God knows how large a force they put in here since we got our nose in it, let alone before. I'm not worried about the airborne assault or the equipment on the seaplanes, but I've a terrible premonition about what we'll run into between here and the Upper Chagres."

"It's mountainous jungle out there, Colonel. The Cats have already started the first leg, and the Skyhooks are on their way to pick up bulldozers and prime movers to leapfrog across the remaining space to the Chagres. By midnight we ought to have the road extensions completed all along the route."

"I *know* the plan!" Watie fired back, then caught himself, alerted by the testiness of his tone. "Sorry, Mick. I work better under pressure. I'm reading something into this that maybe isn't there. Particularly out in that jungle. Odds are you're right. Only be sure there are enough troops sent along for security. Once the enemy finds out what we're up to, with a road and all, you can bet they'll make some response."

"Most likely by air," Orenda agreed. "Blowpipes and Javelins going in first with the construction equipment, then a Century of infantry to each start point."

Watie sighed and produced the first smile since accepting the surrender of the PDF commander at Nombre de Dios. "That should do it. The advance troops for Madden Lake will go in the same birds as their Folbots and field gear. The remainder will progress along the road we're building, hit the river at the first deep point, and make their way to the dam by water. It's a slick plan, if we're given time to make it work."

"Keep it moving," a burly Legion sergeant bellowed as the huge earth-moving equipment came ashore.

By noon of D-day, the first of the gigantic road builders had forged into the jungle, preceded by sapper crews, who blew trees and hauled them out of the way on drag lines. A four-lane dirt road would be constructed through the primeval forest to intersect the Colón highway. Then the Legion's armor and wicked little Panhards would swarm toward the northeastern end of the canal and participate in the relief of the city. The threat of their presence had been calculated to draw the enemy air out in the open, away from their AA protection, where the Marine and Navy pilots on the carriers could engage them. It should, Stand Watie and his staff calculated, insure little attention would be paid to Legion activities on Lake Madden.

Amid the choking swirl of dust and gagging diesel exhaust fumes, Legionnaire Herman Rechter of Alpha Century, Fifth Cohort, paused to wipe a layer of wet mud, which should have been dust, from his forehead. *"Verscheizer!* I joined the Legion to fight, not build roads."

Beside Rechter's large bulk, the short, stocky figure of Legionnaire Pablo Martinez stopped his shovel work and looked knowingly at his big Austrian friend. *"¿Sí como no?* I, too, joined up to kill communists. It was because of my mother."

"Oh? Your mother wanted you to join?" Herman inquired. He had trouble believing the nearly white-haired and prune-faced Pablo ever had a mother.

"Oh, no. She wasn't alive when I got to Guatemala and signed papers for the Legion."

"Then how did you do it for her?" Herman persisted.

"I am from Nicaragua, *comprende*? As a little boy we were at peace with everyone there. Then, when I have thirteen years, the Sandinistas come to our village. They killed the *jefe* and our *alcalde*, also some of the older men. Those between fourteen and thirty-two they take away with them. When the women protested, they were killed and many raped beforehand. M-My mother was one of those. When I attacked and tried to stop this outrage with my little knife, I am shot and left for dead." A wicked gleam glowed hotly in Pablo's eyes as he jerked aside his cammie shirt to show the puckered entry wound.

"I survived and I swore to kill a *comunista* for every hair in my sainted mother's head. *Con la gracia de Dios,* I shall live long enough to do that. To do what I wanted, I joined the contras. For a while we were treated very well by the government of *los Estados Unidos*. We were given arms and ammunition and food, medicine and uniforms. All this we used to help the people and strived to crush the communists so that our land would be free. Then—it was my second year with the contras—we were told that traitors in the *yanqui* government made a law that prevented their President from helping us. For a while things got bad for us." Pablo paused, spat dust from his mouth, and hurled a few shovelfuls of dirt toward a low spot in the roadway.

"Then the supplies began to come again. A private, secret way had been found, we were told, to get what we needed to free Nicaragua from the communists." Pablo's face brightened as he described the fine new arms and vast quantities of ammunition, the badly needed medical supplies for the suffering civilians as well as the contra forces. Then a scowl replaced it.

"All at once the equipment and money stopped coming. The traitors in *los Estados Unidos* had found out about the hidden pipeline and caused much trouble for the President and those who would see Nicaragua free. The *cabrones* of the television and newspapers made a big issue of it and there was a—how you say?—hearing over our getting aid. Once more the supplies dropped to a trickle. For ten long years we hung on and fought with what we had and could get in small amounts. It was then, when I heard of this new President's Foreign Legion, that I decided to join and make good my vow to kill communists."

"*Liebe Gott!*" Herman exclaimed. "My reasons aren't so inspired. I was only bored with my life as a jail guard in Vienna, but my heart goes out to you. This road will harden our bodies, as it strengthens the Legion. *Gott mit uns*, we'll both kill many of our common enemy."

CHAPTER THIRTEEN

Crowd noises surged around him, and the bump and bustle of patrons afflicted with gambling fever provided anonymity to Jason Aldridge as he faded into a quieter cul-de-sac off the lobby of the casino-hotel in Atlantic City. He located the card phone and punched in the eleven-digit number after running his credit card through the magnetic slot. The card was in the name of a nonexistent man who supposedly lived in Fallbrook, California. Jason listened to only two precise rings before the party at the other end answered.

"This is Orkin," Jason announced, using his code name for this operation.

"You are eleven minutes, seventeen seconds late, Orkin," the cool voice at the far end responded.

"The crowds are terrible here. I had to wait for a phone," Jason explained.

"How is the project going?" asked his unseen control.

"Quite well." Jason paused for another question. "Yes, I'm making a careful study of the subject's movements and habits." Another brief hesitation. "Yes, I'm satisfied I can find the right place to do the job."

"Are you properly prepared? Anything you need assistance with?" the icy voice demanded.

"No, all is in readiness except the final location. I'm completely ready, without any help, thank you," Jason asserted firmly.

"Too bad your subject made a sudden move to a distant

place. Will it affect your schedule?" A note of concern colored the neuter tone for the first time.

"Not in the least. Immediately he comes back, all will be taken care of," Jason assured his employer.

Monkeys and parrots competed with insects to irritate the remaining six escapees. Chiquili continued as point man, leading the small detachment in a wide circle around the heaviest concentrations of searching enemy. Wherever possible they left the lush vegetation in an untouched condition, to aid in keeping the PDF and Nicaraguans off their trail.

Paul Challenger estimated it was close to fourteen hundred hours when Chiquili killed the big rattler and hung its headless, still writhing body from the string of his breechclout. After which he wrapped the gape-jawed head in a piece of cloth and dropped it into his pouch. Paul found himself wishing they could spare the time to cook and eat the reptile on the spot.

The Indian insisted on keeping a steep rise to their right. To the left the land fell away toward the hot coastal lowland, the *tierra caliente*. Paul's legs felt wooden from the strain. He concentrated hard to keep from stumbling as often as the other strangers to this country, considering it beneath the dignity of his position as ranker.

Chiquili froze and the Legionnaires shuffled to a halt, vision hazed by stinging sweat. The Indian sank down, then waved them forward as he began a low crawl. Janos saw it first. The whole mountaintop had been cleared, throwing into stark relief the white buildings and the ugly antenna that grew from the top of one.

Even as Paul caught a first glimpse of the *Tres Hermanos* radar site, a door flew open and troops began to spill out. One squad ran straight down the open three-hundred-yard slope toward their position.

"Sensors!" Paul was startled by the sound of his own voice, with its hoarse croak, louder than intended. He tried again: "They've got sensors on the perimeter."

Chiquili had started off on a route that would take them around the clearing. Paul knew that was suicide and took the only action he could think of. Poking the captured FAL through the underbrush, he killed the last Nicaraguan in line.

"Janos! Get the Indian started directly away from here, quick," he commanded.

Machine guns began probing the edge of jungle from concealed bunkers. Paul killed the next soldier in line a moment before Alexis Koropopous, his FAL on full auto, ruined the setup by spraying a short burst into the leader of the charging troops. They immediately dropped, crawling for the nearest cover. Paul finished another scurrying figure before he backed out of his concealment. He jerked at the soft *whump* when the first enemy mortar fired.

Paul crashed through underbrush for the time it took to run ten paces, and threw himself to the jungle floor. There came an earshattering roar and the ground heaved beneath him. Gnats swarmed into his nose and gasping mouth in a cloud that threatened to choke him as he fought clear. Behind him he heard a man screaming in mortal agony and a persistent *whump . . . whump . . . whump,* interspersed with the rattle of Kalashnikovs in his ringing ears. Paul Challenger concentrated on putting distance between himself and that deadly spot on the edge of the clearing.

It was dark by the time Chiquili brought the last survivor to the big mahogany tree. Their FFL pilot, Laroquelle, sported an empty eyesocket, and three fingers from his right hand were missing. Paul assumed he'd been the source of the screams resulting from the first mortar round, and silently cursed the expert mortar gunner who'd fired at the flicker of full-auto muzzle flame and killed with such unerring accuracy.

It was unfair of him, he knew. Particularly since Koropopous received his training from the French. Only the American Legion had realistic training in fire discipline and tactics. He couldn't blame the French Legionnaire, yet he could not suppress a certain revulsion when he looked at the man.

"The black man is dead," Chiquili informed Paul.

"Norbert Settles," Paul said numbly. "Too bad we can't retrieve his body to take back to the Cay. All right, listen up. We're gonna do this by the book."

The after-action debriefing indicated several Nicaraguan uniforms had been spotted due to their brighter green. All the men concluded the reaction to the sensors was more serious than called for.

Paul held his peace on the subject of fire discipline and tried to explain sensors to Chiquili. The discussion degenerated to the level of evil spirits while the Indian built a small fire and roasted the snake. Satisfied at last that he understood about these "sensors," Chiquili assured Paul in his broken English that when men used such evil powers, the spirits would turn on them and extract a terrible price.

For the first time since the plane crash, Paul fought back a grin. "We'll move on about a klick, then sleep for a while," Paul announced a bit gruffly. "Marcel, that hand . . ." Paul didn't even want to think about the eye.

Despite his obvious pain, Captain Laroquelle roused and produced a sardonic tone. "A pilot must make great use of his right hand, so . . ." He gave a sharp snort that Paul figured was accompanied by a typical Gallic shrug. "It appears I shall be making a journey by boat with the rest of you. *C'est la guerre.*"

Their movement in the utter dark under the jungle canopy was restricted and confused. Paul wished fervently for the tiny patrol lights the Legion would normally use under such a circumstance. Invisible at more than thirty paces, the red LED lights clipped to the back of the helmet to allow a proper interval, and prevent men from getting lost. After a seemingly interminable time, Chiquili led them to a small clearing beside a thin ribbon of stream. It ran, Paul noted, in the direction he considered to be east. They slept like the dead for some five hours. Darkness still shrouded them when Chiquili awakened the nearly exhausted Legionnaires.

"I have made something for the pain," the Indian quietly told Paul. "Not sweet like Log Cabin, but it work."

That produced an unseen grin on Paul's lips. "You were at Gulick a long time, weren't you, Chiquili?"

"Oh, yes. I teach jungle to your soldiers, teach brown soldiers, too. They learn much. I learn to like sweet things, like Hershey and Log Cabin. I'll give medicine now, *Jefe*, then we go."

To Paul's considerable relief, the course led downward now and, if his senses hadn't failed him entirely, to the northeast. Cocel del Norte shouldn't be far off. Daylight found them hungry again, yet definitely on a northward course. Relief provided Paul with new stamina. It might be his imagination, but he felt he could detect a slight salt tang in the easterly breeze. Jungle still surrounded the escapees when Chiquili returned and stopped them. Paul estimated it to be two hours after sunrise.

"Make small, hot fire, no smoke," Chiquili instructed after he'd dug a shallow pit. "Fill with coals, put in piqueri, and bury. We eat, then go on."

He proceeded to skin and wrap broad leaves around the small animal he'd produced from seemingly nowhere, while Paul and Janos gathered burnable material. At the edge of a grassy clearing, Chiquili dug up some bulbs, washed them in the stream, and added them, likewise wrapped in greenery, to the fire. Then he covered it all with dirt.

When Chiquili reopened the pit, savory odors caused Paul's stomach to cramp and his fellow Legionnaires moaned and salivated in like manner. Chiquili divided up the roasted tubers and piqueri meat, then dosed Marcel Laroquelle with more of his painkiller before they ate. The welcome repast completed and all signs of it buried, the weary escapees rose and started off. Chiquili spurred them on with a grim reminder.

"Last time we eat before Cocel del Norte. Only safe place."

"Then let's make tracks," Paul urged.

Most of the night creatures had retired to their holes or nests long before the first flicker of false dawn. The day shift of noise makers had not yet made an appearance. Through the hours before, an odd flotilla of small craft had eased along the waters of Lake Madden to predetermined positions near the tiny settlement at the dam. Photo recon indicated a recent addition to the community. A tent city had blossomed, as rebel elements of the *Fuerza Defensora de Panamá*, the Panamanian Defense Force, moved in to secure another of the critical links toward conquest. The clearest photos revealed the rebel flag over the administrative buildings at the dam and power plant, horizontal bars of red, yellow, and black, with a large red star superimposed in the center. Estimated enemy strength, based on these, numbered approximately a battalion.

All of which made the upcoming operation decidedly hazardous. It would be necessary, according to a subsection of paragraph three of the ops order, to initiate the assault with a silent penetration to sever lines of communications, to pave the way for the airborne assault. To facilitate that, the scout platoon of Second Cohort (Third of HQ Second), under command of Ensign David Moreno, had been added to the commando force making a waterborne approach from the southeast—upper—end of Madden Lake.

Chance had settled on them due to the structure of the scout platoons. Each Cohort had a different language or language group specialty. Thus, those of the Second Cohort were native speakers of Spanish, while First Cohort's spoke Swahili and Urdu, Thirds were fluent in Arabic, Hebrew, and Turkish, Fourth a mixture of Asian languages, and Fifth Cohort's scouts were versed in European tongues and Russian. It provided flexibility and, it was hoped, a high degree of penetration of enemy lines. In this particular case, the proof would soon come.

Ensign David Moreno took a moment to peer at the softly luminous dial of his Seiko Legion digital watch. The wristband, though made of a neutral synthetic fiber, itched his arm. This damned jungle grew fungi of a dozen varieties in only hours. It seemed nothing was proof against them. Right then, at 0451 hours local, Dave much preferred to be elsewhere. In San Luis Potosi, perhaps, or Morelos. Somewhere in Mexico, at least, waiting out the gut-tightening minutes before the *clarín* announced the *paséo*, and he and his brother *prácticos* entered the ring to face the horns. Dave blamed his duty with the U.S. Coast Guard for joining the Legion. Though, truth to tell, he loved it. The adrenaline high produced by combat was the only experience he could closely compare to facing a brave and ferocious *toro*. Nine minutes and it would start again.

Exactly on the tick, Dave waved his scouts forward.

Across a three-hundred-meter stretch of low brush waited the sentries of the PDF. A sufficient number of these would be taken out to breach their security and provide access to the radio room. Other members of his team would cut telephone lines and the ancient, little-used telegraph. He had half an hour to accomplish it in, then set out DZ and LZ markers for the airborne assault that would follow. Each cautious step forward in the Taylor Shuffle brought the men closer to detection and the ruin of their mission. Ensign Moreno strained his ears to detect any slight misstep or a start of alarm from the enemy. Two hundred meters more and the first five scouts would be at the outer perimeter.

"José, don't be an idiot. If you light that cigarette we'll both be in trouble." The voice seemed to David to be within a few inches of his ears, causing an angry start at the thought his own men could be so careless. Something shifted in his mind and he realized it was the enemy. Another fifty meters separated him and his main force from the perimeter.

"*Chingada*, Ramón. What need for all of this? Who are we to be attacked by? A lot of starving, diseased Indians?"

"There is fighting at Colón and at Ciudad Panamá," Ramón answered back. "That means we are at war. The *yanqui* Marines have landed, according to Cabo Mendoza."

"*¡Ay caramba!* Ramón. That's all many miles from here. Whatever is going to happen will be long over before we ever hear a shot fired in anger. Win or lose, it shall not affect us."

"We'll feel the sergeant's anger if you don't shu—"

Ensign Moreno's keen hearing caught the rapid yet quiet *fop-fop-fop* of a suppressed Sidewinder. Nearer at hand, José heard the trio of meaty splats as the .45 slugs smacked into his fellow sentry's chest.

"Ramón, *¿qué paso?* Ramón, answ—" José blurted out before another Sidewinder spoke and blew him into eternity.

Two down, at least six more to go, Dave Moreno figured. He sensed, more than saw, his five scouts spread out. To his left a Glaudus made a meaty chunk as it entered flesh. Dave reached behind him and waved his hand twice over the narrow aperture in his Starlight Products patrol light. The tiny spot of red light flickered in the signal for second squad to advance through the opening created. They did so with awesome silence. For a moment Dave wondered if the Defense Force had taken time to put out sensors.

No matter; their silent battlefield shuffle would have defeated those, he concluded. Off to the right soft sounds of brief, violent contact assured him, and he signaled another squad through the perimeter. The next line of guards wouldn't be so easy.

Contact! Four quick flicks over a patrol light spot indicated the location of the next ring of sentries. Moreno halted the advance and slipped quietly forward. He knelt beside his point men and assessed the situation.

"They've got machine guns. We spotted them when a truck drove along that road across the way. They've got good outpost setups, but lousy light discipline."

"Good for us," Dave breathed softly. "I'll go forward with you and we'll take out two adjoining OPs."

"Okay, sir. But if they have night vision equipment, or even old IR scopes, we're fucked."

Dave followed the point, which divided some thirty meters in front of the inner defense perimeter. On his belly he slid into position beside a sandbagged machine-gun emplacement. He held his breath for a long count of five, then sprang up and looped an arm around the neck of a nodding Defense Force trooper. The Glaudus in his right hand pierced cloth and sank into yielding flesh over the struggling soldier's kidney. A hard yank left and right to insure the renal artery had been slashed, and Dave withdrew his blade. A hot gush of blood covered his hand and wrist as he lowered the dead man.

A quick check showed him his silent companion had dispatched the assistant gunner. The ammo bearer, sound asleep at the back of the shallow pit, snoozed on. He never awakened, even when Ascensión Grijalva lopped his head off. Dave withdrew a thin cylinder from his combat coveralls and crushed it. He kneaded it in his hands until it began to ooze quick-set epoxy, then inserted it in the muzzle of the machine gun. It made an effective, if temporary, spike. Immediately he and Grijalva removed their helmets and turned off the patrol lights.

That served as a signal for the platoon sergeant, Manuel Orosco, to bring the remainder forward. Dave issued quick, terse instructions and the dark-clad men faded into the pre-dawn blackness. Ten minutes later, the door to the radio room slammed inward. Before the men inside could cry out an alarm, suppressed Sidewinders trashed them and the radios. Dave Moreno took a turquoise egg from his battle harness. He hefted it in his open palm, then inserted an acid-system-timed detonator through the stiff paper diaphragm in the end of the white-phosphorus grenade. This he left in a pile of paper and broken wooden chairs.

Across the compound, men with climbing spikes slithered up rough poles and clipped telephone and telegraph lines. Dave flipped the light cover from his Seiko and counted down the seconds. When the digital readout reached Mark, he gave the signal to pull out. They had fifteen minutes to put the locator strobes in position and eight hundred meters of ground to cover. Hopefully they would do it undetected. So far the numbers had fallen entirely too easily, Dave worried. There must not be any Nicaraguans among the troops at the dam complex. He'd seen tougher Boy Scouts than these PDF turkeys.

A sudden actinic flare from a large spotlight disabused him of his contempt. "Take it out, shotgun three," he snapped to third squad over the platoon net. To the rest of the platoon he rapidly assigned their revised functions. "Shotgun one and four, to the north side of the compound. We'll hold rear guard there. Designated DZ and LZ security along with shotgun two and three, get lost in the jungle, then proceed to your positions."

That would, Dave fervently hoped, buy them the fifteen minutes they needed.

CHAPTER FOURTEEN

Insects came alive as a faint line of gray split the darkness of the land from the inky sky along the eastern horizon. The buzzing creatures hardly wavered at the drone of the Helio Stallion engine. The small, high-wing bird bore in on a heading for Lake Madden at treetop level, then jinked up to eight hundred feet to release the Pathfinders. The agile aircraft turned off before crossing the defense zone at the dam and buzzed away on a reverse heading for Palanque. With their Paraglide chutes, the Pathfinders slid in to easy standing landings, to be greeted by the DZ and landing-zone-security parties. All in readiness, a brief "squirt" radio transmission went out to the waiting C-130D's. Two Cohorts of the Legion would soon overwhelm any resistance at Madden dam.

Elements of the First came in the lead, Helio Stallions delivering them on the landing zones, along with an air drop of mortars and antiaircraft missiles. With the Blowpipes and Javelins in place, the entire area blanketed by 60- and 81mm and 4.2-inch mortars, the heavies came in, dropping sticks of the First and Second Cohorts at a dangerously low altitude. Surprisingly few injuries resulted.

"We've got a broken leg, eleven sprained ankles, and a couple of knocked heads, Colonel," Second Cohort Sergeant Major Hank Volstead reported to Mark Kelly, the commander.

"Better than I expected," Kelly responded.

"Yeah, ah, sir. Only the stray report ain't so good. Somehow, in less than eight hundred feet, twenty-five guys managed to drift off the DZ," Volstead added in a tone that conveyed his irritation at such incompetence.

"We'll pick 'em up, Sergeant Major," Kelly responded more confidently than he felt. "Or someone else will."

"Yeah. Like those Beaners down there at the dam." Volstead abruptly changed mental gears and went on with the report. "All elements clear of our drop zones, formed up, and ready to move out."

"Very well, Sergeant Major. Pass the word that I want to see Century officers forward in two minutes. We'll get a situations report from the advance party and deploy."

"Yes, sir," Volstead responded, a spreading grin showing his eagerness for battle.

Panic was more than a condition among the *Fuerza Defensora de Panamá* troops at Madden dam. It ws a state of mind. Although reinforced by a battalion of Nicaraguan regulars, they had been badly outthought and outmaneuvered, and by only a handful of unknown enemy. When the initial alarm had been triggered, the volume of fire from their foe had caused a severe overestimation of the enemy's strength. As a result, they hesitated, content on a holding action while assistance was summoned from the aircraft at Darién and Gamboa. Then they discovered that the radios had been destroyed. The telephone and telegraph lines had likewise been rendered inoperative.

"Whole sections missing, *Capitán*," an excited Sergeant Alvarez reported to the communications officer. "The wire has been cut away from pole to pole in three different places, leaving strands standing in between. The splices alone would take hours. And we have no wire to replace that cut down and taken away."

"*¡Burro!* You see only the difficult. Don't talk to me of these things. Tell me how we're going to fix it . . . *at once*," Captain Bustamante demanded.

Alvarez made a helpless gesture. "There is no way we can fix it at once, Captain. The radio sets are so much twisted scrap metal and broken circuit boards. They were shot to pieces, as were the operators. What I don't understand is why we heard nothing. . . ."

"They used suppressed weapons. These are some sort of elite troops. I must see *Coronel* Archuleta at once. These invaders couldn't have eaten that wire, Alvarez. Get some men on locating it immediately. Then . . . do the best you can."

Captain Bustamante seemed a sea of calm in an ocean of turbulence compared to the scene in the headquarters building. Excited NCOs ran to and fro, hurriedly making reports as they received them from the perimeter and internal units. Officers shouted orders. Colonel Archuleta appeared ready to explode. His round, heavy-jowled face had turned scarlet and his small, black eyes bulged in a danger signal of a possible stroke. Bustamante reached him after only minimal chain-of-command delay.

"Do you have more bad news for me, Bustamante?" the obese colonel demanded.

"Yes, sir, I'm afraid I do. But first let me tell you what we've discovered that might help."

"Oh? Someone comes to me with something positive for a change?" Archuleta asked with a note of sarcasm.

"Yes, sir. Do you have anything so far to positively identify the attackers?" Bustamante inquired.

"Ah . . . not exactly," his commander responded.

"Well then, from the nature of the damage done to our communications and the way it was accomplished—what I mean is, ah, *silently*—I believe that these invaders are from the American Delta Force, or perhaps their Foreign Legion," Bustamante declared.

"The Foreign Legion? ¡ *Mierda!* They are mercenaries. They fight only for money. And who is there to pay them now? Moldinado, our former president, is in exile in Costa Rica. His government is fragmented. Some are dead, most in hiding, and none with a hand on the purse, eh? Within hours our dear comrade and friend, Manuel Noriega will be returning in triumph from Nicaragua to assume his rightful place as ruler of the country. So who would pay this fight-for-hire Legion?"

Bustamante produced a stern but sorrowful expression. "Don't underestimate them, *Coronel*. It might prove a fatal error."

"¡*Paracaidistas!*" came a shout from the open doorway.

"A patrol sent out to fight the rear guard of the raiders reported sighting parachutes descending three kilometers from here."

"Where and when?" Bustamante demanded before anyone else could react.

"To the north, some twenty minutes ago. Since then we've lost contact."

A ghastly moment of silence gripped the assembled officers and noncoms, then glass shattered and a loud whoosh filled the office as a 3.5 rocket round roared into the room and exploded on impact with a filing cabinet.

"Right down the alley," Captain Harlan "Alkey" Seltzer enthused as he slapped his Alpha Century rocket gunner on the shoulder.

White smoke and intensely bright spots of light mushroomed from the PDF headquarters building an instant after the WP rocket round sizzled into the office and detonated. The 81mm mortars in Alkey's sixth platoon had opened up and small-arms fire rose to a steady crackle. The bedlam drowned out the hideous screams and wails of agony from the burning structure, where sticky blobs of white phosphorus clung to wood, metal, and flesh, searing and igniting all that would burn.

For a while the Panamanian and Nicaraguan troops outside the headquarters did not realize they had been deprived of leadership in the inferno created by the single blast. The company-grade officers, noncoms, and privates had enough on their hands not to consider it. Additional Centuries of the First and Second Cohorts came onto line and added their deadly rain of accurate fire to the tumult that castigated the rebel forces. Caught between the lines of invaders, the Panamanian search patrols died without a chance. The Nicaraguans had brought along two Soviet BMP model MICVs, and their crews now raced to get their 73mm smooth-bore guns in action.

V-six diesel engines rumbled to life and settled into high idle to warm up while the crews scrambled aboard, along with the eight infantrymen assigned to the lightly armed vehicle. One of the drivers engaged the gears and the pitch of his engine changed as the 12.5 ton, tracked BMP edged forward. It made some fifty feet and then locked one tread while the ponderous hunk of steel pivoted to bring the main gun into line.

Instantly the 7.62 PKT coaxial machine gun opened up, spraying the unseen targets protected by jungle. The low-pressure main gun belched flatly and a round sped from the tube. Immediately, three laser beams touched the slant face of the APC. A moment's pause came while the 73mm reloaded. Then came the soft thump-*whumpf* of a mortar propellant igniting, followed by a short, high-arcing flight for the 81mm "smart" round. At the last second the BMP driver lurched the vehicle forward a few feet. The mortar bomb landed on the thin shell covering of the roof to the passenger compartment. It penetrated with the ease of a hot needle in butter, a *clank!* followed by a dull thud of an explosion. A rear hatch flew open and a shrieking man, his uniform afire, stumbled blindly out of the smoking inferno of the BMP's interior.

Mercifully a rifleman in Alpha Century's first squad shot him through the head and spared the burning Nicaraguan a considerable amount of misery. His companions didn't do so well. Their writhing bodies could be seen in the troop compartment, illuminated by the unholy fire that consumed their clothing and flesh. The Dantesque scene lasted only a smattering of seconds before another smart mortar round pierced the thin top of the turret and detonated the ammunition.

Bits and pieces of BMP, crew, and passengers flew through the air in democratic indifference. The other BMP driver chose to enter battle in reverse gear and slithered backward to position its main gun, firing the moment the armored vehicle stopped. The gunner got off a second and third shot before laser target designators settled on it and a single mortar round reduced it to smoldering rubble. All around, Panamanians in the PDF were laying down their weapons and raising their hands in surrender. The Nicaraguans, better disciplined, highly trained, and more experienced, fought tenaciously against overwhelming odds.

A mere nine hundred now against over two thousand, they gave ground slowly until pressed against the lake shore. There, to their horror, they discovered a flotilla of small boats, armed like pirates of old, closing in with even more of the camo-clad warriors, faces alight with battle lust. The desperate soldiers died like ants at a pest control company picnic.

Forty-five minutes after the battle began, it ended.

"I am Major de Silva of the People's Liberation Army of Nicaragua," an officer standing under a big white flag announced. "We are willing to surrender, given acceptable terms, and demand appropriate treatment under the Geneva convention."

"Our terms are simple," Asiro Tachikawa, CO of the First called out. "Unconditional surrender or die to the last man. As to the Geneva convention, your kind apply its protections only to yourselves and we're not a signatory, so we aren't constrained to abide by its dictates. So you can surrender now and take your chances or die where you stand."

"With whom am I speaking?" the Nicaraguan commander demanded.

"Lieutenant Colonel Asiro Tachikawa, commanding First Cohort, the American Foreign Legion."

"*¡Hijo 'tu madre!*" de Silva spat in vexation. He found himself trapped and unable to do the least to mitigate the circumstances. The Legion. He had no idea that they would mix in. He might as well fight to the death. It would be better than returning to Managua after this insulting defeat. On the other hand, the troops might not see it his way. Under these conditions had he the right to risk their lives?

"On behalf of my men, I accept your terms and surrender. For my own part, I desire to face one of you in single combat to satisfy the question of my courage and my honor," de Silva called out at last.

"Single combat?" Tachikawa answered scornfully. "Get ahold of yourself, man. This isn't fourteenth-century Spain, there's no Rozinante, and you make a poor Don Quixote."

"You are a scholar, sir," de Silva shouted back, thinking fast. "Come now, doesn't the prospect excite your samurai soul?"

Tachikawa's face took on a pained expression of longing. He struggled to produce all his recollection of flowery diplomacy. "More than you'd ever believe, I assure you. Unfortunately for you, I consider those who serve the morally bankrupt communist cause to be beneath honor. As such, bushido precludes wetting my sword on your worthless self. We're on a tight schedule. You must consent to these terms at once or suffer the consequences."

Silence held for a long minute. "My men will begin to turn themselves in and surrender their arms by platoons. I shall await your pleasure as to my personal treatment."

Where were all the frothing-mouthed, fanatic commies? Tachikawa wondered. This Nicaraguan major talked more like a college professor than a Moscow-trained menace. He watched with growing puzzlement as the defeated enemy streamed in to give up their weapons. In the distance, while the parade of prisoners passed by, Tachikawa heard the drone of heavy engines. They grew in number and closeness, and the Cohort commander realized these must be the cargo aircraft with the knock-down barges, heavy mortars, and more small boats. He would have a full-scale staging area on his hands rather soon now and no certainty that all would work properly to employ the forces gathered.

"Demo teams have arrived, Colonel," CSM Whitaker reported to Lieutenant Colonel Tachikawa at 0834 hours.

"Good. Send Lieutenant Siegel here right away," Asiro responded.

"Yes, sir."

Lieutenant Scott Siegel reported with a frown on his high, usually smooth brow. "I'm sorry to lay all of this on you, Colonel," he began. "But I have it by VOCO that I'm to load this dam and blow it out in three sections so as to maintain three successive flood crests of from twelve to twenty-four feet in height. The secondary objective is to preserve the footings and abutments and to facilitate rebuilding of the dam, while containing maximum water reserves. It'll take three days to be ready. Colonel Watie sent us along to get started ASAP."

"Vocal order to the commanding officer," Tachikawa mused aloud. "I've no doubt why he didn't want this one in writing," he added dryly. "I asked to find out why you came up so soon. Now I know. Well, you'd better get started at once. And, ah . . . just a minute." Tachikawa called to his

CSM. "Sergeant Major, send someone for Major Poe. I've got another little job for him."

"Right away, Colonel."

While they waited, Tachikawa explained to Siegel the reason for summoning the water specialist. "I want him to go over every move you make and verify the precise fracture points he drew into the Op plan. Now that Watie's decided to go for it, we don't dare make an error. Do what you're here for, Lieutenant, and do it properly, because as of now, you have us all by the *ume-ishi*."

"The, ah, *ume-ishi*, sir? I don't quite understand," Siegel stammered.

"It's Japanese for plum stones, Lieutenant Siegel. Seeds. In other words, you've got us by the balls. Now get on with it," Tachikawa snapped, anxious to obtain other, more pleasant prospects to contemplate.

Major Martin Oliver Poe indeed knew what was expected of him. He'd managed to get himself written up by *National Geographic* magazine for his expert handling of a revolutionary water reclamation project in Lakeside, California. Reservoirs and flow rates were his brand of duck soup. Fully equipped with the original plans for Madden dam, he showed Lieutenant Scott Siegel precisely where he needed sections blown out, and the necessary time sequence.

"Goddamn it, Major!" Siegel eyed the roly-poly little officer accusingly. "You knew this had to be done nearly a month ago."

"Sure," Poe grinningly assented, "but Congress didn't."

Carried by his own momentum, Siegel continued, "Don't you staff types know it takes time to work out stuff like this on the tables. I'll have to determine which areas to seal off, and how..."

"Easy son, Bill Emsly says you're the best seat-of-the-pants blaster in any man's army. What's more important, the chance of screwing up the dam or having the Legion stranded and cut up for lack of water under their keels because some snooper exposes a story about what *might* happen?"

"Hmm, your point is well taken, sir. Still, it *is* risky."

* * *

Captain Lloyd Harshman tossed an area map on the small folding field table in front of his second in command. "Donald, me boy, we've a fine and humanitarian task to undertake, that we do."

Whenever Lloyd Harshman—a Swede with white kinky hair—started into his Auld Sod act, Lieutenant Don Hoover knew he was bent on conning someone. That someone usually turned out to be one Don Hoover. All the same, he glanced at the colored belts of contours and noted red circles around the villages.

"Don't tell me we got stuck with that job?" Don complained. "Hell, that's Girl Scout work. We're supposed to be assault leaders with our jet skis, not Red Cross rescue workers. Why not put some of the those guys who nearly flunked out on the Folbot course on this?"

"Ah, Donald lad, ye've no appreciation of the finer points. The Old Man wants pros ta do it. It's to be a hurry-up job, with no slipups. For the most part, these are friendlies in these villages. Colonel Watie wants to keep 'em that way. Also, speed prevents discovery by the enemy. So, okay?"

Don Hoover pulled a long face, then his gray-ringed blue eyes twinkled merrily. "I'll tell you what I think of it when we get done."

"Right." Lloyd's blue eyes sparkled with humor. "Now, Charlie Century moved out ten minutes ago to blow the bridge over the Gatuncillo River, they'll establish a blocking force on the highway to Colón. Alpha is rounding up the villagers of Madronal, Nueva San Juan, and Guayabalito to bring them up here." The captain rubbed his bristly chin and leveled his gaze on his officers.

"Our job is to evacuate Gatuncillo and Santa Rosa. The people will be loaded on barges and moved to the staging area here. The beach master will take it from there." Lloyd's long, slender finger indicated a point of land that formed a sort of cul-de-sac cove in the river channel.

CHAPTER FIFTEEN

Their mission did not get off to an auspicious start. Transport was not available, and fifteen minutes after the briefing, the first elements of Bravo began trekking down the steep, traffic-clogged macadam road. The four-man boats, folded into compact bundles, proved heavy and awkward when added to full field gear and weapons. Stir in humidity in the high nineties, temperature around the same, lots of bugs, all of which bit or flew stupidly up the nose or into eyes, and the fact that no breeze reached below the rim of the canyon and one had a fair portrait of human misery.

Bumper to bumper, trucks fouled what little fresh air penetrated, while making it most hazardous to stagger out of single file. When they finally reached the Chagres River, Bravo had to continue down the road beyond the village for nearly half a mile before finding a spot Harshman considered suitable for launching.

"Goddamn it, Franco," Don yelled in exasperation. "Stop those men from crowding. We don't have room to open the boats."

First Sergeant Frank Miner blew an earshattering blast on his whistle, which halted the great bulk of Bravo Legionnaires in place alongside the road, while the crews quickly unfolded and launched the first twenty boats. Then the next twenty were admitted to the clearing. Lieutenant Donald C. Hoover fumed at the delay.

"Take it easy, Lieutenant." Harshman grinned, "I'm going

out with the next batch. We'll wait for you at the staging area."

"Dammit, sir, there's no sign of the truck with the jet skis."

"He's not due for another . . ." The captain checked his Legion watch. "Uh, thirty-five minutes. It'll take at least that long to get the rest of the Century on the water."

True to the schedule, Don, Frank Miner, and four other designated skiers splashed their speedy craft into the Chagres, and soon began to overhaul the swift Folbots. They roared around a short bend and closed on the leading elements waiting for them by a small island. Harshman immediately pushed off.

"One klick ahead," he called, "make a decoy run."

Don cranked the operating handle on his automatic grenade launcher, charging the piece while speaking into his boom mike. "Lock and load and follow me, boys."

He twisted the throttle full open and felt the sudden squat as 600cc's of power booted the ski in the tail. Although faster, with their lighter ordnance the other skis formed a rough arrowhead and held it. Gatuncillo appeared on a high bank to the left and Don felt his skin crawl as they roared past. No way he or any of the ski gunners could elevate enough to answer fire from the bluff.

None came. Don swooped left, past the docks, then slid into a sharp one-eighty, cut power, and drifted toward the floating dock. He kept a wary eye on the boats tied up there. Shy children who'd watched the pirouetting skis in fascination began to fade toward the village and the sanctuary of its big pink church. Adult faces showed in the windows of ramshackle, rusty tin huts festooned with fishing nets.

Sergeant Frank Miner hit the quick release and cradled one of his twin CETMEs in his arms, ammo belt dangling. Don heard hard-driven paddles and noted with relief the lead elements of Bravo arriving. He motioned in the first boat and began to dismount the grenade launcher on his bow.

"What is the meaning of this, my son?" a soft voice asked from the shore.

Startled, Don looked up to see a priest at the head of the stairs leading to the wharf. "There's danger of a flood,

Padre" he replied in his imperfect, hastily learned Spanish. "We've come to help you get the people to a safe place."

The priest thought, scowling, for a moment, then spoke with determination. "Then we must hurry. Sergeant Gonzaga won't like this," he added tightly. "We're supposed to be a rebel village and answerable only to their orders. But he is only one man with a squad of soldiers. Nothing you can't handle, I'm sure."

Their confrontation lasted less than twenty seconds. Sergeant Gonzaga saw the plethora of weapons and recognized the wisdom of cooperation.

The village of Santa Rosa proved an even easier conquest. Bravo began to expect a cakewalk as villagers boarded their fishing boats and loaded onto the barges, then followed the skis into a steady stream of craft that hauled cargo from the trucks downriver. The line of barges and Folbots held to the left as the channel opened into what appeared to be a small lake, but was actually a backwater caused by the convergence of what had once, before the dam, been another river.

Don steered left and overtook Harshman's boat, cutting his throttle. He stared at the staging area high up on the point of land between what had once been two river systems.

"Why the hell are they stockpiling that shit so far above waterline?"

"Ours not to reason, Lieutenant." Harshman shrugged. He nodded to the 40mm grenade launcher on the bow of Don's specially modified ski. "You get the spare ammo and ratons?"

"Last dozen boats, sir." Don's head jerked upriver, and he held out a hand. "Pass me the rope."

Don busied himself with making the line fast with a slip-knot to the stern of his ski, then powered up and hauled the captain's boat ashore. Moments later he was red-faced with indignation when he learned his men had to haul all the boats and skis some two hundred meters above water.

White-orange flashes preceded the gut-shaking blast and roiling smoke and water as the bridge at the Gatuncillo River disintegrated at each end and a single span hung precariously in the center. Charlie of the Second put a heavy rifle platoon

and half of their weapons platoon ashore, along with half of
Delta Century, to form a blocking force which was tasked
with preventing the enemy from rebridging and later cutting
off the Legion's lines of supply and communication or forming a counterattack on Madden dam. With well-wishes all
around, Captain George "Tex" Ade and the remainder of his
command set out by road for the villages of Buenos Aires
and Calzada Larga. Elements of the Fifth, already en route
down the river, would join them for the final mission, to
take Madden Field, while Bravo went on to blow the bridge
at Chilibre. Ensign Dale Pryor, six foot four and lean, with
the long face and aquiline nose of a Down Easterner from
Maine, sat beside Ade in the lead truck.

"Tex, any odds the resistance is going to get a whole lot
stiffer as we go farther?" the young officer inquired.

Ade snorted derisively. "Are you kidding? So far we've
only had a little stroll in the sun. Intel says we've got a
battalion of antiaircraft and two of infantry at Madden Field.
Maybe some armor. 'Stiffer' isn't exactly the word."

"We've got a whole Cohort behind us," Pryor stated confidently. "That should do it."

Ade suppressed a smile at Pryor's inexperience. Entering
his first combat in a command position, the young ensign
retained the self-deluding confidence of a line soldier. *The
brass made decisions, the troops carried them out.* His earlier exposure in Venezuela should have shown Pryor more,
Ade considered. Yet, when the world turned to shit, so to
speak, Pryor had acted with distinction and valor and saved
the day, thus his field promotion to ensign. Soon now, Ade
thought with a certain sadness, the awesome truth—that the
officers didn't know a hell of a lot more than the troops,
once the first shot had been fired—would descend on Pryor.
His commanding officer could only hope that he would react
as before.

"That's a Cohort minus one Century and all the armor,"
Ade reminded his junior. "Absence of those three hundred
could cost us a lot if we ran into something . . . unexpected."

At five hundred meters outside Buenos Aires, Charlie
Century met its first heavy resistance. Fast-moving scouts
had silenced distant observation posts, so that the first warn-

ing reached the enemy when Charlie's vehicles came into view. Hasty, unaimed mortar rounds and machine-gun fire searched for them. Small geysers of black, rotted jungle floor erupted in fascinating lines that converged on the lead truck.

"Brake!" Ade shouted at the driver and hit the door handle on the passenger side.

He bailed out, followed by Pryor, an instant before a 12.7mm slug spiderwebbed the windshield and splashed the driver's brains all over the cab. "Halt the trucks," Ade shouted through his Century net helmet radio. "Hoodoo-seven, bring up the 106 jeeps."

With the precision of a ballet troupe, the trucks faded back while the two awkward-looking 106mm recoilless rifle–fitted jeeps came to the flanks and forward. The feisty little vehicles had barely stopped rocking on their carriages when the 50 caliber semiautomatic spotting rifles *blanged* out ranging rounds. Evidently the gunners were satisfied in their split-second decisions, for they slammed in the trigger and both 106mm guns spit projectiles ahead of flat *BLAM!*s that punished ears despite protective plugs. At once the heavy machine guns opened up. The remaining heavy rifle platoon leaped from truckbeds and took advantageous positions. The light infantry made ready to spearhead an advance if ordered.

"Shit, we can't stay out here and slug it out with them," Captain Ade spoke almost to himself.

"I've got to get back to third platoon anyway, sir. Let me take them around to the left and hit the enemy flank," Pryor offered.

Captain Ade gave a decisive nod. "Do it."

By a circuitous route, the light infantry covered the five hundred meters at a dead run, dodging vines, fallen trees, and underbrush. Sweat bathed the Legionnaires, and several, despite rigorous training, panted like dying dogs before more than half the ground had been traversed.

"I never could run the hurdles," Private Larry Link groused in a gasping whisper. "What's all this gonna accomplish?"

"Hell, I don't know. Ask the ensign. Officers always

know what we're up to," came a reply from Legionnaire Quinn.

A quartet of Panamanian soldiers appeared suddenly from behind a low wall. With short, controlled, three-round bursts from their M-16s, Link and Quinn cut them down. Without pause, they closed on the wall and dropped down behind its cover. Hands automatically sought grenades, which they activated and tossed over the neatly piled stones.

"How about that?" Larry Link asked after the sharp detonations. "We're the first ones here. That means we get the prize."

"Yeah," Quinn agreed sourly. "All their shit gets tossed at us."

Half a dozen more Legionnaires appeared at the edge of the jungle and charged forward. Link and Quinn joined them, vaulted the low fence, and ran in among the buildings. Ahead they saw a mortar position and Link popped a 40mm round from the M-203 launcher under the M-16's barrel. A moment later, Tommy Quinn grabbed his arm and jerked him down.

"There's a goddamned tank over there. I hope they've got the mortars laid. I'm gonna put a spot on it."

He spoke over his squad net helmet.

"Hoodoo Three, this is Inca One-six, I have a spot at Golf one-fiver, Papa niner." He raised his LTD-equipped M-16 and triggered the laser by squeezing the soft bulb attached to the rifle's forearm.

Invisible infrared light flashed over the intervening space and tagged the tank while an LED inside the *Aim-Point* scope blinked on to indicate the Laser was functioning. Now if only they had the mortars set up and registered. . . . Hell, they had to. That main gun had been firing in the direction of the highway. An audible rattle of Spanish followed and the turret ponderously began to rotate in their direction. The 7.62mm SGMT coax machine gun wobbled to life. To Tommy Quinn it seemed the black hole of its muzzle pointed directly at him. All the same, he nailed the T-54 with another laser spot. The coax and the bow gun opened together.

Solid thumps struck the mound of refuse behind which Quinn and Link hunkered. The vibrations seemed worse than actual hits. Each could imagine the slugs penetrating, smashing into their fragile bodies. They wore Softcorps vests, but no help against these armor-piercing rounds. Their scrotums tightened and their penises shriveled into secondary belly buttons. Quinn had an awful desire to urinate. More 7.62 rounds ripped away at garbage and broken utensils. Then Tommy Quinn heard a soft *whump* off to his right. He raised up and spotted the tank again.

Human reactions betrayed the tank gunners. Tommy dropped out of sight before they could center on him and fire a burst. A second later the smart mortar round clanged into the turret hatch, burst through, and demolished the Nicaraguan crew along with their T-54.

"There's gotta be Nicaraguans here," Larry Link surmised. "Panama hasn't any Soviet equipment."

"Oh, shit," Tommy lamented. "What's it gonna be like when we get to Madden Field?"

"You joined the Legion to fight, didn't you?" Larry asked scornfully.

Buenos Aires fell after a twenty-minute firefight. The superior technology of the Legion, coupled with superlative training and esprit, easily carried the battle. Rebel air from Madden Field came in high and ran into the Legion Hawk missiles. They changed tactics and came within easy striking distance of the British Blowpipe and multipurpose Javelin SAMs the Legionnaires carried.

By that time, elements of Legion Juliet were on the scene with the deadly quick Marsh COIN birds and their dogfighting Kukri missiles cleared the sky. Charlie of the Second moved onward to Calzada Larga. The highway remained clear, though rutted and potholed in places. After the set-to at Buenos Aires, the march order had been changed, with the 106 reckless jeeps backing up the vanguard. It made nasty surprises more difficult to pull off.

"Church up ahead," Hoodoo Seven announced over the radio. "Must be Calzada Larga."

"Slow 'er down, Hoodoo Seven," Captain Ade responded. "Any sign of our advance screen?"

"Negative, Kiowa One. Makes a feller wonder."

"Hold five hundred mikes short of the village, Hoodoo Seven."

"Roger five hundred mikes, Kiowa One. Out."

Seven tense minutes slid by as the column drew up, the 106 jeeps out front at five hundred meters. When they received no incoming, Tex Ade ordered the Century forward. Well spread out, the infantry units passed through the 106s and entered the village first. So far not a shot had been fired. Dust boiled up under feet and tires. Unimpeded, the entire Century entered the confines of Calzada Larga.

"I don't believe it. I fucking don't believe it," an awed voice came over the radio net. "Hoodoo Seven, this is Kiowa One. Come on up and take a look. Our scouts and point men are swigging beer with the local garrison."

"I am *Primer Sargento* Ignacio Jesús y María Calderón, *a su servicio, Señor Capitán,*" the portly, smiling, bibulous noncom greeted Captain Tex Ade and his officers in the Plaza de Armas at the center of Calzada Larga.

"How . . . how did all this come about?" Ade demanded. "There were Nicaraguans to the east of you at Buenos Aires, and . . ."

"Oh, *sí*, and more to the west at Madden Field," Calderón cheerfully agreed.

"So? How is it you escaped their attention? You're right on the highway."

"*Correcto.* They left a small—how you say?—detachment here. We are a company in strength, with only our officers on the rebel side. The rest, we are loyal to our *Presidente* Molinado. So last night we get the Nicaraguans and our *cabrones* officers *un poquito de fuego* and . . ." Calderón shrugged expansively. "Zzziittt! No more Nicaraguans. *¡Viva Panamá libre!* We are at your disposal, *Señor Capitán.*"

Unfamiliar with the Panamanian slang, Ade shook his head. "You got them what?"

"A leetle dronk. Then we cot their throats. Now we fight to free our country again, no?"

"Shit! First Sergeant Griggs."

"SIR!"

"We'll take volunteers from this, ah, loyal PDF unit to serve as an advance screen and guides from here to Madden Field . . ."

"*Oye, Señor Capitán*, so that everyone knows we are loyal to the true Panama, why don't you call us Moldineros?"

"Okay by me. Griggs, see that these, ah, Moldineros are outfitted properly and we'll move out when the Fifth links up. And for Christ's sake, sober up our own point people."

CHAPTER SIXTEEN

Clouds of butterflies performed spectacular aerobatics in the shafts of gold and black created by the jungle canopy. Parrots squawked their disapproval of the massive invasion of their territory and small creatures burrowed or fled before the swift advance. Even before the linkup with Fifth Cohort, after talking with the ranking NCOs of the loyal PDF company, Tex Ade knew that spotty intelligence had betrayed them in regard to Madden Field.

Located in such a strategic position in relation to Madden dam, the Nicaraguans clearly saw the sense of fortifying the small airfield. Even subtracting for alcohol, *macho*, and normal native exaggeration, Ade reckoned they would be facing close to a reinforced regiment of Nicaraguan regulars, plus at least a battalion of rebel PDF. He reported accordingly when he turned overall command over to Lieutenant Colonel Bob Skimin.

"Aw, shit, thanks, buddy," the short, black-haired Skimin responded. "If we don't play it damned close, we could walk into a death trap. I'd rather be addressing the last tee on the course at Fort Bliss, looking forward to a tall, cool one in the nineteenth hole, than this."

"You get us out of this, Colonel," Tex Ade said sincerely, "and I'll buy you all the booze you want."

"Make it Perrier with a twist of lime and you're on," Skimin said through a grin.

Ade, a dedicated devotee of Jack Black, grimaced. "God, that sounds awful."

"It's like eatin' pussy," Skimin quipped. "Once you get past the first one, you've got it licked." Then he turned serious. "I'd like to put some of your PDF assets with our RTOs. Let them monitor the enemy frequencies. Might fuck 'em up a bit."

"I'll see to it, Colonel. Funny, but I'm beginning to feel better already."

Radios crackled in the intercept van situated in a revetment back under the trees at Madden Field. A young Nicaraguan officer stepped from the dim interior, a light tan message form in one hand, and walked briskly to the command post. He entered and rapped on a divider at the forward end that delineated the commandant's office.

"Entrarse," the gruff voice of the CO commanded.

Captain Lupe Ramirez pushed aside the blackout curtain and stepped beyond. He entered the cramped space, taken up almost entirely by a small field table strewn with maps, with more on the wall, and a postage-stamp-sized desk. He saluted and extended the message form.

"Enemy radio traffic, Comrade Colonel. A force of undetermined size has taken Calzada Larga and is approaching from that direction. Transmissions in the clear refer to a unit designation of a Century."

"*¡Hy!* The Foreign Legion of the norteños. So, a Century, eh? How many of them, Captain Ramirez?"

"Six . . . perhaps seven," the communications officer replied.

"Six or seven hundred. *¡Qué bueno!* We shall crush them like the vermin they are. On the way out, tell my staff I want to see them at once. Also have Major Bruno notify all units."

Exactly three minutes after beginning, all radio communication cut off on Lieutenant Colonel Skimin's command. Hopefully their simulated "approach" by radio would put the Nicaraguans on alert far too soon, keep them tense and watchful for longer than advisable, and deaden the expectation of an actual attack. A cocky bantam rooster, Skimin waited an entire hour before the first units pulled out of the assembly area, only half a klick from Calzada Larga.

"We ought to have the pipes skirlin' for those Nicaraguan bastards," Lieutenant Colonel Skimin quipped to his CSM, Rattlesnake McCorkel.

McCorkel grinned wickedly. Come to think of it, Bob Skimin reflected, McCorkel *always* grinned wickedly. "Jim O'Borney's birds are equipped with loudspeakers. They can play any fuckin' thing you'd like, Colonel."

Skimin took him seriously. "How about the 'Cutthroat Song'? I hear Lucy Growland paralyzed the Cubans with it in Zalambia."

McCorkel nodded. "Yep. Can do, Colonel. O'Borney's also got 'Ride of the Valkyries' and *William Tell Overture*."

"Hi-yo Silver, eh? Good enough. How soon before they join up?"

"An hour or so, sir. Got to get the wings bolted in place."

"When they do, have 'em cut loose with all they've got."

Three BM-21 launchers rippled off their forty 122mm rockets in series. As each Nicaraguan crew in turn began the ten-minute reloading sequence, the other half of the battery fired single rounds every thirty seconds. The total effect amounted to some 4.44 tons of high explosive delivered on target every ten minutes.

To the Legionnaires trudging down the road from Calzada Larga, it was wave after wave of devastation interspersed with periods of mere hell.

Ta! Ta-de-dah! Sharp and clear the bugle notes splashed around the sweating Nicaraguan crews as they labored to load 101-pound rockets into the forty-tube launchers aboard ZIL Ural-375D trucks.

Flashing low over the jungle as they slid out of the ravine, Marsh Falcons, with their loudspeakers synched on the "Cutthroat Song," opened up with minigun pods. Strafing run complete, they arced up in perfect Immelmann turns and came in on rocket runs with the happy, crystalline notes of the "Deguello" warning, "No quarter."

Nicaraguan antiaircraft people raised their Grail missile launchers and watched vainly for the red light that signaled the IR system had locked onto the plane's heat signature. Surviving riflemen flopped onto their backs and opened up with AKs.

TOW rockets streaked from hardpoints to trash the pride of the American-built factories in the Soviet Union, as one Ural-375D after another erupted in thunderous explosions. Jim O'Borney sent a smoking Falcon home, then went to have a look-see at the damage caused by the Russian rockets.

He arrived in time to find Legionnaires filtering back onto the demolished road to continue the advance across fallen trees and cratered earth. He switched the music to the *William Tell Overture*, wiped a nervous backhand across his round, sweating cheek, mumbled, "Hi-yo Sil-ver, Awaay!" and turned back to rearm.

"Christ!" Bob Skimin exclaimed in their departing wake. "For little bitty airplanes, they sure bring down a lot of scalding pee. They're not much more than the L-5's and L-19s I flew before I joined the forces."

Ed West, his executive officer, chuckled. "You old-timers give too much away. I let these kids guess about how old *I* am."

"It don't matter in the Legion. Get a check on our losses. It's on to Madden Field."

A deep frown of confusion and worry creased Colonel Antonio Carvajal's face. "They're closing to assault range as though the rocket attack caused no casualties at all. Where did those aircraft come from that destroyed our mobile launchers?"

"They had the crested helmet insignia of the Legion, Comrade Colonel," Major Ocampo, the S-2, informed him.

"*I* could have told you that," Carvajal snapped back. "What else do you have to report?"

"In spite of injuries sustained in the rocketing, there appear to be close to three thousand troops advancing on our position."

"Impossible! That's more than they had to begin with. Six or seven centuries comprise six or seven hundred."

"Perhaps their century is a bit larger than the old Roman one, sir," the S-2 suggested dryly.

"If they are, we could be in for a great deal of trouble," Carvajal observed, tight-lipped.

"Look over there," Kurt Wessel, one of the scouts in fourth platoon of HQ Century of the Fifty, said in an awed tone as he pointed toward the Nicaraguan defenses at Madden Field. "There must be a dozen T-54s over there. And those, *Verscheissen in mein Hut*, are T-72s." Quickly Kurt keyed his helmet radio. "Santee One, this is Stamper Four. Over."

"This is Santee One. What have you got? Over."

The crump of mortar rounds, incoming and outgoing, made hearing difficult on both ends. Wessel quickly outlined the ponderous might of Soviet armor arrayed against them. He concluded with a puzzling observation.

"What I don't understand is why they're not firing. Over."

"Waiting for us to show ourselves, then crush us like bugs," Jeff Short, the company commander, opined. "Give us coordinates and we'll get some LTDs up to your position. Over."

Within forty seconds a platoon of light infantry, with half their M-16s dedicated to Laser Target Designators arrived. Swiftly they fanned out and began spotting the Soviet tanks. Smart mortar rounds blooped from their tubes and fell in a rain of destruction on the iron monsters. Machine guns opened up, spraying the heavy foliage along the fringe of the dense rain forest, though doing little damage. The mortar barrage continued for five minutes. Kurt Wessel checked his Legionnaires. Their main assault would start in ten minutes.

A moment later, everything the Fifth Cohort had opened up. Above, the sky filled with the Marsh Ag Cats of Legion Juliet and the frisky OV-10Ds of Legion Foxtrot. Continuous cataclysm descended on the rebel and Nicaraguan defenders.

Lloyd Harshman's Bravos purred past the flood-crest embarkation point at the confluence of the Chilibre and Chagres rivers. The demo teams, escorted by a pair of armed jet skis, started off to blow the bridge at the village of Chilibre, while the remainder continued toward Gamboa, where the Chagres debouched into Gatún Lake. Arizona Jim's platoon occupied a series of towed barges well back in the flotilla. Their assignment to help take and then hold Gamboa, as a prelude to the close-in on Darién and eventually Barro Colorado, weighed heavily on his mind.

Not so much so that he didn't note, and wonder uneasily, at the rounded-up downriver civilians, their possessions, and Legion supplies stored so far above the banks.

"What're they expecting?" Jim wondered aloud. "A tidal wave?"

Flying nap-of-the-earth, the Legion aircraft avoided radar detection and acquisition by the SAMs at Gamboa, South Gamboa, and Darién, although it consumed more time to and from Madden Field and Palanque for refueling and rearmament. Since his arrival at Madden dam, Colonel Norman Stand Watie fretted and stewed over this situation while finalizing the major assault on Barro Colorado. His primary concern became the heavy armored Nicaraguan force, already landed on the highway at Darién and speeding both directions to reinforce rebel positions in the capital and at Colón. Probes against the Legion had so far been platoon sized and halfhearted, due to few troops and little equipment in the area.

"Cryptanalysis, Colonel," Lieutenant Colonel Stan McDade advised Watie when he brought the latest enemy transmissions. "Looks like the head Beaner at Barro Colorado doesn't believe an attack can be launched from here and has advised his columns to continue to their primary objectives. He considers all our activities to be diversions to the major efforts at the canal entrances."

"Let's not disabuse him of that convenient fantasy, Stan," Watie replied drolly. "You'd think he'd take more heed from what's happening at Madden Field. Damn! How I wish we could spare more help for Bob Skimin. He's taking a hell of a pasting there."

* * *

Fierce hand-to-hand fighting raged over the landing strip at Madden Field. With their armor destroyed or inoperable, the enemy resorted to grenades and small arms as the Fifth Cohort closed inside of mortar range. Careful placement of 40mm grenades had eliminated their 12.7mm Soviet machine guns, while light infantry with M-16s, Jackhammers, bucklers, and Hardcorps vests wiped out most of the PK general-purpose and RPK light machine gun positions. The worst engagement centered around a two-story brick building at the public end of Madden field.

Forty-five Legionnaires died in the attempt to breach the structure before the last defender killed himself in desperation, rather than surrender to the Legion. With his death, a terrible silence settled over the airfield, broken only by the moans and cries of the wounded and dying. Lieutenant Colonel Bob Skimin sat in brooding silence, waiting to get the total on the butcher's bill.

"If Barro Colorado's as hard to take as this, the Legion could be history," he brooded darkly as the toll of KIA and disabled mounted.

CHAPTER SEVENTEEN

Light rain squalls lashed the Caribbean coast of Panama as a new day dawned. Paul Challenger, Janos Vajdar, Marcel Laroquelle, and Alexis Koropopous could smell the sea air distinctly and estimated only two klicks separated them from Cocel del Norte. They slogged along in the fine mist. Paul nearly shot a native when he appeared suddenly at the side of the trail they were following toward the fishing village.

"No, I am a friend," he called out in rapid Spanish.

"Who are you and why did you jump out at us like that?" Paul demanded.

"I am . . . ah, I recognized you. I have come looking for you," the fisherman declared.

Tension increased and the military slack came off the FN/FALs. "Why were you looking for us?" Marcel Laroquelle asked coldly.

"You are from the *norteños'* Legion, *sí*? I work for this Legion. I am called Victor Portales. An *hombre* named McDade pays me to seek soldiers who are from the Legion. You are here and you are soldiers. So . . ." He shrugged expansively, as though that explained everything. "Come with me. I take you where there is a radio."

"We heard a lot of shelling two days ago," Paul inserted. "What is it?"

"*¿Comó?* What is shelling?" Victor asked.

"Big guns."

The native brightened. "Oh, *sí*. There is an invasion. The canal is being invaded by many countries. Hurry. The

143

Fuerza Defensora is close by. We must fool them." Beckoning, he led the way.

In a small clearing within sight of the church spire at Cocel del Norte, Victor Portales ushered them into a small peasant shack. Fishing nets hung out to dry on its outer walls of thatch, and an upturned barque caught Paul's attention. Before they entered, Chiquili solemnly shook hands with each of the escapees.

"My tribe not far from here. I leave now. Go to my home. You hookay already. Sometime send Chiquili Hershey? Log Cabin?"

"You bet, Chiquili. Whole cases of them," Paul told him earnestly.

"You bet, Paulchallenge. You bet, Marcel. You bet, Janos. You bet, Alejandro. Good-bye."

Inside the hut, the native asset produced a tunable-frequency radio set and checked the batteries. Next he produced covered baskets that contained dried salt fish, roasted tubers, and freshly roasted goat meat. The hungry Legionnaires fell to eating with a will. Then Victor turned to a number on the large dial and began broadcasting, clarifying his signal with minute adjustments of a smaller knob.

"Bueno, bueno. Esta Cocel del Norte. Bueno, bueno."

Static alone answered him for a while, then a voice responded in atmosphere-garbled words. At once, Victor began to transmit in the clear. "This is Victor. I have the lost Legionnaires here with me. They are in my house. . . ."

Paul and Marcel exchanged worried looks. Their alarm increased when the reply came through.

"Keep them there and we will send someone for them. Good work, Victor."

Paul realized the import a fraction of a second before the wounded French officer. Janos had done likewise. The two unwounded Legionnaires jumped Victor in the midst of their grateful pig-out on native fare. Their speedy action interrupted any response to the instructions. Janos held Victor rigid while Paul pounded hard bony fists into the man's midsection and chest.

Victor went limp after a sharp crack to his jaw. Janos wrenched his head sharply, feeling the sharp crack with satisfaction before lowering the body to a grubby sleeping mat. "It feels weird punching out a guy while chewing his food," Paul reflected aloud. "Search this place," Paul instructed Janos and Alexis. "He's bound to have an SOI, SSI, and code book somewhere."

The spartan arrangement of the small, dirty shack made discovery easy. Janos located the signal operating instructions and code book and handed them to Paul. A quick study revealed the worst.

"Damn!" Paul exploded. "They're Nicaraguan. The son of a bitch is a double agent.'

"Was," Janos corrected. "I broke his neck when I put him down."

"Look what I found," Alexis called out as he rummaged among some wooden crates at the rear of the hut. "A marine locater beacon. A big one. This Victor must have a larger boat than that barque. All we have to do is find it."

"Good work," Paul congratulated the French Legionnaire. If he kept up like that, Paul considered, Alexis might make up quite a bit for his screw-up under fire. He had hardly spoken when a young man, a mid-teenager in fact, poked his head inside.

"¿Que es estó?" the boy demanded in a high voice.

"Come on in and sit down," Paul invited in Spanish, the muzzle of his FN/FAL pressed into the side of the newcomer's head.

Paul quickly learned that this was Fidel Ernesto (named for Castro and Guevara) Portales, eldest son of the double agent. He had lived some fifteen years and, like his father, was a strong supporter and agent for the Nicaraguan Sandinistas. Janos and Marcel alternated questioning the youth, playing good cop–bad cop. Soon they ascertained that the other Portales children were in school. Their mother had been dead some five years. Also that Victor had a much larger boat down at Cocel del Norte.

Paul decided to leave at once for the larger boat. "We'll take the kid along, make him show us the right one. That way he can't give any clues to the Nicaraguans or PDF who show up here," he decided as he spoke. The others agreed with him.

Before they departed, they arranged Portales to appear t be taking a siesta. The radio they destroyed. Fidel Portale began to cry when he realized his father was dead. He stum bled along when forced to help launch his father's fishin boat. All fire gone from him, Fidel took his directions fror the Legionnaires. The Legionnaires piled into the bottom c the boat except for Janos, who sat in the bow with the dea agent's straw hat pulled low over his features.

"Take her straight out to sea, Janos, then double back an we'll switch to the larger boat. If that punk doesn't stee exactly where you tell him, I'll kill him."

Paul lay on his back, the muzzle of the FAL resting on th board seat above his head, nearly touching the boy's groin He kept his fingers on the trigger.

Weeks of wrestling small boats through the Atlantic su off Corsair Cay had nearly inured American Legionnaires t the actions of wind and wave. Not so the Frenchmen. Al ready weakened, Marcel was the first to lose the recer meal, most of it in a hot, wet mess against Paul's knee Alexis explosively followed suit.

The sickening smell, blended with rotten fish and salt ai soon had Paul in a cold sweat. He longed to simply pull th trigger and put an end to the swaying figure of the frightene boy, if for no other reason than to sit up and breathe fres air. Paul seemed to hear Janos command from far away.

"Hokay, back her down some." The hand signal was un mistakable, and the whiny outboard faded.

They'd reached a small, protective jetty in an inset cov by a roundabout course, and Janos watched from the bow c the boat for any sign of an alert. When none materialized Paul urged Fidel forward.

"No. I will not," the boy answered in a surly tone. "Yo can't make me."

"I can break your fingers one by one," Paul suggested "Or slice off your toes. What if I blow off your *gusano* an feed you to the fishes?"

Fidel involuntarily clutched at his groin and shrank away Janos looked back over his shoulder.

"Keep away from him, you animal," Janos snapped i Spanish. "I'll not let him harm you, Fidelito. I'll see you ar treated nice and let go soon. Once we're safely away, why, we have no use for you. You can go on your way."

"Really?" the frightened youngster inquired in a shaky voice.

"My word on it," Janos assured him. "First, though, you have to take us to your father's boat."

"A-All right," Fidel relented. He twisted up power, then steered toward the ramshackle pier and lay alongside one of six small inboard fishing smacks rocking beside it.

"Everyone aboard," Paul commanded, helping Marcel.

Fidel turned anxiously to Janos, small face contorted with fear. "But you said . . ."

"Once we're safely away," Janos reminded him. "See that little point of land to the northeast?"

"No one lives there," Fidel answered in a sinking voice.

"Good. Then we'll put you ashore there and you can walk back here. That should give us time," Janos explained.

Alexis already had the small wooden "house" over the inboard motor raised and the little Chinese diesel engine ready to start. "Full of petrol, Paulus," the Greek-born French Legionnaire called out cheerfully.

Paul nodded as Janos and Fidel came aboard. The engine sputtered to life. Lines cast off, the fishing boat made its way out around the jetty.

At fourteen hundred hours, D+2, Don Beisel, along with Legion Foxtrot and Juliet, landed at Madden Field. Don went about establishing his headquarters and had the tower manned. The Juliet Marsh Falcons armed with eighty-five percent South African CB-470 cluster bombs and fifteen percent Kurki missiles. Fully refueled, the OV-10D's of Foxtrot took on loads of GP and anti-PAM bombs.

"I'm still not convinced that this is the right time for a preliminary air strike on Barro Colorado," Don complained to Major Orenda by way of radio.

At the operations office at Madden dam, Mick Orenda pushed back his boonie hat and wiped at a thick layer of perspiration that matted his forehead. "Look, Don, it's a simple matter. We've got to keep the enemy off balance.

I've another day before we can blow this dam." Th‹ scrambler gave his voice a tinny quality.

"Mick, considering the lethality of our cargo, and that ‹ least one of the barracks areas is occupied by slave labo from the preserve support community, the crews of the cap tured ships, and our own people, aren't we risking a hell of lot?"

"It's the way the colonel wants it, Don. Compared to th‹ effect of having the canal closed even for a week, let alon‹ possibly permanently, their lives can't amount to a nickel. ‹ would cripple world commerce, represent a staggering blo‹ to the United States' strategic defense, endanger the non communist countries in Central and South America . . . Do have to go on? If you strike there, then hit Darién, strafe th‹ highway . . . you know the drill. Legion Juliet has the abilit‹ and the skilled pilots, to drop everything with pinpoint pre cision. Don't bitch about it; just go out and do it."

Three loudly laboring air conditioners did little to reduc‹ the appalling humidity inside the command and contro center at Barro Colorado. CD Juan Corrales stood before large situations-map board, which he studied with frownin‹ concentration. Female soldiers, in the green uniform of th‹ Nicaraguan Army, moved small symbols around, indicatin‹ the positions of their own forces and of the interlopers. Th‹ thrice-damned American Foreign Legion. Worry line‹ formed on his face as two subordinate commanders ap proached.

"Comrade *Comandante*," the lean shadow of a brigad‹ commander addressed him as he stopped in front of the map "The Foreign Legion has apparently brought in at least si‹ thousand men, their own air support and tactical bombin‹ command. They present a real and damaging threat."

"Quite true, comrade. Yet, look closely at the map." Coi rales strode over and picked up a pointer. With it, he ticke‹ off each point he made.

"Notice our troop dispositions. Artillery, some armoi heavy machine guns, six regiments of infantry to hold th‹ riverbanks. And the terrain is on our side. No force can cu‹ through all this, climb steep banks, and fight a decisive bat‹

tle once they do arrive. Barro Colorado is secure. The antiaircraft batteries, the SAM sites, our hostages. Even if I worried about a direct attack, your own unit has fast-moving elements only an hour and a half to the eastward. I would be reinforced before any real danger could present itself. My concern is with these multinational landings at the ends of the canal. They won't be so easy to dislodge. It will require all of our resources to do it. That's why, no matter how pressing this Legion development appears on the map, we must not be fooled by what has to be a diversion. I want both of you to concentrate on reinforcing our comrades and the rebels at each end of the canal."

"But, *Comandante*," the other brigade commander injected, "what if the American Legion waited until we were fully engaged at Colón and Ciudad Panamá?"

Corrales scowled a moment. "Leave it to you, Humberto. You strike upon my greatest concern. Exactly how much knowledge does the enemy have of our setup here? If they realize nearly all of our troops are committed to the defense of our holdings at each end of the canal, mightn't they attack here anyway? Get me an answer to that one and I might be able to rest a little more easily."

CD Corrales got part of his answer twenty minutes later when the Marsh Falcons and OV-10D Broncos of the Legion Air attacked troop concentrations on the mainland sides and island fringes of Barro Colorado, inflicting terrible losses. Portions of Darién blazed with hellfire, and the swift aircraft departed with a loss of only three birds. Shocked and demoralized, though raging at the personal affront of such an attack, Corrales bellowed at his staff.

"Where did they come from? Find out and blast that place off the map!"

"This inactivity is worse than when they made us work," Legion Corporal Albert Denning complained.

"You've got it, Al," his squad leader replied. "Uh-oh, here comes the Old Man. Any bets *he's* got something for us to do?"

"Not for me," Al Denning replied.

Bob Fuller entered the barrack building. With him came young Lieutenant Robert Pruitt, Bob's second in command. Sergeant Sterling Clark called the room to attention. Fuller looked around and nodded with satisfaction. So far discipline and esprit de corps hadn't slipped too much.

"At ease, men. You have all been around enough to realize from the rumbles and thumps we've been hearing that something big is going on. It might be that the countries who use the canal, those who signed the mutual protection pact, have taken a hand. It might be the Legion. Right now we don't know any more than you. I'd say that air strike proves it. The Beaners are catching hell all along the canal. In any case, I want you to be ready in the event there's a rescue effort. Get your hands on anything that can be used as a weapon. Hide the stuff well and be prepared at a moment's notice to get it out and make use of it. We don't know anyone's coming for us, or if anyone even knows where we are. But if this is a heavy enough operation, the shit's going to splatter on our Beaner friends, and that's the time we act for ourselves if necessary."

"What will shovels and machetes do against Kalashnikovs?" Al Denning asked sarcastically.

"It's a simple formula, Denning. Even you can catch on quickly," Fuller responded, matching the defeatist's sarcasm. "One or two machetes can get us an AK. One AK can get us a dozen. Twelve of them can provide a machine gun or damned near anything we want. Remember your Legion Basic, Denning? 'There's no such thing as an obsolete weapon. Only more modern ones.' A rock will kill a man if you chuck it at his head hard enough. So will a pitchfork or a fucking table knife. Use what you've got. That's all for now. Get working on it, right?"

Outside, Fuller's confidence left him for a moment. Eager young Pruitt started off again on what-all they would do to their captors when the Legion arrived. The chatter grated on raw, exposed nerves so that Bob snapped at his junior.

"Where's your guarantee the Legion is going to find us?" Bob, a man of few illusions, demanded. "Precise intelligence is absolutely crucial to launching any sort of operation, let alone one to rescue us. What worries me, and should you, is whether the Legion knows *exactly* where we are and whether they can get here in time before the Nicaraguans murder us all."

Adrift at an unknown location in the Caribbean, Paul, Janos, Alexis, Marcel and their prisoner waited anxiously for the first puff of a breeze. When the engine had run out of fuel, they hoisted a crude lateen sail, only to watch the offshore wind die half an hour later. Of the small band, only Fidel Portales hid a smug smile. His spirit remained high even though Alexis Koropopous had beaten him wildly when it was discovered the fuel had disappeared. There had been plenty, full tanks, before Fidel had opened a drain cock and let it run away.

He'd done this after the Legionnaires refused to set him ashore where promised. They would release him when they reached a friendly landfall, the boy had been promised. That wouldn't do for Fidel, and he'd sought the proper moment to wreck the escapees' plan. His father would be avenged. Retribution came sooner than Fidel planned.

Two hours passed in the calm, heat building so that all aboard suffered from thirst and sunburn. Then a shriek came from over the horizon and a loud explosion as a shell detonated at water level beyond them by a hundred meters. Almost at once the slender mast and radio antennas of a patrol boat were spotted on the horizon. Then Paul Challenger heard the report of the deck gun.

Involuntarily, everyone ducked when another shell ripped close overhead. The bow wave increased perceptibly and the Nicaraguan vessel increased speed. As it drew near, Fidel Portales jumped up in the bow of his father's fishing boat and waved frantically, shouting for them to hurry.

For his loyalty he received a 12.7mm Soviet machine-gun round through his shallow, skinny chest. His body was flung to one side and overboard. Uselessly, the Legionnaires opened up with their FN/FALs. The DShK slammed heavy slugs at them, swept the deck, and trashed the pilothouse. A fine spray of blood misted the air as one 12.7mm bullet ripped through the fleshy portion of Janos's left side.

He threw up his arms, the FN flying overboard into the

gently undulating sea. Alexis kept his weapon on semiauto this time and, as the patrol boat closed, carefully picked off two of the gun crew. Replacements rushed to the mount on the flying bridge as the gunner centered on their antagonist and blew bits and pieces of Alexis all over the fishing boat. With grim determination, the savage crew of the Nicaraguan vessel closed in for the kill, only to explode in a ball of fire and greasy black smoke as the cavalry arrived.

Flapping stiffly in the breeze created by their speed, the French tricolor waved on a staff above the pilothouse of a comandeered Panamanian patrol boat that sped down on the gory confrontation. When Marcel recognized it, he turned, grinning, to the surviving Americans.

"See, didn't I tell you that on the honor of d'Anjou's hand, the *Légion étrangère* would rescue us?"

CHAPTER EIGHTEEN

Captain Salvador Arviles of the New People's Panamanian Defense Order, sat in the command couch of his, new to him, Soviet T-54 MBT, tracking an odd, blind-looking tank with the sight of the big gun. The NPPDO, consisting of the rebel elements of the *Fuerza Defensora* and communist guerrillas trained in Cuba, was an army that blended well on paper, but refused to gel in the field. Arviles let such ruminations pass as he honed his sight picture, confident that to either side he had strong support, including BMP model MICVs with mobile launch units for the advanced—by Panamanian standards—Soviet AT-3 Sagger missiles. Perspiration stung his eyes and Captain Arviles cursed the relentless sun that beat down on Puerto Pelón.

Although shaded by the roof of the mud-walled house he had ordered his tank driven into, the heat and stifling humidity of the day added to the effect of the idling engine. All he need concern himself with, Arviles allowed, was to keep the weird armored vehicle in the center of the calibrated reticle. When the time came, he'd remove it and its occupants from the face of the earth.

When the odd piece of armor advanced a slight bit more, Arviles fired a fraction of a second after one of the BMP's Sagger missiles blasted off its over-gun rail.

How quiet it had gotten, Legion First Lieutenant Luis Inchausti marveled as he looked around the countryside. He recalled how their presence had hushed the usual cacophony of birdsong and monkey chatter, even when they had stopped for a breakfast break some two hours ago. Now, near Puerto Pelón, Lieutenant Inchausti sighed with relief. At last a connection with a major highway system and, perhaps, an end to waddling along dozer tracks and potholed jungle roads. Even better, he could look forward to a scrap at Puerto Pelón. Intelligence indicated that the enemy would certainly oppose them in force at the small village. Luis grinned savagely, in anticipation of something to shoot back at after thirty miles of mosquitoes and an occasional sniper. Suddenly the distinctive roar of a Vulcan gun heard over the steady rumble of engine noise, shattered his contemplations in a sustained blast from the lead vehicle.

The familiar sound simultaneously informed the young lieutenant of several facts. First, contact. Second, a Soviet Sagger missile had been destroyed before it could strike its target. Third, in all probability an attack by Soviet armor was imminent. Luis flicked on the coaxial, coded laser target designator, called for HEAT ammo, and swung the low-pressure 60mm mortar gun toward the most likely source.

He lined up in time to see his choice vindicated when a terrific muzzle bloom erupted from the side of a native hut. Pressing the switch which actually sent the coded laser beam, Luis watched its image appear on the dull-painted hull of a BMP, Soviet armored personnel carrier. The Mechanized Infantry Combat Vehicle burst through the facing wall and began to line up its 73mm smooth-bore main tube on his Panhard.

Shifting the laser spot from the razor-edged hull to the turret, Luis became conscious of elapsing seconds as he tripped the trigger. Flame and smoke obscured the top of the BMP, which continued its charge until secondary explosions ripped the turret askew and brought the vehicle to a grinding halt. Luis expelled the breath he didn't know he had been holding and assessed the damage.

To his right front, gunner and commander of a crippled Legion Sheridan leaped from its hull. Struck by the hardened penetrator of an APFSDS round, it developed a small cratered hole in the bow which wrote finis to the driver.

"Pull up beside the damaged Sheridan," Luis instructed his driver.

He planned to instruct the survivors as to which of the following infantry platoons to attach themselves to. A rippling scream cut short his communication as it announced an incoming. The round exploded loudly though harmlessly, as Luis shouted into his radio.

"Echelon left and form a skirmish line," he ordered the Panhards under his command. "Pick your targets along the facing edge of the village. *Por Dios*, there are enough of them."

At about that moment, Luis noticed he had come under small-arms fire. The armor-piercing bullets clanged dully as they stuck in his armor. A quick survey through the scope showed a muzzle flash from the rear port of the smoking Soviet BMP. Luis selected the remote Skoda and slammed three quick 20mm rounds into the troop compartment before a great gout of dirt rose in the gun sight and concussion from the near miss slammed the sight into his nose.

Luis ignored the blood streaming from his nostrils as he spoke rapidly into the mike. "*¿Mierda!*" he shouted, then reverted to English. "Oh, shit, we've got tanks. I say again, *tanks*. To front and right of our position."

Starved, dehydrated, and bone-weary, but reunited with the Legion, Paul Challenger tried to concentrate on the blowup of a satellite picture of Barro Colorado and the Nicaraguan installations on the island. He and Janos had been flown to Legion HQ at Madden dam and given canteen cups of hot soup, though neither had time to clean up nor rest before attending a grueling debriefing.

"Go over it again, Paul," Major Jay Solice prompted. "These are the SAMs, and over here the fuel depot?"

"That's right. And, uh, no. That's the cruise ship, closest to the SAMs. They have the women and children passengers aboard, along with the female Smithsonian workers. Here, here, here are unarmed cargo vessels. On these two, " Paul pointed to a pair of grounded ships, "the Beaners have set up antiaircraft defenses. Some 12.7 DShK's, Grail and Galen missiles."

"How many troops?" Mick Orenda put in.

"Hard to say. There was a hell of a lot of them. At least seven shiploads and all their equipment. Every time another Soviet ship anchored to off-load, we were put inside our barracks with the big drop shutters let down. From engine noise, I'd guess at least three battalions of tanks," Paul added.

"Did you see or work on the airstrip?" Jay pressed.

"Yes. It should be able to handle high-performance jets before a month is out. Concrete has been poured for only about a quarter mile of strip, but the forms are in place for much of the rest."

Their hard, thorough questioning went on for another hour. Then Colonel Watie entered the G-2 shed and called a halt. "These men need a good, long sleep. By now you must have wrung everything out of them. You'll need the rest," Watie confided to Paul and Janos. "Because you're going to fly back to the Cay and spend the rest of the operation on Carmine's cruise ship."

"On what?" Paul blurted, forgetting the courtesy of a "sir."

"Oh! That's right, you don't know about that. Master Sergeant Carmine Brown is now cruise director aboard a luxury holiday vessel that is currently cruising in the Bahamas with three hundred lovelies aboard. There's a casino, a Las Vegas floor shows, haute cuisine—if I pronounced that right—and tropical nights for romance. So you have good reason to conserve your strength."

Eyes aglow over this bountiful description, Paul and Janos conferred with wordless glances and reached agreement. Paul served as spokesman. "Ah, that sounds great, sir. But, ah if it's all right, sir, if you've no objections, we'd like to stay on. It's only right we join the rescue op for at least as long as it takes to get Bob, ah, Major Fuller out safely, sir."

Astonished at the crackling sincerity of their request, Colonel Watie took the easy way out and glanced over at Doc Tortora. "Well, Mike, what do you say?"

Lieutenant Colonel Michael Tortora shook his head slowly in a negative gesture. "I've been here to supervise their condition during the debriefing. From what I've seen, they need total rest and relaxation for at least two weeks before we can even consider returning them to full-duty status. Sorry, boys, I guess you'll just have to content yourselves with wallowing in acres of silky, feminine flesh and gorging on gourmet meals. It's back to the Cay for you, then on to Carmine's boat."

"Aw, Doc . . ." Paul started to protest, then cut it off at the hard, determined expressions of his commanding officer and the chief medical officer of the Legion. "Whatever you say, sir," he concluded with a shrug.

At nineteen hundred hours, D + 3, Lieutenant Scott Siegel entered the command center in a rush. His face registered what might have been interpreted as great worry, and the Legion rumor mill immediately began to generate speculation that the mining of the dam had gone sour. LSM Henderson waved him through and he entered Colonel Watie's office at the trot.

"Colonel, I have good news and bad news," Siegel began.

"Give me the bad news first," Watie growled, resigned to yet another delay in his overall plans.

"The dam is ready for blowing," Lieutenant Siegel responded flatly.

"Uh-huh. So what's the good news?"

"The dam is ready for blowing. You see, depending on your point of view, it's either good or bad news."

"Siegel," Watie began in that storm-flags-blowing tone, "a comedian you are not. But I gather what you're telling me is that I can begin the invasion of Barro Colorado at any time I choose?"

"That is essentially correct, sir. I'd like half an hour to get the rest of my men out of the dam complex, but basically it's ready, sir. God, I hate to do it to such a beautiful piece of work," Siegel added, frowning. Then he beamed with a boyish grin. "But it'll be a magnificent blow."

Thirty minutes later, a series of muffled *whumps* announced the detonation of the primary series. Dust rose from the dam face and cracks appeared. Spurting jets of water erupted, grew with a roar into a dozen gigantic Old Faithfuls, then sections of concrete slid away like so much mud.

A wall of water rushed outward, to crash resoundingly in the riverbed and rush off madly down the gorge.

Nervous Legionnaires kept watch while the staff stood above the tumult, surveying the handiwork of Lieutenant Siegel and his demolitions crew.

"By *Yoa*, what a sight," Colonel Norman Stand Watie was overheard saying in an awed tone. "Let's get ready, boys. We're gonna take a wild river trip."

At sunset, a few minutes after nineteen hundred hours, Spanish-speaking Legion radio operators, acting as supposed natives, broadcast panicked warnings of a huge flood crest. When the dam blew, their act grew to purely hysterical outpourings. If anyone failed to respond, they had no one to blame but themselves. With tight discipline, Legion units entered the water to ride the back of the crest toward Gatún Lake and their appointment with the Nicaraguans. As the boats and barges filled, the eternal voice of the universal sergeant could be heard above the roar of the water.

"All right, all right, keep moving. Watch your step, stupid! Shuffle up, shuffle up, men. Hold that boat, Stevens. What the fuck you think this is all about? Keep moving. All right, all right, keep moving."

The next day, at 1910 hours, Legion Juliet received its briefing and manned aircraft for a strike at Gamboan and South Gamboan SAM bases, timed to coincide with the arrival of the flood crest at 1940 hours. Forward air controllers, already in position, awaited them, to direct the raids against the most critical and best-hidden targets.

"Fledglings, this is Oglala One," Major R. C. "Dick" House said softly into the boom mike after the squadron completed its climb-out. "Let's keep it low and slow. After this run we won't have to sweat radar, except from Barro Colorado. We want to be TOT at nineteen-forty exact. Watch your mixture and throttle. Should pick up our FAC at nineteen-three-five. Oglala One, out."

Major House's Marsh Ag planes droned along, skimming the treetops, the pilots lost in the serenity that comes from perfectly trimmed aircraft. At precisely 1935, their headphones crackled to life with the voice of the forward air controller.

"Oglala One, this is Blackhawk One-seven. I have multiple targets for you, bearing two-six-zero relative. Hardstand missile sites at four-zero-niner-seven, under standard camouflage net. Your initial point will be the riverbank, release point at the line of trees ahead of target. Over."

"Blackhawk One-seven, this is Oglala One. I copy target and heading. Be advised we have a mixed load of HE and tank busters. Over."

"Rog-o, Oglala One. Couldn't be better. Second target is tank park one klick west of town, on your initial heading. Third target is headquarters complex, three vans, one two-story brick building, and a large bunker. Bearing two-five-seven relative, one-half klick southwest of town. We'll put a star shell on target at your request. Over."

"Roger, Blackhawk One-seven. Copy targets two and three. Copy star shell on my call. Here comes the cavalry. Over."

Major Gustavo Barrios breathed expansively, thankful for the first hint of coolness wafting in from Gatún Lake as evening came on. He strolled along the riverbank, enjoying his evening constitutional. At his side frisked a lively black Scottish terrier. He whistled to the dog and threw it a stick to fetch.

"*¡Mierda!*" Major Barrios exclaimed aloud. "Who are we to believe? The local radio traffic says there is a huge flood crest rushing down the Chagres. The People's Defense Order headquarters says it is a ruse by the enemy. What enemy?" Barrios asked the tail-wagging Scotty who pranced at his feet, the stick clinched in sharp, white teeth.

"The coup is no more than taken place and we are attacked at both ends of the canal and even here in the middle of water and jungle." Barrios belched prodigiously, enjoying the aftertaste of his ample repast of roasted pork, fried bananas, beans, and rice. A faint rumble attracted his attention and he turned around to look upriver.

"*¡Por Dios!*" he blasphemed.

The rumble had become a fearful rushing roar and Barrios's eyes settled their nervous flickering on a huge wall of oncoming water. Too late his feet obeyed the command to hurry. With a yell of alarm, he ran toward the headquarters bunker.

"It is true!" Major Barrios shouted. "The water is coming. Secure the base, secure the missile sites. *¡Darse prisa! ¡Darse prisa! ¡Adelante pronto!*"

Alarms sounded and men rushed to protect the most valuable military equipment, hauling their asses for high ground. Few survived to find shelter as the roiling, muddy waters boiled up over the banks and spread out like a thin blanket. For a moment it appeared to have reached equilibrium. Then the gigantic surge crashed down, inundating everything for a kilometer around. The underground bunker flooded, generators shorted out, radar vans lifted on the flood and floated away momentarily, only to turn turtle and slowly sink below the surface, the operators trapped inside. Sparks made blue-and-orange spiderwebs over the metal skins and inside the delicate circuit boards of the SAM missiles, as the water level rose inexorably. Major Barrios and some of his staff found refuge in the two-story brick structure that had once housed a rope works.

They rapidly retreated to the second floor when the water rose to six feet inside the building. Frantically the RTOs attempted to open communication with the surviving units around the tank park on the far side of town, the infantry and artillery people, and the outside world. Only faintly did Major Barrios recognize the drone of propellers above the tumult of the flood.

Almost at once the antiaircraft guns at the tank park opened up, as did the AA missiles unaffected so far by the rising water. Enemy air activity? Barrios shuddered at the thought. The radio nearest him crackled to life as the Panamanian pilots at the small airstrip took to the air to defy the invaders.

"*Estandarte Uno*, this is *Cóndor*. We are engaging enemy aircraft. Over."

Barrios grabbed up the mike. "Vulture, this is Standard One. Designate one plane to assess damage to the area while the rest engage. Have your pilot report directly to me. Over."

"We will comply, Standard One."

Don't let it be too bad, Barrios willed. "If they follow this with an assault, we're doomed."

CHAPTER NINETEEN

Ignoring the ground fire and missiles, Juliet's Marsh Falcons lined up on the primary target and unloaded long streams of high-explosive bombs. Designed to penetrate concrete for a distance of several feet before exploding, they did maximum damage to the unflooded SAM sites, destroying SA-2 Guideline and SA-4 Ganef missiles in their hardstands. The volume of AA increased from below as S-60 57mm and ZU-23 23mm antiaircraft guns opened up.

Two Falcons wavered, spurted smoke, and side-slipped to oblivion in the marshy ground outside Gamboa. Another Marsh erupted into a bright orange ball. Trails of green Soviet tracer ammo made weird streaks on the sunset. The second flight of Falcons began their run on the SAM sites.

"Vindicator One, this is Oglala One. Break fast. There's lots of AA down there. Over."

"Roger on that, pappy. We copy and do. Vindicator One, out."

"Oglala One, this is Avenger Three. We've got bandits at niner-o'clock low. Look to be Foxtrot-fours. Must be Panamanians. Over."

"Roger, Avenger Three. Avenger One, break off bombing runs and take cover mission against the fast movers. Over."

"Rog-o, Oglala One. Copy and wilco. Avenger One, out."

Vicious Kukri missiles began to take a toll among the inexperienced and unprepared Panamanian pilots. F-4 Phantoms blew apart in the sky, showering the ground with flaming wreckage. Fires started in the palm thatch roofs of the town and general panic set in. Faced by a choice between a watery death and another form of mortality from the sky, the civilian populace jammed the streets, creating further complications for the military.

"Standard One, this is *Cóndor Dos*. We've lost seven aircraft. Over."

"Where is Vulture One?" Major Barrios demanded. "Over."

"He . . . just blew apart, Standard One. So far we haven't even seen what it is that's killing us. We're climbing to twenty thousand meters to shake off the enemy pursuit. Over."

"Stay down here, Vulture Two!" Barrios shouted. "You'll leave us at the mercy of the enemy. We need air cover. Over."

"Ah, acknowledge, Standard One, but they're blow—" Static replaced the voice as the Panamanian pilot who had assumed command of the F-4's vaporized in the white flash of a Kukri missile.

"*¡Condenación!*" Barrios shouted.

It might have been that the battle had functioned on his say-so, given the abruptness with which the Marsh Falcons of Legion Juliet broke off contact and sprinted for home to rearm at Madden Field. A crackling and gurgling silence replaced the bedlam of combat. Major Gustavo Barrios breathed a sigh of relief and began to direct a restoration of order. They might yet survive this madness. Particularly so, he decided when he saw the rapid approach of the MiGs from Darién Air Base. How magnificent! How right it is to end like this!

"How . . . how can this be?" he cried aloud, then continued. "Those aren't MiGs. They are the en—" Barrios and his discovery disappeared into oblivion when a Legion five-hundred-pound bomb detonated right in his makeshift headquarters.

Turboprops burring, the OV-10D's of Legion Foxtrot roared over, unleashing death and destruction from missile pods and bomb toggles.

* * *

Troops started landing at Gamboa at 2015 hours. Their small boats swiftly cut over the flood crest to the newly defined banks. Machine gun–firing jet skis led the way, slashing at the pockets of resistance in taller, isolated buildings, and the distant flicker of enemy fire inside Gamboa. In the forefront of the invasion, as on the Orinoco in Venezuela, Legionnaire Lester "Pearlyman" Fagin raced along beside Lieutenant Don Hoover. The little Cockney turned his head sideways and his voice crackled in Hoover's helmet receiver.

"We'll give 'em a right proper dust-up this time, eh, gov?"

"Bloody too right, jock," Don replied, affecting a Cockney accent. "Unless they up and do us first."

"Gor—never thought of that, gov'ner," Fagin came back, straight-faced.

At extreme operating range for the skis, Hoover and Fagin smashed into the stunned and demoralized resistance. About a company in strength, the Panamanian and Nicaraguan soldiers stood waist deep in water, their ammunition exhausted and resupply lost under the flood. The sight of the hell-belching 40mm auto grenade launcher and twin Ameli LMGs crushed their last vestige of defiance. They threw up their hands and waited docilely for instructions.

"Who's in command here?" Lieutenant Hoover queried.

From the midst of the defeated troops, who withdrew from his proximity, emerged a bedraggled, wild-eyed captain. "I am, I suppose," he answered in Spanish. "Major Barrios is dead, the war room destroyed, and all communications with the People's Defense Order command are cut off. We have no means to fight, without relief."

"I take that as an offer of surrender?" Don Hoover responded.

A blank stare answered him. Slowly, the disconcerted officer calmed slightly. He took a deep breath and looked around. His glazed eyes focused on the crested helmets of the men facing him, their unusual battle dress and outlandish weapons. Shaking his head as though in denial, he at last realized that he was not reporting to comrades sent to their relief but to the enemy. Galvanized to new energy by this revelation, he swiftly drew his Obregón pistol.

His being flashed out of existence in the loud burst from Fagin's righthand Ameli. "Bleedin' starkers, 'e was, gov'ner. Best to put 'im out of 'is misery, what?"

With the roaring whoosh of their huge Tumanskii R-29B turbofan engines, the MiG-23s came back. The air over Gamboa came alive with the swarming fast movers, boosted by 27,500 pounds of thrust at max augmentation, which unloaded thousands of pounds of ordnance on the Legion below. For the first time, the Legion came under heavy, serious air attack at twenty-two hundred hours. Puffs of smoke and the yellow-white flickers of rocket fire twinkled on the two AS-7 Kerry long-range ASMs on glove pylons on each MiG-23. Their snaky trails glowed through the sky as they sought out ground targets.

Explosions trashed Legion barges, fortunately not loaded with personnel, wrecked the surviving trucks and tanks of the defending force with equal unconcern, and went on to smoke buildings and Legion supply dumps. The presence of Hawk missile units kept the MiGs down on the deck, which met with the instant approval of the Blowpipe and new-generation three-tubed Javelin gunners. Such a concentration of fast movers, arriving far too late to aid the now-deceased Major Barrios, chased the vulnerable OV-10D's out of the area.

That meant little regarding their own life span. Blowpipes and Javelins began taking a brutal toll. MiGs flashed out of being. A pair collided in an unplanned maneuver designed to let both escape pursuing AA missiles. Captain Lloyd Harshman called frantically for air support. The Marsh Falcons were being serviced, he was informed.

"Like a fucking gas station," he shouted in frustration. "Like a fucking stud farm. They're getting serviced, for Christ's sake."

"They'll be back," Lieutenant Don Hoover told him reassuringly.

"If we don't have this son of a bitch under control by then, it won't matter much," Harshman told him. "Hell, we're the advance element. The whole show's coming right behind us. They'll get creamed, man, creamed."

At 2215 hours, Legion Juliet returned. Spitting their highly maneuverable dogfighting Kukri missiles, the Marsh Ag Cats played billy-be-hell with the old BN and MF model MiG-23s. By the time they arrived on station and began unleashing the speedy killers, the air war had nearly been won. Then a small flight of newer MiG-25U's came blowing in at Mach 3.2 and their turbulence literally threw the light, fragile Marshes out of the air. Three pilots died before the squadron could take effective diversionary maneuvers.

Then the Kukris began to eat MiG-25s. With the enormous speed advantage, several MiG pilots tried to outturn the Kukris. Two of them blacked out from superhuman G levels, and one flashing speed machine splashed into a hillside to the north of Gamboa. The other cartwheeled along the flood crest for a ways as it broke up into huge chunks of junk aluminum honeycomb.

The remaining MiGs, their weapons systems exhausted, opted for the safety of Darién. In the wake of their departure, Dick House summoned his surviving pilots.

"Avenger One, Vindicator One, this is Oglala. I want the three aircraft with the largest reserves of ammo to remain on station. The rest of us will head for home and reload. Report. Over."

Quickly the list ran down, each pilot giving a reading on his ammunition status. Dick assigned the twenty-percent cover under Staff Sergeant Jim O'Borney and led the rest away to Madden Field.

"Let 'er rip!" came the command over the special air-to-ground net in the command-center vehicle of the Fourth Cohort.

Overhead, rigged as gunships, the entire Legion complement of Helio Stallions led out on the road to Darién. The Legion had every intention of bringing their particular brand of hell to the home of bellicose MiGs, and, if intelligence could be believed, assertive armor.

With their departure from the Gamboa staging area, it left the First, Second, and Third free to ride the second flood crest down the Chagres River. As they passed under the Gamboa bridge, led by scouting jet skis, they received hearty cheers from above by the Fifth's security detachment and attached units.

"Get a load of them, will you?" Staff Sergeant Darrel Williams of third squad, Charlie Century, of the Fifth told his squad. "From this angle they look like a bunch of bum boats and Hakka scows in Hong Kong Harbor."

Three of his Legionnaires followed Williams's pointing finger and nodded. Below, anything with an engine towed anything capable of floating supplies, interspersed with units of hundreds of Folbots loaded with Legionnaires, which in turn were escorted by the busy little jet skis. Seen like this, the controlled madness took on the aspect of a Chinese fire drill. Then the voice of his assistant squad leader, Corporal Koi Suginaga, came to him, rich with a Hawaiian beach boy accent.

"Yeah, the lucky dogs. They're gonna bring a lot of scalding pee down on the Beaners at Barro Colorado, while we just sit here."

"You want to go with 'em? Just jump over the side," Williams riposted.

"What? And miss the overwhelming pleasure of your company?" Koi shot back sarcastically.

CHAPTER TWENTY

Lieutenant Luis Inchausti listened to the chitter of insects, the nocturnal hum of mosquitoes, and the haunting banter of coatis. From a distance came the hissing snarl of hunting jaguars and the frightened hoots of fruit-eating monkeys. He dabbed delicately at the thin pencil line of mustache beneath his long, straight, aristocratic Castilian nose. Then he dug a spoon into the still-steaming contents of the thick plastic bag. Quite a deal, these reconstituted rations of the Americans. *Chicken and Rice*, the label read. *Portion, Individual, one each*. With a bit of personal seasoning, some garlic powder, a dried chili pod, and some sliced onion—from a bag he'd conned a Navy cook out of before the landing— Luis had managed to turn it into an almost passable *arroz con pollo*. If only he'd had some saffron and diced tomatoes, Luis lamented.

His crew had heated their meals on the manifold of their idling Panhard, like most of the unit, and took advantage of the break to chow down. For all the violence they had encountered with the unexpected Soviet armor at Puerto Pelón, they had fared well, Luis reasoned. He took another prodigious bite and set his meal aside as the briefing appeared about to get under way. Quiet washed like a tide over the assembled officers as Major Gordon Rounding approached the head of the field table, where a portable map stand had been set up.

Luis did consider Legion Charlie's commander to be a bit flamboyant with his twin Bisley Colts, when the tough little

Englishman swaggered into position before them in the temporary headquarters in Silver City. *¡Mierda!* He was tired and being unfair, Luis chided himself. The Limey had already proven himself one hell of a fighting commander. Still, a really modern weapon like his own fine Star PD was a comfort.

Was he perhaps being emotional simply because he'd spent a number of years in the junior-executive program at Star Bonifacio? A powerful wave of nostalgia nearly brought tears to his eyes as Luis recalled the mad impulse that had turned him from an advantageous marriage and promising career into an officer in the Royal Army of Spain. Ah, his beautiful and beloved Estrella. She of the sparkling green eyes and trilling laugh. Given his native ability and the support of such a wife, his career at Star Bonifacio, or anywhere else, would have been assured. What little-boy fantasy had generated the image he became obsessed with, of himself in a flashy uniform?

Worse still, what imp of satan had caused him to fall in love with the damned Panhards? Luis recalled the moment he'd first seen them at the *Veinte-ocho de Marzo* parade in Bilbao to celebrate the anniversary of the Nationalist relief of the capital back in 1937 during the Civil War. Before the day was out, he'd signed up with the Royal Spanish Army, his *bachillerato* and completion of third-cycle studies guaranteed, along with admission to Officers' School. And, before he knew it, he was posted to Morocco. So much lost so soon, he sighed, for a man who could still consider himself young and handsome.

"Lieutenant Inchausti!"

The forceful mention of his name snapped Luis out of his fatigue-induced reminiscences and into the present. He saw before him Major Rounding's leathery face, the brown brow puckered into wrinkles as he glared at the young lieutenant. Luis swallowed hard when Rounding started to reprimand him, then thought better of it and rapped the map of Colón instead.

"Everyone put down whatever you're eating and take a look at this. As I was saying, Lieutenant, you will take your command on a dash through the lines and secure a perimeter around the Hilton Hotel . . . here." Gordon Rounding indicated the exact spot. "I suggest you mark it on your map."

Embarrassed, Luis matched streets and located the intersection, then worked out an approach route from the outskirts into Colón. With a satisfied nod, Major Rounding continued.

"G-two says the hostages are all quartered above the ground floor. There are flash grenades, Hardcorps vests, extra bucklers, with spare Sidewinders and Jackhammers for your crews, if you need them. Don't get fancy. You are not—I'll say again—*are not* rescue specialists. If you do not see hostages on the ground floor, smash in and kill anything that moves. Better draw a half-dozen Jackhammers for that stage. But *make sure* they don't go upstairs."

Luis shuddered at the thought of Jackhammers in a rescue operation. The deadly full-auto shotguns would slaughter nearly everything in any given room of a building before the operator could sort good guys from bad. With a mental jerk, he returned to the briefing.

"Each commander has a specific location, what? There's Soviet-made armor in the railroad yards. Skip, that'll be yours. We have to secure the water system to make it available for fire fighting later on. Reggie, that's your baby. The police central and jail complex I'll handle. The rest of you cover our asses while we nail our objectives. Any questions?" There were none. "In that case, we're dismissed. Good luck."

With a grateful sigh, Luis Inchausti grabbed up his chicken and rice and headed for the supply depot.

Lieutenant Colonel Chuck Taylor looked like a grim character from the battle scenes in *Julius Caesar* with his crested Legion helmet. From a slight rise, where he'd ordered his command car halted, he watched the action below. At 0030 hours, his Fourth Cohort hit Darién from the south. Tracers made a Christmas-light display, red outgoing, green incoming. The solid BLAM-BLAM-BLAM of the 50s and light chatter of the 7.62 LMGs provided the rhythm and melody of this symphony of death. A radio crackled to life and announced the counterpoint.

"Lummee Zero-zero, this is Chickasaw One, over." The familiar voice of Colonel Don Beisel announcing the arrival of Legion Foxtrot and the OV-10 night fighters eased Chuck's mind.

"This is Lummee Zero-zero. Welcome to the party. Over."

"We've got our night eyes on, so all we need is a few star shells to mark targets, Lummee Zero-zero. Over."

"You've got 'em, Chickasaw one. Good hunting. Lummee Zero-zero, out."

Down on the shore of Gatún Lake the thump and crump of battle drowned out all other sound. Serving as the major of two disbursal points—Frijoles being the second—the Nicaraguans had left Darién well defended. Their artillery and mortars ripped into the ranks of Fourth Cohort, spreading wide swatches of wounded. First-timers, unaccustomed to the benefits of Second Chance's Hardcorps and soft body armor, marveled at being alive after taking multiple hits from shrapnel. When the word reached Alpha Century to fire star shells over enemy positions, it greatly heartened Captain Jason Black. Stony knew help was on the way.

"Get 'em out there," he told the 4.2-inch mortarmen. "Make sure you mark the gawdamned bunkers and the gun emplacements covering the highway. We're gonna run right in under that shit after we get the air strike."

"What air strike?" a kid-faced Legion mortarman asked.

"The birds are on the way," Stony Black told him calmly. "That's what the star shells are for, dummy."

Illuminating rounds belched from the tubes and arched over the two lead Centuries, and the Nicaraguan defenses came into stark relief under myriad new suns. At once, Legion Foxtrot streaked in at treetop level and unloaded cluster bombs in a long string that sowed the deadly seeds in batches, which pounded and pulped the Nicaraguan infantry on the MLR. Having spotted hardened targets on the bombing run, the OV-10s doubled back and engaged them with rockets.

Although great gaps appeared in the main line of resistance, the Nicaraguan and rebel troops put up fierce opposition. Here and there Grail 7 missiles streaked into the air, and as the third sweep over the target area began, two

OV-10D's turned into balls of flame and ruin. Whistles shrilled along the Legion line and a determined advance began.

From the far side of the city, a battery of Soviet 180mm S-23 field guns slammed 194-pound shells at the gaps in the line. AH-64 Cobra gunships struck at the muzzle flashes within the one minute required to reload.

Under a devastating hail of mortar and light-artillery fire, the soldiers of the Legion swarmed over the enemy, following the soft red glow of their leaders' patrol lights. The range closed to a hundred meters before the first Nicaraguans broke.

We're on the lake! The exhilarating realization struck Lieutenant Don Hoover as Bravo of the Second rode the dissipating second flood crest into Gatún Lake and circled around Darién in their small boats and jet skis, to come ashore to the north and cut off any retreat toward Frijoles. Overhead, Legion Juliet—not equipped with the excellent night-fighting electronics of Foxtrot's OV-10s—flew top cover. Don spared them a glance as he directed the other skis to provide escort for the small boats. More star shells burst and the speedy Broncos made another pass over Darién.

So far they had been lucky, Don Hoover considered. Both squadrons had such low IR profiles that they were immune to the big, long-range SAMs at Barro Colorado and most of the medium missiles the enemy would have. Still the Legion air could take casualties. Another OV-10 fell even as Don considered it. Something inside shriveled a bit as its flaming parts spun lazily toward the ground. A pervading, familiar rush of air claimed his consciousness.

There, to the west, darker shapes against the star-clustered night. Fast movers. The Panamanian F-4 Phantoms.

"*Halcón* leader, this is *Halcón* Three. I have visual contact with the enemy, over," a voice crackled on the Panamanian squadron net.

"Then you're too close, *Halcón* three," the flight leader rapped out. "Pull back. We will attack in echelon right. Fire missiles first. *Halcón* leader out."

With the thundering power of their jet engines, the F-4's bore in on Legion Foxtrot. At five thousand meters they released their missiles in a flat arc that would take them down toward the unsuspecting OV-10 Broncos. A moment later hotly burning decoy flares blossomed and led many of the slender, finned projectiles off on useless pursuits. Instantly Legion Juliet leaped on the jets from above with a volley of Kurki missiles.

Forced to take evasive countermeasures, the F-4 pilots gave off their attack run and jinked away into open air space in an effort to avoid the determined air-to-air killers. They likewise released flares. As the Panamanian Phantoms powered upward it soon became obvious their gamble didn't pay off. Four out of the six birds burst into flaming rubble, which rained down on the defenders of Darién.

Another flight of six Phantoms followed the Hawk squadron, and the surviving pair joined them. Immediately, the once orderly formations became a mad scramble. Enemy AA gunners and missile units on the ground could not fire for fear of hitting their own. Not so the three-tube British Javelin missiles of the Legion. Each murderous projectile carefully preselected its target, then scooted away to deliver a mortal blow.

The sky rained Phantoms. Three out of the fast movers disintegrated or burst into flame, trailing bits and pieces. Two pilots managed to eject before the fateful encounter, drifting down serenely over the wild scramble of combat below.

Chuck Taylor listened with a frown on his face to the excited report from the advance elements of Alpha Century. Acknowledging it, he got on the command net to the headquarters Century Javelin team.

"We've got another target for you. Prepare for ground targets and fix on a platoon of T-72 tanks moving out from the eastern end of town. They're trying to flank our advance and wipe up from the rear."

"Roger, Lummee Zero-zero," came the acknowledgment.

Three minutes later the earth shook to the detonations of internal explosives when the T-72s took direct hits from Javelin missiles. The impact of the inertial warheads turned hardened steel to liquid that became white-hot shrapnel inside the forty-thousand-kilo Soviet-made tanks. It ruptured fuel and hydraulic lines and started fires. Exposed ammunition took care of the rest.

With the bulk of Bravo Second ashore, Captain Lloyd Harshman issued new orders.

"The jet skis are to conduct interdiction operations to the north. Chop up anything coming by water to relieve the garrison at Darién. Don, keep 'em tight and keep 'em primed. I'll be running land ops, pushing outward toward Frijoles. . . ." Harshman paused a moment. "Who'd ever call a town 'Beans'? Anyway, that's the picture. So far we've got the numbers on our side, but the resistance can only build from here on. Now let's go out and do it."

"*¡Diez milliones de demonios!*" Juan Bautista Corrales shouted when he read the few words on the message form. "Darién has fallen to elements of the Legion," he informed his staff.

Comandante de División Corrales had called a hasty gathering when word first came of the approach on Darién. It put the enemy dangerously close. Now, with the city in Legion hands, he had little doubt of their eventual goal. Things were decidedly *not* going as they should. He felt vulnerable, exposed, even betrayed. Bitterly he outlined the situation to his staff.

"As you know, our combined air forces were compelled to abandon Albrook and France Air Bases. They fell back on the only alternative strip that could handle them, at Darién. With Madden Field in the hands of the mercenaries, there was insufficient fuel, armament, and maintenance support available. We were lucky to get a couple of unarmed MiG squadrons started back to Nicaragua." *Comandante* Corrales wiped his heavily perspiring brow, then continued.

"The Panamanians managed to lose their Phantom aircraft as well. Our ground forces were left alone, after the initial assault, to stand off the enemy. They were defeated by overwhelming numbers of missiles, aircraft, and smart mortar rounds. The Legion, when its infantry attacked, came like *los indios* in the *yanqui* Wild West cinema.

"These cowardly mercenaries have blown Madden dam and drowned many of our soldiers like rats, rather than face them in open combat. Now our SAM missile sites are flooding and artillery emplaced to cover the channel approaches is underwater. The hostage ships we ran aground are in danger of floating off and we do not have indigenous personnel with the expertise to prevent this in the event of more flooding. In light of this recent and rapid development, I am open to suggestions."

Several ideas were put forward, none of which appealed to Corrales. At last he silenced his fellow officers. "This is but one course I can see. We must contact our main troop deployments along the Trans-Panama Highway and have them return some trailing elements to smash this impudent thrust by the Legion. Second, the ships' crews must be sorted out from the prisoners and forced to drive their ships further aground."

General agreement followed. With a sinking feeling that he had done too little too late, Corrales ordered the radio message sent. Yet, a fierce determination flared in his breast. Now the Legion would come to him and he would smash them between his mobile force and the defenses of Barro Colorado.

CHAPTER TWENTY-ONE

More bad news awaited CD Corrales in the black, early hours of the new day. At 0148 hours he received a report that a third flood crest was heading his way. If that didn't constitute enough to worry about, his engineering officer's hasty announcement capped the night of woes.

"Three of the beached ships have gone adrift, Comrade *Comandante*. Including the cruise vessel."

"Why weren't they put under power so that could be prevented?" Corrales demanded.

"By your orders, Comrade *Comandante*, all had been stripped of crews for the labor force. There are only token watches aboard."

"I am aware of that, dolt. Those orders were remanded this very night," Corrales raged.

"Yes, sir. Uh, sir," the engineer responded. "Uh, there's more. The imperialist dogs refuse to identify themselves, and our records were so badly water-soaked in the initial flooding they're nearly illegible, sir!"

Corrales accepted this bit of news in silence, fighting hard to contain his temper. The engineer took the quiet as encouragement.

"With the ships afloat, the women hostages are now removed from the immediate vicinity of the missile stands. Worse, Comrade *Comandante*, the missiles are themselves endangered by rising water. What this third flood crest will mean, I haven't yet calculated."

"I can tell you one thing," Corrales answered coldly. "It

means the Legion commander is still blowing holes in Madden dam. Have any of the rest of you something to report?" His eyes settled on the G-2.

Shamefaced, the intelligence officer rose, a thin sheet of paper in his hand for reference. "Comrade *Comandante*, a small bridge on the Trans-Panama had been blown and a blocking force installed to isolate the defenders of Ciudad Panamá."

Damn! Corrales thought. He'd sent all of their bridging equipment along toward Colón, due to the possibility that loyal Panamanian forces might demolish the bridges to buy time.

"Is there no good news?"

His G-2 heaved a hearty sigh. "Yes, comrade, there is. Trailing elements of the Colón task force have turned around and are on the way back toward Frijoles. They will engage the Legion there."

Lights flashed and whistles shrieked in the prisoner compound on Barro Colorado at two hundred hours. Nicaraguan sergeants yelled in shrill Spanish. Slowly the fatigued prisoners responded.

"Out! Everyone out!" the noncoms bellowed. "Turn out for work."

"What's all this about?" several voices complained.

They soon found out. Once formed into ranks, a rumple-uniformed captain addressed them in English. "There are reports of another rising flood crest on the way here. You are to fill sandbags and place them along the shores to the south and east. You are working to save your own lives, as well as for the liberation. Ship's crews will be excused from labor, take one step forward, face right, and fall into separate ranks."

No one moved.

"Imperialist peegs!" shouted the frowsy officer. "We have your names, remember. Step forward or be shot as you are identified."

The bluff worked, very slowly. The merchant seamen managed to draw it out for half an hour.

Fuller scratched at the stubble that had grown on his face

nearly as long and thick as his drooping mustache. The moment floodwaters had been mentioned, he realized such an excessive flow this time of year could only be the Legion's doing. While the files marched to the work area, he sought out Andros Kalamantiano.

"Andros," he asked in a side-of-the-mouth whisper. "What could cause a flood like this?"

"I haven't any idea. A great tidal wave, perhaps Captain. But the locks should tame that before it reaches us. The portion of the island we're shoring up is interesting. There's nothing in that direction except the Chagres River, and at its head, Madden dam. Opening the floodgates might...ah, but no. The volume they could handle would not account for the rise in level we have already experienced." Andros pointed to the swirling, oily-black water to their left, its surface dotted with flecks of foam.

A wild light glowed in Bob Fuller's eyes. "Thank you very much, Andros." Then his enthusiasm completely overcame him and he threw back his head to shout. "Watie, you crazy bastard, you've blown the damn dam! The Legion is coming! The Legion is coming!"

Electrified, the prisoners produced a cheer that grew to a roar. Before their guards could react, those closest snatched the weapons from the Nicaraguans' hands and cracked skulls with glee. Spontaneous joy became feral riot as the word spread.

"*¡Socorro! ¡Socorro!*" a young soldier from Managua bleated a moment before his own AK's butt smashed his jaw and eager feet trampled him into the mud.

Shots crackled near the rear of the column and the armed prisoners hurried in that direction. There they brought down some fifteen soldiers who sought to contain the outburst. Scooping up their arms, including hand grenades, the howling prisoners continued on. Four men veered to one side and appropriated the entire contents of a mortar installation. Two French Legionnaires grabbed a light machine gun and four metal containers of ammunition. Well armed now, they led the way across the compound, shooting any opposition, and disappeared into the jungle.

"Head for the center of the island," Bob Fuller shouted to those around him. "We can hold them off there."

Like a swarm of gnats, small boats wove around the dock at Gigante, the former support town for the Smithsonian staff. Behind the village, hardy Legionnaires did rolling leaps from grass-skimming Helio Stallions. Quickly they formed up and advanced on the rear of the small force holding the lakeside community. Grenades crunched and the heavy slam of Garands filled the night. Here and there men screamed and died or expired horribly in the blast of a mine. As the Legionnaires dashed ashore from the Folbots, two entire squads of a light-infantry platoon went down in an avalanche of machine-gun fire and bursting 30mm grenades from AGS-17 Plamya AGLs.

Mortar fire from the airborne insertion began landing on the enemy MLR and the AGS-17s grew silent. One by one the machine guns ceased to chatter and thump. Yelling fierce war cries, the Legionnaires overran the primary defenses and pounded into the village. For a moment it appeared that the increased volume of desperate fire would drive them back.

Then roofs began to blaze and terrified PDF rebels ran screaming from the burning buildings. Legion riflemen cut them down with methodical calmness. Five minutes after the assault began, the battle ended. A tiny pocket of resistance remained in a small chapel built for the native workers on the project. A squad of heavy infantry started in on the thick front doors.

Ten minutes of unproductive fire indicated that the ornately carved pieces were not made of any ordinary wood. "Damn," Sergeant Mike Presley exploded. "That must be fuckin' ironwood. Two of you, come around to the side with me."

Garands opened up again a minute later, to the accompaniment of tinkling glass. Inside, the altar screen flew apart in chunks and the huge crucifix above it took three mortal wounds in the chest and head of the Christ figure. Cries of alarm arose and the front doors swung wide. The occupants rushed out, bayonets fixed and their FN/FALs blazing. Two went down at once, ripped by .30–06 rounds from the squad's M-1 Garands. Then the opposing soldiers closed and steel rang on steel.

Horrible shrieks came from first one, then another of the Panamanian rebels as the wide leaf blades of the Legion Glaudii slashed their bodies, opening them from rib cage to crotch. Spilling coils of intestine, the fatally wounded rebels sank to their knees, then fell in the welter of their own gore. The remainder, shaken, three wounded, gave up.

"Back to the boats," Captain John Dyer, CO of Charlie of the First commanded. "Sergeant Inman, pick three craft to guide the rest in. We're ready for the jump off to Barro Colorado."

A soft, red glow illuminated the LCD numerals on Lieutenant Luis Inchausti's Legion watch. It read 0236 hours. Not bad time for reaching Colón, considering they had met sporadic resistance all along the highway. None, however, like what waited ahead, Luis judged, based on the sounds of fighting from the outskirts of the city. He ordered his Panhard scout cars to button up and gave the advance as he snapped the safety cover shut on his watch.

"Up ahead, Lieutenant," Luis's driver's voice crackled in his ears.

Luis sighted the low-pressure main gun on the glowing figures of an RPG crew that loomed behind sandbags at an intersection two blocks away. When the rangefinder settled down, he tripped the trigger and hurtled a round in that direction. The rocket gunner and his assistant disappeared from the face of the earth.

Clangs and *plocks* registered strikes by small-arms fire on the outer hull of the Panhard. As the formation roared through the streets toward the Colón Hilton, Luis risked a sideways observation in time to see two squads of harassing infantry ground into hamburger by the external-mount antimissile Gatling on one of his vehicles.

Nasty weapons, the straight-casing 20mm, six-barrel Gatlings fired a load of shot that effectively put 75,000 rounds downrange per six-second burst. Although not ordinarily approved for antipersonnel use, they had served well in this case. The enemy troops had four rocket launchers with them, and one of the dying men managed to get off an RPG-7 round before he fell from loss of blood.

The Soviet-made flying bomb wavered erratically toward its target, only to disappear in a bright flash when a second burst of the Gatling slapped into it. Beside Luis, his RTO and loader worked the dial of the Panhard's set, seeking the Legion command net. A Mickey Mouse voice warbled at them in and out of frequency until a fine touch of clarifier steadied it into a human voice.

"A little update for all troops FYI. Another wave of Marines has landed at Panama City and resistance is crumbling. Additional U.S. Marines and their British counterparts have landed to the west of Colón and are closing on the city as our own forces advance through the outskirts. Heavy resistance is reported."

That last brought a laugh from everyone in the Panhard. Luis slapped his loader on the shoulder and nodded toward the distant silhouette of a T-54. It waited like a deadly spider some four blocks ahead, the turret as yet turned away from them.

"Let me have a smart round. I'll spot that monster and take him out before he knows we're here."

"At the rate we're going, this won't take long," Mike Rupp, the gunner, said glibly.

"*A ver si podemos ir a Cuba este verano,*" Luis quipped back in Spanish.

"Huh?" Mike asked as he shoved in the 60mm shell.

"I said, 'Let's see if we can go to Cuba next summer.'"

"Oh, sure. *That'd* be a lot of fun." Mike emphasized his meaning by slamming the breach.

Luis's index finger touched the small white button in the target-control stick and an unseen laser beam struck the tank. A moment later he tripped the trigger and sent a smart round after the telltale spot. It found the mark with a shattering roar as the T-54 blew up like a movie car crash.

"That did it," Luis breathed out. "We should have a clear path from now on."

Taller buildings flashed past the roaring Panhards. Legion India closed in on the plaza, where they came in sight of the tall tower of the Hilton. At Luis's direction the scout cars spread out into intersecting streets and signaled their arrival at the indicated positions.

"Now all we have to do is knock on the door," Luis declared.

"This is impossible!" Captain Santos Arvelos shouted at the gathering of troops in the spacious lobby of the Colón Hilton. "Damn you all for fools, cowards, and whores' sons! What do you mean you can't stop them?"

"We have no more ammunition for the rocket launchers, *Capitan*," a burly sergeant explained with a shrug. "Rifle fire bounces off the vehicles these Legion *cabrones* drive. We are helpless."

"I shit on your helplessness, García," Arvelos ranted back. Yet a part of him acknowledged the truthfulness of Sergeant García's words. They had only two RPGs to begin with. Against even light armor, their assault rifles and light machine guns were nothing.

"The sergeant is right," an aging lieutenant offered. "We can do nothing against them. It is wiser if we flee the building, *Capitán*."

"We fought hard enough to take it," Arvelos snapped back. "Now the people in here are our hostages. The *Yanqui* mercenaries out there will not fire their big guns. Man for man, we outnumber them. They *can* be beaten. Give me that voice amplifier."

With the bullhorn in hand, Arvelos strode purposefully up the curved stair to the mezzanine. There he went to a window facing the front of the hotel and raised the amplifier to his lips.

"American capitalist dogs! Do you hear me? *Yanqui* mercenaries, listen well. We have many people here as hostages. Do not attack this building or we will begin killing them. There are members of the Moldinado government here, American businessmen, tourists, women, and children. The children will die first and we will throw their twitching bodies onto your bayonets. I demand that you withdraw immediately and join with the *Fuerza Defensora* and our Nicaraguan comrades to prevent the *norteño* Marines from entering the city. Only this way will you pay for your lives.

Otherwise we will kill the hostages, then we will kill you."
Arvelos paused a long moment. "What is your answer? You
have five minutes."

Luis Inchausti gave him an immediate answer. At point-
blank range, his 60mm gun slammed a direct hit into the
front of the hotel facade. It blew away the small balcony and
shredded the body of Captain Santos Arvelos, who stood
behind the windows. At once, Luis spoke into his Century net.

"Ironman Two, come with me."

With that, Luis led a two-car charge that circled to the
right and then rammed through the side of the building, into
the lobby. The second car sported an antimissile Gatling,
which Luis directed to sweep the interior. The roaring,
snorting multibarreled weapon trashed everything. At such
close range the volume of shot stripped the plaster from the
inner walls, dissolved the reservations desk, and killed
nearly all the enemy troops still rooted by shock to their
places. Again, Luis spoke.

"Sheepskin fiver-two, fiver-three, and fiver-four come on
in."

Three Bradley fighting vehicles, their 90mm guns re-
versed, smashed through another outside wall and fifteen
Legionnaires spilled out of them, Pancor Jackhammers and
Sidewinder SMGs at the ready. The special crash crew wore
Second Chance Hardcorps body armor and carried bucklers.
Through the dust and flying debris caused by the forceful
entry, the Sidewinder-armed Legionnaires hit the stairway
while their Jackhammer-toting buddies mopped up in the
lobby.

Feeble cries for mercy and wails of surrender faded under
the basso profundo roar of the 12-gauge full-auto guns.
Blood, flesh, and feces splattered the walls and ceiling, and
pools of crimson gore formed on the floor. Although not so
well protected in his soft vest, Luis bailed out of his command vehicle with a Sidewinder. Over the helmet radio he
instructed his driver to pull all the vehicles out and resume a
perimeter patrol. He switched to the command frequency
and spoke again.

"We have the ground floor secured. Jackhammer men,

move out to the attached parking garage. There's bound to be more enemy there. I'm going upstairs. If there's trouble, reach me on this frequency through your squad leaders."

Luis took to the stairs, bounding up the first two flights two at a time, to the occasional thump of flash grenades and frequent short barks of automatic fire. Through the shattered windows in the wall to his right he could hear the echoing detonations of Jackhammers in the parking garage. Between the mezzanine and second floor he encountered a dazed and frightened knot of rescued hostages.

"Keep going down. You are not wearing uniforms, so you won't be hurt. Move on out of the hotel. There will be someone to care for you there," he instructed them in English and Spanish.

Around the bend in the stairwell one story higher, he came upon the grotesquely sprawled corpse of a former hostage who hadn't fared too well. Ahead he heard the stutter of controlled three-round bursts from Sidewinders and realized the terrorist bastards were still resisting. Luis put on a spurt of speed and reached the fourth-floor landing in the middle of a brief, nasty firefight.

Hardly had he rounded the doorjamb when stinging pain ran up his arm after a stray steel slug from a Soviet AK trashed his Sidewinder. Grimacing but game, Luis ducked back and drew his Star PD. With a leap, he cleared the doorway and bounded off the opposite wall. He came up with the muzzle downrange.

"*¡Pan y libertad!*" a wild-eyed rebel shouted a moment before Luis put a .45 slug through his left nostril.

"There's your bread and liberty, *cabrón*," Luis growled.

Znnap! Another AK round snapped past Luis's head and he heard a grunt behind him. The stray had taken a Legionnaire in the neck. His mind on the melee before him, Luis reached out and snagged the dead Legionnaire's buckler. He turned back to the fight in time to see a Soviet-made M-10 grenade rolling along the corridor directly toward him.

Luis barely had time to drop to the floor behind his buckler when the shield slammed against his head and shoulder. Dazed, bleeding from nose and ears, Luis rose unsteadily to his knees. A quick glance showed him to be the only living Legionnaire in the hallway. An instant later the dust-laden air filled with automatic fire as three Panamanian rebels charged line-abreast behind flaming muzzles.

Cool, detached, and operating in an apparent time warp, Luis gunned down each of them with the PD. The first he gave a head shot. Then he waited impatiently for the gun to come down and line up so he could tick off the next round. All movement seemed to be in congealed gelatin. Suddenly he looked around in a vast silence, surprised to find there were no more targets. Again Luis tried to stand and found his ankles would not support him.

Puzzled, he glanced down to find the cause, and discovered a red ooze from shrapnel-shredded boots. With a soft sigh, the fierce warrior from Castile passed out.

CHAPTER TWENTY-TWO

Soft wavelets lapped against taut rubber skins as Captain Henri Chaud gauged the height of the setting moon and judged it would settle into the jungle on his left flank within the hour. His orders read, 0430 hours. That's when he was to attack. It must be three o'clock now. Ahead of him, distinct tracers arced erratically skyward and flashes, underlined by long belated thunder, told the gruesome story.

A grimace of humor bent Chaud's craggy features; it was brought on by an old folk saying that crossed his mind. "Swatting flies with a sledgehammer." Why not? If the Nicaraguan bastards were throwing that heavy stuff at the fire-spitting little jet skis that harassed their shores, it would be exactly what they were doing. Henri took a survey of his flotilla of rubber dinghies and a low, bitter bark of laughter escaped him.

That miserable giant of an Indian had relegated his elite French Legionnaires to these toy boats. Arm-weary, and beginning to straggle, they plied their flimsy craft into battle. A slight disturbance from behind caught Chaud's attention. Then a voice hailed and long, sleek boats slid in among them, each paddled by four men of the American Foreign Legion. Instantly recognizable by their arrogant crested helmets, the Legionnaires passed with silent, powerful strokes, leaving the Frenchman envious of both their craft and skill. Muttered comments from his men, the dregs of a dozen nations, indicated they didn't share his contempt.

"*Bon chance, Amérique,*" whispered one French Legionnaire.

"*Vive les Légions,*" called another.

"*Très bons batteaux,*" one remarked on the passing boats.

Those boats! Captain Chaud recognized them as Folbots. Sleek and sturdy in the water, their odd name derived from the fact they could be collapsed for easy storage and transport. Henri Chaud heard a derisive voice from the last canoe and belatedly translated it.

"Get a horse."

What the hell could he do with a horse out here? the French commander pondered. Then he shook his head. He must have been mistaken.

Bill Kane tried to count the foaming wakes behind him as the semicircle of waning tropical moon touched distant tree-tops. Kane preferred daylight for almost everything but screwing. Here he was, out on the water at 0345 hours on the fourth day after the initial invasion, skimming along in a silly little boat while the horizon ahead sparkled and flared with the ghastly lights of battle. For all of that, Bill feared there would be too little illumination to pass through the wakes of slower boats in front of him once the moon was entirely gone. Abruptly his craft veered, and muttered curses came over the powerful drone of muffled outboards.

"Watch where you're fuckin' goin'," a Bronx accent snarled.

"Up yours, Jack," an unseen reply came.

"At least you ain't no Beaner," the boy from the Bronx retorted.

In the next minute, Bill's inflatable craft wove through laboring Legionnaires in shadowy, paddle-powered life rafts. Then they pulled into the clear and Bill breathed a sigh of relief. Head swiveling, he tried to count his craft again. Worry over possible collisions eased when he recalled no shouts of surprise or anger. At last he could relax.

Then they set to dodging again, the moon nearly gone, yet light enough to show snags and snarls in the flowing water. It also provided enough illumination to recognize Legion crests on the helmets, and this time, as they pulled away from the rafts, Bill heard jet skis on a high-speed run far ahead. From the briefing he knew, it would be Bravo of the Second's scouting contingent, coming in from Darién to join the main battle. Bill checked his watch and grinned.

Right on time. Jesus, maybe they could pull it off after all. Suddenly the inflatables were among another wave of life rafts. As expected, the helmets were round in contour and triggered an angry response in Bill's thoroughly Legion breast. After two campaigns, he'd come to recognize any helmet without the crest as the symbol of a probable enemy. The reaction caused instant resentment that the Froggies had been given the honor of leading the entire life-raft contingent ashore. He instantly regretted his uncharitable thoughts.

After all, the French Legion had been around a hell of a lot longer than their own. They'd had a lot of hairy fighting in well over a hundred years. It wasn't their fault the politicians pulled the plug on them at Dien Bien Phu, or that de Gaulle had betrayed them in Algiers. He was waxing almost lyrical in their support when to his right one of his inflatables suddenly porpoised and capsized as it overran a French dinghy.

Bill's gut clenched and his balls retracted painfully in sympathy for the screaming men as his flotilla powered steadily on. God, someone had to have been badly hurt in that. Bill made a vain effort to take satisfaction that the French Legionnaires were more in harm's way than his own people. The rationalization didn't work. Hell, the poor bastards were only doing a job. The same job he and his men were doing. *They* had prisoners on that fucking island, too. Silently he hoped someone would be able to rescue every one of the dunkers.

Absolutely vital that you achieve a successful conclusion to your current project within the next forty-eight hours.

The unsigned note had been delivered to Jason Aldridge's Manhattan townhouse by messenger service during his absence. Now, in the early morning hours, his infrequent lust sated by a rousing encounter with a talented young girl from Harlem, he felt too world-weary to consider business. Perhaps, Jason pondered a moment, he should throw this one over. It represented the greatest danger for him. All odds indicated he would be detected, apprehended, and exposed, successful or not. Yet... the challenge. Ah! That was it. The absolute to which anything could be reduced. If it challenged enough. Jason sighed and walked through the empty townhouse to his bedroom.

In the morning, he decided, he would pack his equipment and make ready to depart for his ultimate kill.

The arrival of Bravo of the Second's thirty-five jet skis at 0430 hours coincided with Legion Juliet's first morning air strike on Barro Colorado. Terrible destruction was evident wherever they went, and the fading drone of the strike aircraft could still be heard when they throttled back. Flames leaped high into the air and illuminated a scene out of wartime London. Or perhaps Dresden or Hamburg, Lieutenant Don Hoover thought as he wet dry lips and spoke into the small mike of his helmet radio.

"We'll swing around that peninsula," he informed the tiny fleet. "Keep wide of the shore and be ready for an immediate response. You are free to engage targets of opportunity. Blackhawk One-two, out."

Beyond the finger of land, the signs of destruction became awesomely worse. As their eyes adjusted to the intense light of the fires and awesome explosions, the Bravos saw a tempting target materialize in the form of a tugboat. It labored sturdily to shove the helpless cruise ship and its cargo of screaming women back toward the raging inferno that had recently been a SAM base. A wisp of smoke and steam rose from one of the fairing-enclosed stacks, indicating an effort to get up pressure and power the ship. It couldn't be the regular black gang, Don Hoover figured, or they would have it done by now.

"Let's take that tug," he ordered crisply into the mike.

Forty-millimeter grenade launcher blazing, Hoover led the charge. Bits of the taffrail, pilothouse, and decking flew in sprays from the small craft. In seconds it became evident that the tugboat captain had seen all the jet skis he would ever be interested in. Still being ripped by punishing lashes of 5.56mm rounds from the Ameli LMGs, the tug sheared off and began to run.

"If I get this one, I win the big stuffed bear, right?" Don said aloud to himself as he placed a track of explosive fireballs along her waterline, while his men sent sheets of tracers splintering into the superstructure.

No answering muzzle blooms came from the dying tug, yet gouts of water soaked the Legion skiers from small-arms fire. Red mist appeared where a Legionnaire's head had been and his uncontrolled ski rammed another. Lieutenant Hoover swung his attention shoreward in an attempt to locate the source of their trouble. He found it, only to throttle back and gape in amazement at what suddenly developed.

Yelling obscenities and words of defiance in Spanish, a group of Panamanian soldiers, distinctive in their faded khakis and tiger-stripe cammies, mutinied and attacked their Nicaraguan counterparts. In a combination of frenzy and methodical skill, they cut down the troops who had fired on the Legion.

"Over to the left," Don Hoover advised his command. "Seems like those fellers decided to join us."

"Son of a bitch!" Franco Miner's voice came to him. "Look at that."

Assured the situation was well in hand, Lieutenant Hoover circled back toward the liner in time to see more Panamanians swarming aboard from small boats. As he drew nearer, he heard a flurry of reports, dulled by his earplugs and helmet. Then the winners thronged the rail, rifles raised over their heads in both hands. When he drew nearer, they began to shout something at him and the other skiers. Unable to make out the words, Don shrugged, gave them a friendly wave, and powered off in search of prey. He felt confident the hostages were no longer in danger.

Rising waters of the third flood crest transformed Bill Kane's "beachhead" into a swamp, with the swirling mass surging through liana vines and heavily buttressed tree trunks. The dense vegetation blocked out light from the inferno raging on the peninsula. Bill could only guess at the results. At first the Low Cost Night Vision Goggles had helped them navigate through the maze of vegetation. Eventually even they lacked sufficient light to amplify. Far ahead, Bill heard small-arms fire that told of a fight being conducted by the Folbot crewmen.

They had managed to slide their slender craft through openings too narrow for the inflatables, with their awkward wide bows. It had been nearly a half hour since the sleek little craft had passed through their lines to become the Legion vanguard.

A sudden lurch that nearly took Bill off his narrow seat underscored his reflections on their clumsiness. He checked and found the right bow snagged on a liana.

"Ed," he called softly to his coxswain, "kill the engine. We're hung up."

"Oh, shit," Ed Travis replied. "Not again."

Resigned, Sergeant Kane slipped over the side, speaking softly to the crew. "Let's unass this thing and get it clear."

Hip deep in the inky water, the Legionnaires worked together in stygian darkness to free the craft. Then they began to haul it and its precious cargo of a 4.2 mortar and the new GRM-20 ammo by main strength and tight-lipped determination toward the firefight. Splashes and curses all around gave them confidence they were not alone in this seemingly endless endeavor.

At times events conspired to make a man appear prophetic, Captain Bob Fuller mused as he peered through the trailing vines and broad leaves of the underbrush. The prisoner riot he had initiated might have been timed to perfection. He had led the men in a wide circle deep into the jungle, then turned back, to create diversions and sabotage parts of the installation. That had allowed his men to break the other Legion prisoners out. With increased strength and more harassment, the entire compound had been emptied by 0428, only moments before Legion Juliet's strike on the SAM base.

Panamanian and Nicaraguan troops, dazed and blinded by tons of ordnance, stumbled for shelter in the trees, only to die under the concentrated fire of captured weapons and the picks and shovels of their former slaves. By 0502 hours, all but those few who had seriously curried favor and collaborated with the Nicaraguans had reached freedom. Bob Fuller assessed the usefulness of the gathered force and decided to move off on an independent operation.

By daybreak, after small skirmishes with scattered enemy troops, the Legionnaires among the former prisoners, both French and American, were well armed, a cohesive fighting force under joint command. While they squatted at the edge of a small clearing, Bob Fuller outlined their alternatives.

"The way I see it, we have two options. First, we can escape from the island by boat. We can do that by setting off on our own or by identifying ourselves to the invading force. The trouble with that is whoever it is out there might think we're the enemy and blow us away. Or second, we could do something to get a little pay-back."

"How's that?" Major Gaston Fouchet of the French Legion inquired.

"There's a radar installation on the top of that high point. If I remember the map correctly, it's Hill 537. We can attack, take it, then hold it until relieved by our forces."

Fouchet frowned. "Don't we again run the risk of being attacked by our rescuers?"

"We do," Bob Fuller answered shortly. "Only, this way we will have accomplished something and they're bound to have radios up there. We should be able to talk our way to safety."

To Bob's immense satisfaction, both contingents volunteered to a man to take the radar site.

His defenses a shambles around him, *Comandante de división* Corrales was tempted to pull off the island to await the expected reinforcements. Reason told him, though, that any retreat at that time would be harshly dealt with by his superiors. He had to wait it out, he decided. Gather his forces again and counterattack the Legion—that was what he had to do. He had at least a reinforced battalion of infantry, as yet unharmed by the bombing or initial light landings. With them he could push these arrogant Legionnaires back into Gatún Lake.

"Comrade *Comandante*," the staff intelligence officer called from the doorway. "We have another little problem."

Pulled back from his desperate planning, Corrales snapped, "*¿Que es estó?*"

"The reinforcements we were expecting, *Comandante*...? They have been recalled to Colón," the halting answer came.

"'Recalled?' *¡Por amor de Lenin!* Is nothing to go right? Why were they recalled without my authority?"

"The commanders in the field came under additional attack by another Legion force. The armor and mechanized infantry are needed to strike them in the rear, Comrade *Comandante*," the G-2 explained.

"*¡Mierda en la leche de sus madres!*" Corrales screamed, beside himself with frustration. "Is there anything else?"

"The prisoners, Comrade *Comandante*. . . ."

"Yes, I know. They have rioted and escaped. That is not new."

"It is believed that they are forming a cohesive fighting force, comrade," the hapless officer informed Corrales.

"*¡Hijo de tu madre!* Here in Panama we don't *have* any *little* problems!" Corrales exclaimed in vexation. "Now that you've told me, don't stand there. Go do something about it."

"*S-Sí, Comandante*," the intelligence officer stammered as he made a hasty departure.

He took with him his superior's explosive rejoinder, which soon became the watchword of the beleaguered Nicaraguan soldiers. *Aquí en Panamá no tiene pinché problemas*.

CHAPTER TWENTY-THREE

"We are unalterably opposed to the insane, barbaric plan to actually *fight* like...like *disgusting* soldiers," the pouting-lipped young ornithologist lisped heatedly at Dr. Tucker Abbott, as the escaped Legionnaires waited close by.

"You won't have to risk your curly blond locks, Seymour. This is a call for volunteers. If you haven't balls enough for it, stay with these other '*women*.' For that matter," Abbott went on, "some of you who might want to go along but are a bit over the hill should keep back a couple of AKs to protect the noncombatants. That's all I've got to say. What do the rest of you plan to do?"

"We intend to be sensible about the whole matter, Dr. Abbott," Seymour began, to be cut off by Dr. Myron Smythe.

"Shut up, Seymour. You're nothing but a whining little twit. On the other hand, I'm opposed to the plan on moral grounds. These are freedom fighters seeking to liberate their homeland from an oppressive government. As such, I can't oppose them. I'll wait until the outcome."

Acid exploded in Tucker Abbott's gut. He could not contain himself in the face of this sanctimonious mewling. "Your 'freedom fighters' are Nicaraguan regulars, in case you hadn't noticed, Myron. Foreign invaders bent on conquest, not liberation. I suggest that if you want to test the issue scientifically, you should trot out there and try spouting some of your parlor-pink liberalism to them, like you have to us for the last eight months. My hypothesis is that they'll blow your shit away so fast you won't know what happened to you."

"Wh-What about the Panamanians among them?" Smythe spluttered.

"What about them? Assuming your 'liberators' won, how long do you expect they would survive? Look at their own country, look at Cuba, or even Russia itself. Traitors can't be trusted. The communists know that a hell of a lot better than we do. After all," Dr. Abbott added parenthetically, "who's the expert at suborning loyalties? Traditionally, all those not previously in the Soviet—or in this case, Panamanian— Communist Party get sanctioned after the victory. Why do you think those PDF troops turned on the Nicaraguans?" Tucker stopped abruptly and raised his hands in a gesture of helplessness. "Forget it. Nothing I say will change your thinking. I asked what plans you might have. I'd still like to know."

"We, ah, we thought we might, ah, just hide out in the jungle until it was over," a mousy little man who, uncharacteristically, made a study of predators in the wild, suggested.

Abbott considered that awhile. "The landings we've seen or heard have, naturally, been along the beach. Might I suggest that instead of cowering in the interior, you make your way toward the landing site farthest from the compound until you are overrun by friendly forces?"

The majority of scientists and assistants nodded agreement. Before he started off, Tucker called the mousy little predator specialist aside.

"Charlie, it's damned important for the landing force to know what the Legionnaires are up to. I'm charging you with the responsibility to see that they learn it at once. I'd do it myself, but I'm going off to play Legionnaire for the duration."

Clouds gathered on the far horizon, their leading edges tinted pink by the low, rising sun. It had taken better than an hour for CD Corrales to effect a calming and reorganization of the scattered, demoralized troops. Many could not understand why their Panamanian comrades had fired on them. Others bore psychic scars from the horrendous bombing and rocket attacks. The final count, given him by his adjutant, numbered some 1,597, including infantry, armed technicians, cooks, mechanics, and missile crewmen. Not an auspicious figure around which to plan an attack.

All the same, Corrales outlined his plan and ordered the troops deployed. No sooner had his counterattack schedule been put in effect than a new source of headache appeared. The communications sergeant poked his head out of the makeshift radio room and saluted tiredly.

"Comrade *Comandante*, surveillance radar on the radio, sir. They report troops on the slopes below them preparing to mount an attack."

"*¡Al lado de la barba de Lenin!* Half of our troops are already deployed to attack the Legion invaders. Where did this new force come from?" Corrales asked rhetorically. "Quickly, radio the field commanders to turn their advance by ninety degrees and prepare to attack enemy on *Colina Cinco-tres-siete*."

Within ten minutes, fierce fighting broke out to the rear and on both flanks of the Nicaraguan attack group. CD Corrales quickly learned the error of his tactics as confusion broke out among the ranks when the seaborne invaders employed brief, fierce attacks and quick withdrawals all along the line.

"Somebody's reading our minds," Captain Bob Fuller called out. "The Beaners are getting hit from the rear and both sides. Now's the time to push the last five hundred meters."

"There are no trees up there," Major Gaston Fouchet observed, disturbed by their lack of support arms.

"So we create good cover fire. We make one mortar and a machine gun into a battalion of them. What do we care if we burn a barrel out or warp a tube, so long as we get the job done," Fuller riposted.

Two of the French Legionnaires turned out to be accomplished mortarmen. Bob agreed to assign them to the weapon. They managed to put five bombs in the air before the first one struck. Fuller dropped his hand in a signal and the 7.62 RPK LMG began chopping up concrete wall and sandbags at six hundred rounds per minute. He turned a grinning visage to the French officer.

"They're good, Gaston. Damned good. Only trouble is there's just six mortar rounds left. Before they fire them, we'd better be on the move."

Under the sparse but accurate protective fire, the combined Legion force surged forward, yelling fierce defiance. The lightly defended radar site proved no difficulty. With mortar rounds still crashing down, the vengeance-hungry ex-prisoners charged a handful of troops at a low perimeter fence.

Hard, close, hand-to-hand fighting erupted as the Legionnaires closed with their enemy. The machine gun ceased fire and moved to another place. Its rhythmic *pat-pat-pat* began once more, driving reinforcements back inside the building. With a wild rebel yell, Bob Fuller slammed the butt stock of his rifle into the face of a Nicaraguan soldier, spun, and emptied the last two rounds into the belly of a fat, knife-wielding sergeant. His ragged gasps for air sounded loud in the sudden silence that followed.

"*¡Entregarsenos! ¡Entregarsenos!*" came a weak cry from inside the radar structure.

Captain Fuller and Major Fouchet exchanged beatific grins of relief and solemn handshakes. The surviving Nicaraguans had surrendered. "Jeez, only seven men lost. I don't believe it," Fuller breathed out in a pent-up sigh.

"Believe it, *mon ami de guerre*. We were—how you say?—fokking locky."

Now the problem became one of avoiding being fired upon by friendly forces. Bob Fuller addressed the question directly.

"I suppose we could wreck the radar dish. But that would take too long. If only we have some flag or banner to show and let them know we're in charge and there's no need to attack the place."

Fouchet's self-conscious grin grew into a full-blown smile as he reached inside his shirt. "As it happens, *mon ami* Major, for the glory of the Legion and of France, we all sacrificed bits of cloth to produce this." He drew out a folded square of cloth which showed blood red. Slowly Fouchet opened it to reveal the tricolor of France—blue, white, and red.

Eyes fixed on the crudely sewn banner, Bob Fuller summoned two men. Taking his instructions, they located some field-telephone wire and climbed to the top of the installation, where they hoisted the handmade flag of France over the building on a tall radio antenna.

Ten minutes later, the officers and men of the American and Foreign Legions stood at rigid attention over the covered bodies of their fallen comrades, hands at their brows in salute, as the final words to the French anthem rang out in the silence of Hill 537.

"Allons enfants de la patria, le jour de gloire . . ."

Any minute now. The taut silence told him more than anything heard on the radio. The final assault would come damn soon. Master Sergeant Bill Kane had linked up with elements of Bravo Third, and was back under command of his own Century, vetted to work with Captain Otis Helton, the Legion's mortar wizard from Delta Three. Bill could feel it in the breeze that ruffled the hair on his forearm. The Beaners would be history in half an hour, he anticipated.

What could come along and kick over their apple cart? Colonel Norman Stand Watie, who had arrived on Barro Colorado with the second wave, wondered that as he looked at their rapid advance and phenomenal successes illustrated on the situations map in his command center. One by one he ticked them off. By minutes it seemed, starting at 0430 the vaunted Nicaraguan invasion force crumbled before the onslaught of high water and battling Legionnaires. By 0600, Legion Air, in the form of Helio Stallions, mounting sidefiring 7.62mm miniguns, OV-10s with their deadly rocket pods, and AH-64 gunships, controlled the air over Barro Colorado. What little air the enemy had left—a handful of YAK-36 jump jets—was tied up over Panama City and Colón by Marine and Navy fighters. It all seemed too easy. Watie accepted another message slip and read it quickly.

"Gentlemen," he announced to his hardworking staff, "despite all predictions to the contrary, British and Argentine air elements are cooperating beautifully over Colón. The Argentines are flying top cover while the British use Harriers to bust antiaircraft batteries all over the city. It looks like all we need is another strong push here on the island and it's all over."

"Shall I give the word to open the mortar barrage?" Major Orenda asked expectantly.

"Yeah. Yeah, why don't you do that, Mick?"

Captain Otis Helton's cherubic face was wreathed in smiles and his little blue eyes sparkled with anticipation as he surveyed the 4.2-inch mortars, whose ugly snouts rose above the rims of their firing emplacements like so many chimneys leaning with a high wind.

Inside the pits, men hunched over piles of black-fused green mortar bombs stacked in readiness. Grim-20s as they were called by the Legion gunners, for the GRM-20 designation assigned them by their manufacturer, Pyrkal, the Greek Powder & Cartridge Company. Otis walked past the row of pits, then dropped into his command hole as the radio began to squawk.

"Seeker Zero-zero, this is Cherokee Zero-six, over."

"This is Seeker Zero-six. Go ahead."

"One round, Willy Peter at seven-niner degrees, seven-one minutes. By niner degrees, niner minutes. Fire when ready."

"Yes, sir, Major Mick."

Otis switched to his helmet mike and instructed his number-four tube on azimuth and range, then gave the order to fire one white phosphorus for range. Moments later he had a correction.

"Seeker Zero-zero, this is Cherokee Zero-six. Down seven, right four. Fire Grim-20 for effect."

Moments later over a hundred pounds, in the shape of four mortar bombs, arced through apogee and began the descent toward communist lines. At a mere eight hundred feet, the fuse charges burst and scattered eighty little bomblets over an area greater than a thousand square meters. At that instant, there were sixteen Grim-20s in the air, with more to follow. The dug-in Nicaraguan troops who would have merely been decimated by a normal barrage, were doomed to annihilation.

In the pits, Bill Kane worked grimly while his coxswain of two hours earlier, Ed Travis, boon companion and drinking partner, who doubled as assistant third squad leader, handed him freshly peeled rounds. Bill bent to stack them neatly in the ready pile.

"Tell those bastards to slow down, Ed. We're gettin too much shit in here." Bill puffed as he added the most recent Grim-20 to the pile the loader worked from.

"Ha! Maybe you think an incoming round will kill us any deader?" Travis quipped.

"Goddamn it! Don't joke about it." Bill huffed, accepting the next mortar bomb. "It's bad luck. Their one-twenty mike-mikes have our range, you know." He glanced back as his buddy stretched upward to receive the next round.

"Horseshit! Ya wanna live forev. . ." Ed's head and arms disappeared in a white-hot fireball, along with the Legionnaire passing ammo to him. A gigantic fist slammed Bill to the far side of the pit and he recalled with horror a slow-motion sequence of the GRM-20 bomb spinning like a top on the bottom of the pit.

"—on't know, Cap'n. He's been like that since the damn thing bounced in here, huggin' that damn bomb and cryin' for someone called Ed. He jumped on it while it was still spinnin', prob'ly kept it from goin' off." The voice came through a weird, unnatural silence, accentuated by strange animal sounds.

Bill blinked, focused on the blood-smeared, gritty bomb in his arms. Slowly he realized the voice was referring to him. He tried to control the sobs in his breathing.

"Better get a medic before all hell opens up again," Otis Helton suggested. "Any of you guys know him?"

"I've seen him around, a platoon sergeant from Charlie that got caught up to fill in a shortage."

"A . . . I'm a'right. Just gotta get back to my outfit." Bill had himself under control now. Jesus, had that really been him groveling on the ground? And for how fucking long?

Goddamn, he'd have to get a transfer someplace no one knew him. He got his knees under him, then shakily his feet.

"Yeah, Captain. I'm fine now. Musta been knocked silly, eh?" Bill turned and swiped furtively at a tear. Faces swam into view, white and staring under the camo paint. Master Sergeant Bill Kane, feeling naked and exposed, made his way to the ammo crate that served as a step out of the pit.

"What the fuck are you people starin' at?" He swiped blood from his nose and felt more dripping from his ears. Voices held a tinny ring. "Get the hell outta muh way. Ain'cha ever seen concussion before?"

CHAPTER TWENTY-FOUR

At 0610 hours, Major Jay Solice interviewed Smithsonian Charlie. He quickly verified his report by visual observation of the highest point on Barro Colorado. To his astonishment, the man on the Celestron scope informed him that the French flag flew over the radar site and the structure appeared to have suffered considerable damage.

Immediately he got on the radio and called off the scheduled Juliet strike on Hill 537. With nothing specific to do, Dick House and the Juliet pilots cut lazy doughnuts and figure eights around the island, looking for targets of opportunity. It came as no surprise then, when at 0635 he received a hail only a short time before they would have to break to refuel.

"Oglala One, this is Cherokee Six. I have a target for you, over."

"You're just like my wife, Cherokee Six. Always wait till the last minute. What's the target? Over."

"Mortar positions at the base of fiver-three-seven are putting rounds on our boys up there. Troops are counterattacking under their cover. Locate and terminate all. Cherokee Six, out."

"Roger, Cherokee Six."

It took little effort to locate the targets. While the conquerers of Hill 537 tensely sweated out the building damage of the counterattack effort, Legion Juliet lined up and made continuous passes through the squadron. In seconds they turned the jungle immediately around the offending mortars into a bubbling caldron of napalm and the hillside into a red mudslide of shattered bodies.

"Good work, Oglala, over." The praise came from headquarters.

"We aim to please, Cherokee. Over," Dick quipped back.

"Sometime you oughta aim too, please," a disgruntled, unidentified voice came on the net. "Ya fuckin' near roasted us with that anti-PAM."

"Ooops! Sorry about that," Dick gulped. Chastened, Legion Juliet buzzed away to fill thirsty tanks and rearm.

Within five minutes of the fresh assault, Panamanian troops began to filter to the rear, fingers laced behind their heads. Guarded by Legionnaires who would far rather be up fighting with their buddies, they cast wary glances at the sullen-faced men in crested helmets. Not a PDF soldier doubted that, given the slightest excuse, these demons of the Legion would gun them down and hurry back to the fighting. This realization did wonders for their mood when Jay Solice began to interrogate them.

It had been daylight for two hours. Jason Aldridge had meticulously gone over every detail. The room had been rented by another person using a false name. The key was passed to him far from the site. The window had been left open all night. Thin curtains, which screened details of activity inside, would be no impediment to the speedy bullet. The Sako rifle rested on a sturdy tripod five feet back from the opening, clamped in place by the wooden stock. Considering the thickness of the walls and the distance to the target, the three-foot-long suppressor would perform acceptably. His timing would have to be perfect.

He'd have to abandon the fine weapon, scope, and suppressor. Immediately after the shot, he would leave the room, walk directly to the elevator bank, and summon a car. Then he would run down the stairs two floors and do the same thing. If all went well, he would be out of the hotel and well away before the search concentrated there. At 7:50 A.M., Eastern Daylight Time, Jason eased into position behind the rifle and searched the grounds for his target.

There he was as usual, jogging around the grounds in sweats and Reeboks. The family dog trotted at his feet. Exactly as always, after ten laps he stopped to play with his eleven-year-old son. A smile of supreme confidence illuminated Jason Aldridge's face in his fourth-floor room of the Mayflower Hotel in Washington, D.C., as he watched intently through his powerful sniper scope, lined up the cross hairs, and began his squeeze. . . .

"There's heavy enemy activity around Fort Gulick, Major," Gordon Rounding's RTO informed him.

Rounding and the rest of Legion Hotel had linked up with Luis Inchausti's spearhead at 0550 hours. The Britisher had personally seen to the wounded young officer's care. Medics had cut away Luis's boots and began the tedious project of removing the tiny steel balls from the M-10 grenade. They also started a transfusion of whole blood—only the Legion, and carefully screened volunteers, gave blood for the Legion's use—to replace the large quantity lost. He would be air-evacced to the Cay before noon, the medical officer from Mike Tortora's staff assured Gordon. That out of the way, Gordon Rounding looked for something to do. His RTO gave it to him.

"All we can spare is Legion Hotel. Get Captain Grenier of Hotel to the CP on the double."

Captain Steve Grenier, affectionately known as Grenade, due as much to his short fuse as the spelling of his last name, wasted no time in arriving. He'd served in a Sheridan in Zalambia and become Bob Fuller's XO by the Venezuelan campaign. Short, heavily muscled, and aggressive, Grenade and the Panhards were made for each other.

Fierce resistance greeted them at a thousand meters. The Nicaraguan column, minus two battalions of tanks and an infantry brigade turned back for Barro Colorado, had already arrived and deployed around the old U.S. military base. Accurate fire from the 125mm smooth-bore guns of the T-72s, and 100mm D10TG guns of the T-54s, slashed into Steve's lightly armored Panhards. Vehicles and their crews died all around while he struggled to make a hasty withdrawal.

Safely out of sight and effective fire, Captain Grenier opened up with the 60mm low-pressure mortar guns. From a low ridge, crewmen with hand-held LTD units spotted the Soviet-made equipment at Fort Gulick. Gunners loaded and made ready.

"Casualty check," Steve ordered before engaging.

The result staggered him. Better than twenty-five percent wiped out in the first, brief encounter. The unwelcome news caused a quick revision in plans.

"There's infantry mixed in with that armor. I want crews out with claymores. Also get some chain saws from the equipment vans and stand by to fell trees. We'll fire two volleys with the sixties, pull back five hundred meters, fell trees, and fire again. Then place more claymores and fell trees as we retrograde another five hundred meters and continue fire."

Quickly the Legionnaires carried out the orders, returned to their vehicles, and signaled the commander. "On my command . . . Mark! Execute!"

Twenty-three low-pressure tubes belched projectiles as the LTD men spotted targets to the rear of the Nicaraguan battle formation. With all the speed they could muster, the loaders fed the 60s.

"Fire!" Grenier commanded.

Mortar guns spat high-arcing rounds and an instant later went into reverse and backed away. Chain saws growled to pugnacious life and raw white sawdust began to appear around the trunks of a dozen trees. Black smoke rose boiling from the destroyed armor. More tall trunks fell, interlacing to form a barrier across the road and precious little firm ground. The mortars fired again. Then again.

The chain-saw men ran back and began cutting more trees. Once more the Panhards drew back. Observers radioed that the Nicaraguans had started an advance. An infantry screen out front crested the rise and observers tripped the first claymores. The invaders went down in clusters, like blitzed bowling pins. Another salvo of 60mm smart rounds arced overhead. One more, Grenier figured, and the laser spotters would have to be withdrawn.

"Fire!" he commanded. "LTDs pull back. The enemy will be over the lip in a moment. When they come, all units spot and fire at will." Nervously, he checked his watch. It was 0710 hours. Too bloody damned early to die, Steve thought recklessly.

Like animated sewer pipes, the ugly snouts of 125mm guns appeared along the ridge, followed by the looming bulk of T-72 turrets. Immediately the 7.62mm coaxial machine guns opened up on the fleeing laser men. One, two, three, a fourth one fell, legs sprawled at grotesque angles. At near point-blank range, the 60mm guns fired, their smart rounds answering spots projected from integral LTDs on the Panhards. A swarm of infantry appeared behind the advancing enemy.

Abruptly, a Panhard two removed from Steve's command vehicle on the left exploded into so much fiery trash. Then the Nicaraguans halted. Engines idling a moment, they took ferocious fire from the beleaguered Legionnaires. Then, slowly, they began to back up. Steve Grenier watched in amazement as they rolled up the facing slope and over the low ridge.

"What the hell," he exploded aloud. "They had us cold. What happened?"

"I have the Nicaraguan frequency, sir," Steve's RTO informed him. "I can't understand the Spanish."

"Pipe it through to me," Steve requested, his grammar going to hell as it always did in combat. "Bloody hell," he breathed out a moment later in an awed tone. "They're being told to pack it in. To get the hell out and surrender to troops they haven't been fighting. All right, boys, let's encourage them a little. Send them along with a few more smart rounds, eh?"

Fighting ashore had dwindled to sporadic stutters of small-arms fire as the trapped, and often recalcitrant, Nicaraguan soldiers paid with their lives for their leaders' folly. Tragically, Lieutenant Don Hoover knew, they took the lives of too many good Legionnaires in the process. He and his jet ski command cruised lazily around the island's hot spots, seeking opportune targets, finding few. Then, at 0645 hours, while paralleling the west side of Barro Colorado, the point man spotted a Canal Authority cabin cruiser pulling out from the small bay formed by crab-pincer headlands on the north end.

"Let's check it out," Don ordered. A touch to the throttle surged his jet ski forward.

Aboard the speedy craft, CD Juan Bautista Corrales, the surviving four members of his staff, and Colonel Enrique Gonzales Gorman of the Panamanian Defense Force, attempted to make their escape. Bitterness filled Corrales, who saw in his defeat a future appointment with a pock-marked wall and twelve soldiers with rifles. Perhaps, he considered, he could escape into Costa Rica and assume a new identity. The money carefully salted away in those three secret numbered accounts in a Swiss bank would help him in that endeavor. He looked with disgust at Colonel Gorman.

Enrique Gorman pouted. All his great plans had fallen into ruin. Why had that idiot Corrales asked the Russians for the Foreign Legion prisoners? If the Legion had kept out of this, they might have won. No, he sternly corrected himself. That was only self-pity talking. What they had failed to take into consideration, what even Manuel Noriega had not foreseen, was the impact seizing the canal would have on the rest of the world.

In particular they had underestimated the Americans. No matter the attitudes and policies of the majority in their Congress, they were compelled to submit to the demands of other nations and their own people. The participation of U.S. forces had broken the back of the revolution. He ceased his deliberations when his eye picked out small, fast-moving dots out on the lake.

"What are those?" he inquired of no one in particular.

"They look like those sport vehicles," the boat's captain responded. "Water—no, jet skis."

Flickering orange light flashed at the front of the lead jet ski. Although the shots went wide of the bow, Gorman ducked instinctively. "They're shooting at us!" he bleated.

"Shall I heave to?" the captain inquired.

Gorman blanched. "*¡Por Dios, no!* Those cursed Legion-naires. They make weapons of anything. Full throttle. Hurry."

A wicked grin of battle lust distorted Lieutenant Don Hoover's face as his small command closed on the cabin cruiser. He triggered a blast from his 40mm grenade launcher that blew off the bow pulpit of the speedy vessel. As it reflexively altered course, the stream of egg-shaped grenades trashed the port light, chunks of foredeck, and rubrail.

Growing closer, he saw the side windows of the cabin opaque, then shatter inward under blasts from the twin Ameli LMGs of his wing men. From the rear cockpit, a puff of smoke indicated the firing of an RPG. The 85mm, 4.95-pound projectile sizzled along above the water and impacted with a horrendous roar. Small chunks of the jet ski and its rider flew in every direction. Don Hoover felt a familiar sickness growing in his gut. Small-arms fire answered them now from the flying bridge and cockpit.

Don let go another string of grenades, then swung away to allow the machine gunners free play. Half a dozen bursts at the waterline and the crippled cruiser slowed to a crawl. The CETME Amelis trashed the port side. A man appeared on the flying bridge and lowered the Canal Authority pennant, hoisting in its place a white flag.

Twenty minutes later, Lieutenant Don Hoover and five of his Legionnaires personally delivered their prizes to Colonel Watie. The sullen enemy officers stood before Watie's desk aboard the grounded freighter he chose as temporary headquarters. Watie glowered at them with icy distaste. His words left no room for debate.

"You are going to get on the radio and broadcast a formal, unconditional surrender. You will tell all troops to cease firing and lay down their arms. Then we will make a joint announcement to my troops. They're to be the last to know in order to prevent any treachery. You are going to do that, or by Christ I will skin every one of you alive."

"Oh, Jesus! Oh, God, no!" The impassioned shout of the radio operator on the Gamboa bridge roadblock silenced even the ubiquitous monkeys, birds, and insects.

"What is it?" Captain Frank Tall Bear, CO of Charlie of the Third, demanded in his usual ursine growl.

"It's . . . it's the President, sir," the white-faced RTO responded.

"On the horn?" Tall Bear snapped, incredulous.

"N-No, sir. He's been shot, sir. An assassin, sir. It's . . .

oh, God, it's awful. Massive damage to his chest, arm nearly torn from his shoulder, his son, Tommy, hysterical. No complete report. There'll be more later," Corporal Lance Waller repeated as he listened to the crackle in his phones.

"Aw, shit!" Tall Bear responded. "All hell's gonna break loose now, fellas. Those rotten Red bastards. I don't know what the Old Man's gonna say, but I'm tellin' you right now. No prisoners. We take no prisoners from those scumbag Nicaraguan filth." Uncharacteristic of his usual calm, Frank Tall Bear threw back his head and howled his anguish at the startled jungle creatures.

"Hu ihpeya wicayapo!"

Race memory sent chills up the spines of several Legionnaires who had ancestors who had witnessed the Fetterman Massacre and survived the Wagon Box Fight. "Jesus, Captain, what's that?" one asked timidly.

Released from his spell, Tall Bear grinned a bit foolishly. "It's an old Sioux war cry. It means we're gonna take those Beaner bastards and punk 'em in the ass till their noses bleed. No quarter, you understand?"

"¡Madre de Dios!" the inquirer exclaimed, crossing himself.

"You're not going to believe this, Captain, but there's a train coming," a Legionnaire from third squad reported.

"Let's get ready for them, then," Captain Tall Bear replied calmly. "We'll derail that son of a bitch and blast 'em all."

Fortunately, a moment before the planted charges were to be detonated, an outpost reported from the perimeter. "There's an American flag on the locomotive. No joke. It's a whole fuckin' train of Marines."

From the lake side of the roadblock, the maneuvering horn of a U.S. destroyer hooted at them as it passed by. Whistles and shouts rose from the blockading force and a mighty cheer answered them. Only belatedly did the Legionnaires and Marines recall the tragedy in Washington.

Over the rumble of engines, which made the announcement unnecessary, Pops Henderson stuck his head in the command van and informed Colonel Stand Watie, "The Ace-deuce-treys are comin' in, Colonel."

"Already? They're a day ahead of schedule," Watie muttered.

"I . . . ah, don't think they're ours, sir," Henderson added in scant enlightenment.

"Well, let's go see."

On the landing field, hastily smoothed out by Legion Caterpillar operators, Watie was saluted and greeted by a spiffily outfitted young Air Force captain. "Air Transport Command, sir. We're bringing in supplies for the occupation forces. And a set of orders for you. From the President, sir," he confided. "He must have . . . must have signed them last night."

Well, he warned me about blowing that dam, Watie thought resignedly. Probably my recall as commander in there, as well as hauling the Legion out. Put the best face on, it's all that can be done.

"Yes. And God damn to hell the son of a bitch who shot Hunter," Watie growled. "Any news on that situation?"

"Only that the President is still in surgery, sir. His chances aren't—aren't very good."

Watie exploded with a string of expletives. Then he tapped the stiff cardboard folder. "What's this about occupation forces?"

"They'll be arriving in Darién by train soon, along with airlifted elements coming in this afternoon, sir."

"What about us?" Watie queried.

"I don't know, sir. I think it's in the orders. Now, with your permission, sir, I have a lot to attend to."

Watie returned the salute. "Go ahead." The fly-boy's coolness only fed his preternatural suspicion as to what the orders contained.

Right enough, he discovered five minutes later. The President directly ordered him to evacuate the Legion *at once.* Damn. His foreboding did nothing to diminish his consternation at seeing it for real.

"They're kicking us out, Sergeant Major," the suddenly old and tired Watie announced.

CHAPTER TWENTY-FIVE

By 0715 hours, the hilarity and jubilation over the Nicaraguan surrender had calmed down in Bob Fuller's old Legion Hotel. The men went happily about repairing and replacing parts for their Panhards and few tensed, as their commander did, when the sound of rumbling diesel engines returned from down the road. Over the rise came the Nicaraguan armor and Steve Grenier consigned his soul to whatever Grand Master there might be in the afterworld, resigned in body to total destruction.

When the T-72s and T-54s drew nearer, Steve saw white flags on their radio antennas. The infantry marched empty-handed, their weapons gathered and transported on trucks. The long column slowly wound over the road and halted some fifty meters from Steve's Panhards. An officer, *Comandante de Brigada* Uvalde Blancanales, came forward, a frown growing as he drew near enough to recognize the Legion's crested helmets.

"Where are the Marines?" he demanded peremptorily.

After the pasting his Panhards had taken, the appalling loss of life, Steve Grenier had little humor left for this strutting capon. "On the east side of Colón, kicking ass on your comrades."

"Impudent *gringo cabrón!*" Blancanales blurted, then thought better of it. "I will make my formal surrender to no one other than the Marine commandant. See to it I have a safe-conduct pass to reach him."

"Colonel, the circumstances dictate that I should reason

with you," Steve began in a tightly controlled, civil tone, which belied his rising fury. "To which end, I'll tell you this. Since you refuse to surrender to me, you must be considered to still be hostile. In which case, I shall give orders to kill you to the last man."

"Y-You're bluffing!" Blancanales spluttered.

"Listen to me, you Marxist pig son of a bitch! You will surrender to me immediately, or I shall take inordinate pleasure in shooting you where you stand."

A summons to Colón deprived Steve Grenier of the necessity to blow away Colonel Blancanales. Before he departed he gave orders for the newly arrived prisoners to be taken to French Field where another surrendered column had been confined. Then he sped off in his Panhard.

When he joined Gordon Rounding at French Field, he found all the enemy armor a smoking ruin. Although personal arms had been surrendered, the Nicaraguan troops managed to use thermite to destroy the heavy equipment.

"On whose authority was this done?" Rounding coldly demanded of the gathered enemy officers.

"*C-Comandante de Brigada* Blancanales," a timorous voice responded.

Rounding sought out the pompous, defiant officer. "I will deal with you later," he told Blancanales coldly. "For the moment you are all to remain here. When I return, Comandante Blancanales will be treated according to the severity of his crime."

In the command van, Rounding contacted Watie by radio. Quickly he outlined the situation.

"Son of a bitch!" Colonel Watie exploded. "Blancanales must be KGB. The smart bastards have found our weak point. They're going to try to destroy us economically. After Venezuela, I should have expected it. But so soon? This can blow all our future plans for expansion."

"What do you recommend I do about it, Colonel? Blancanales, I mean?"

"Right now I don't give a damn, Gordon. How in hell are we going to find a way around this? I'm due on the last plane out of here in fifteen minutes. I'll see you back at the

Cay for debrief. After that, we'll see. Cherokee Zero-zero, out."

Gordon Rounding walked from the van in deep thought. Troubled by this revelation, he glanced abstractedly at the assembled Nicaraguan and Panamanian officers. Suddenly his anger surged upward again. He turned to Steve.

"Find *Comandante* Blancanales's sidearm, if you please. His or anyone's will do."

When the trooper returned, Gordon took the pistol belt and walked over to the smug-faced Nicaraguan. "You didn't do that on your own," Rounding snapped, not needing to refer directly to the subject of his accusation. "This is the work of the Kay-gay-bey. You're one of their bloody toadies, what?"

"What if I am? You are nothing but a piratical mercenary, a strutting Limey fool stupid enough to think your paltry band of brigands, this *fine* Legion of yours, could challenge the might of the Soviet Union and its friends. We are the wave of the future and no motley assortment of criminals and gutter scum is going to stand in our way."

Major Gordon Rounding had anticipated many sort of replies. This one took him off guard. His patience evaporated, his cool heated to an inferno. Thrusting the belt forward, he shouted into Blancanales's face.

"Put it on!"

"W-Wh-What are you in-t-tending?" Blancanales stammered.

"I had planned to display your sidearm in front of your fellow officers and lay claim to it as personal spoils of war to indicate how thoroughly and utterly you have been whipped. Now I have another use for it. Put—it—on!"

Hastily, and therefore sloppily, Blancanales strapped on the brown leather belt and flap holster for his Makarov 9mm pistol. "What's the purpose of this?"

In reply, Rounding drew his left-hand Colt Bisley and shoved it in the fat gut of the Nicaraguan officer. "Draw. Pull that pistol of yours. Fill your hand, you son of a bitch!"

Hesitantly, *Comandante de Brigada* Uvalde Blancanales let his right hand drop toward the holster. As he did, Gordon Rounding took a quick step backward and drew the right-

hand Colt. A loud blast drowned out Blancanales's shriek of
terror and a large cloud of smoke formed around the six-gun
in Rounding's hand. Blancanales seemed to cave in from the
center and pitched forward onto his own weapon, which
went off with a blubber-muffled *whump*.

The smoke had hardly cleared when a Marine Corps general arrived to take command of the prisoners. "What happened here?" he demanded.

"That bloody bastard destroyed all this captured equipment and tried to take a shot at me. I killed him, sir," Gordon replied with a straight face.

"What a mess. Well, can't be helped, I suppose," the general responded. "By the way, you are officially relieved. You
are to prepare to load your vehicles and men on the transports that are unloading ours right now. I'm sorry, old man,
for the loss of that captured equipment and for the quick
shuffle out of here. I truly am. 'Ours not to reason why,'
eh?"

Back on the Cay, gloomy though victorious, the Legion
listened to the media describe their campaign as a brutal
rampage against innocent civilians. They sat in silence, not
bothering to comment or protest. They'd heard it all before.
The same old scurrilous clichés taken out, dusted off, and
mouthed over and over by the same crop of empty-headed,
pretty-faced automations. Not until a new twist was announced did anyone comment.

"Congress today announced that they will conduct a complete investigation into the destruction of Madden dam and
the wanton murder of a neutral observer, Brigade Commander Uvalde Blancanales of the Nicaraguan Army. A full-
scale hearing is planned to follow."

"Neutral observer, my ass," Arizona Jim growled. "Way I
hear it, that fat Beaner took a shot at Major Rounding."

"It's the same old shit," Charlie Smith declared. "But
watch out, boys. For this one they might take Hanoi Jane out
of mothballs and have her crusade for the firing squad for
the Old Man and Major Rounding."

"How'd those fat-cat Congressmen like ten thousand Le-

gion Glaudii up their asses?" threatened another Legionnaire.

"Ya know, it's a funny thing you should mention that,"
Arizona Jim began. "I've been giving it a lot of thought
lately and . . ."

"Aw, get out of here, Jim!" a dozen voices called, the
mood broken into easy laughter.

Unfortunately, Colonel Norman Stand Watie had no ready
laughter to soothe him. Training resumed for the fit, hospital
for the wounded. In Washington Colonel Watie found many
former supporters unwilling to speak to him. The final blow
came a week after the Legion's return to Corsair Cay. Colonel Lew Cutler entered the commander's office with a scowl
about to turn into rage.

"Norm, Congress just announced that they're cutting all
funds to the Legion, pending their investigation of the dam."

"Shit! That ties it. We're through. Between the KGB and
their allies, we've got our pocketbook stolen. What Zalambia and Venezuela are paying won't buy us beans for three
months."

"There is some good news. The President's condition has
improved considerably. He sat up and took solid food this
morning. He also said the Legion did a damn fine job, then
added that he'd not meant any pun."

"*You* spare me from amateur comedians," Watie feigned
agony.

The depression that settled on the Legion extended to
every aspect of their life. Accidents on the training ranges
increased. Sick call had record numbers of minor complaints
every day. Stan and Sam also found out that the Legionnaires weren't partying anymore. The Beyerisher Hoffbrau
stood nearly empty every evening. Only the hard-core of
music and strong brew buffs put in an appearance. Although
never admitting it, everyone knew the whole thing was
about to go bust. The Legion would be no more.

Then the first contributions began to arrive. Some came
from private sources, from the Canal Zone Citizens' League,
and endowments by wealthy, anonymous donors. Larger

amounts came from small governments grateful for the existence of the Free World Liberty Corps to help in their time of need. Then the avalanche started with donations from governments not so small. Great Britain in particular showed appreciation with a ten-million-dollar bounty paid for freeing British subjects captured on board vessels taken at Barro Colorado. An unreported ground swell of public opinion favored the Legion. Not since Ollie North's conquest of Congress had so many spoken out so boldly for what they saw as right.

Doubtful of their future, Legionnaires listened eagerly to the earliest sign on radio talk shows. "Okay, go ahead," a nationally noted talk host declared.

Peep! "I don't know why you guys are still kickin' the Legion around," the caller responded. "The canal's open and there're American troops on guard." *Peep!* "With Americans runnin' the show again, that's okay in my book."

"But, sir, consider this. We aren't supposed to be there. And the job could have been done without the Legion."

"Bull!" *Peep!* "Those Legion guys went right to the heart of it and captured the leaders behind the revolt. As to the Legion being in the Canal Zone at all, until we gave up the zone as a U.S. territory, every person born there is an American citizen, just like Puerto Rico and the Virgin Islands, right?" *Peep!* "So the Legion was only protecting U.S. citizens' lives and rights, while our *government* let that Red puke Noriega slip back to his commie buddies in Nicaragua." *Peep!* "But the *real* government's in charge again in Panama. Someday they'll be able to handle it. Until then, let's keep the Canal American." *Peep!* "An' say, why don't Congress go hold their hearings in Managua? They'd get told what they wanted to hear that way."

"Uh-uh, thank you very much, sir. Next? Hello?"

Colonel Stand Watie listened to the broadcasts, too. Within another week, the major newspapers began to cave in to threats of withdrawing advertising. Pro-Legion articles, letters to the editor, and editorial comment began to appear once again. Watie predicted that the networks would be last to concede. Then the greatest surprise came when Sweden wrote off the Legion's debt to Bofors for their 155mm guns. Great jubilation erupted around headquarters and the Hoffbrau sold out of beer that night.

"More good news, Colonel," a fresh-faced young aide announced as he entered the office with a long box. "You're even getting personal presents. This just arrived."

Inside the brown cardboard container lay a fine rosewood presentation case containing a high-quality commemorative rifle, shipped direct from the factory in Czechoslovakia. Watie scowled at the address label while his aide removed the rifle from its velvet liner.

"This is sure some fine shooting piece, sir," the aide remarked as he hefted the rifle and placed his finger on the trigger.

"Yeah. Only why would a client state of the Soviet Union send me a present?"

"I, uh, never . . . uuuhhh, ne-nev—" Ashen, the aide dropped the rifle and clutched feebly at his chest. With a pained gasp and jerky gesture of helplessness, he fell forward to where his face struck the corner of Watie's desk before he bounced onto the floor.

"Get an ambulance here at once!" Colonel Watie shouted to Pops Henderson.

Help came too late. The young aide was DOA at the Legion hospital. Three hours later, Jay Solice, now confirmed in the G-2 slot, entered the office with a manila folder containing the autopsy report.

"I think the KGB has finally overstepped itself. Dr. Dunklee did the post and found a small brown smear on Graham's index finger. He did a workup and identified the substance. Graham died of nicotine sulfate poisoning. It had been applied to the trigger of that rifle your benefactors sent you."

"And the fucking FBI won't submit a recommendation for a prosecution of Gulyakin!" Watie exploded. "By God, this is enough. From here on out, we take care of our own messes. We should have all along. We owe it to these kids. By God, we owe it to ourselves."

"But how can we possibly defeat the KGB's silent war?" Jay Solice questioned.

"George Patton had an answer to that. And from now on, that's the way we're doing things around here. 'To win battles, you do not beat weapons—you beat the soul of man, of the *enemy* man.'"